Kathleen Anne Kenney

GIRL ON THE LEESIDE

Kathleen Anne Kenney is an author, freelance writer, and playwright. Her writing has appeared in *Big River*, *Coulee Region Women*, and *Ireland of the Welcomes*, as well as other publications. She has had numerous short plays presented in Minnesota theaters and has published the play *The Ghost of an Idea*, a one-actor piece about Charles Dickens. Her play *New Menu* was a winner in the 2012 Rochester Repertory Theatre's national short-play competition. She is currently at work writing her next novel.

www.kathleenannekenney.com

D1366374

GIRL ON THE LEESIDE

GIRL ON THE
LEESIDE

· A NOVEL ·

KATHLEEN ANNE KENNEY

ANCHOR BOOKS
A DIVISION OF PENGUIN RANDOM HOUSE LLC
NEW YORK

FIRST ANCHOR BOOKS EDITION, MAY 2018

Grateful acknowledgment is made to the following
for permission to reprint previously published material:

Carcanet Press Limited: Excerpt from "Her Voice Could Not Be Softer"
from *Collected Poems* by Austin Clarke. Reprinted
by permission of Carcanet Press Limited.

Farrar, Straus and Giroux, LLC, and Faber and Faber Limited: Excerpts
from "Poem," "The Wishing Tree," "Bog Oak," "Relic of Memory," and
"Sweeney in Flight" from *Opened Ground: Selected Poems 1966–1996* by Seamus
Heaney, copyright © 1998 by Seamus Heaney. Reprinted by permission
of Farrar, Straus and Giroux, LLC, and Faber and Faber Limited.

The Library of Congress has cataloged the Doubleday edition as follows:
Names: Kenney, Kathleen Anne, author.
Title: Girl on The Leeside : a novel / Kathleen Anne Kenney.
Description: New York : Nan A. Talese, 2017.
Identifiers: LCCN 2016034555
Subjects: LCSH: Women poets—Fiction. | Americans—Ireland—Fiction.
| Family secrets—Fiction. | Self-actualization (Psychology) in women—
Fiction. | Ireland—Fiction. | Domestic fiction. | BISAC: FICTION/Coming of
Age. | FICTION/Family Life. | FICTION/Literary. | GSAFD: Bildungsromans.
Classification: LCC PS3611.E6667 G57 2017 | DDC 813/.6—DC23
LC record available at https://lccn.loc.gov/2016034555

**Anchor Books Trade Paperback ISBN: 978-0-525-43265-4
eBook ISBN: 978-0-385-54240-1**

Book design by Pei Loi Koay

www.anchorbooks.com

Printed in the United States of America
10 9 8 7 6 5 4 3 2 1

lee *n.* 1. The side that is sheltered or turned away from the wind.

GIRL ON THE LEESIDE

The west coast of Ireland, late twentieth century

Countless women throughout millennia have known such a night of birthing, the fortunate ones landing in a sheltered place where kindness and friendship awaited. Galway Gwen was fortunate and knew it. The Leeside Pub on the shore of Lough Carnloe was such a sanctuary now that her time was near, the Doyles having been friends of the travelers for generations.

Maeve Doyle shooed away Gwen's husband as she wrapped a sturdy arm around the pregnant woman's waist. "Off with you. We're not needing a man in this." As she guided Gwen up the stairs Maeve continued briskly, "The bar's the place for you. Drink to good luck for your woman and God's own blessing on the baby to come. And stay out of my kitchen, I just cleaned in there."

Gwen felt a heavy aching pressure in her lower belly and a giddiness that came from joy. This one had come to term, this one would be all right. Maeve settled Gwen in her own bed, bustling about calmly and chatting away as if the two women were having tea by the fireside.

"There, now. You're looking grand. I'm thinking this one will be no trouble at all. What a mercy that Maureen's away on

a school trip. No need to worry about her being underfoot."
Maeve coughed harshly then, a smoker's hack.

"That sounds bad," Gwen said. "Are you not well, Maeve?"

"Oh, well enough. I'm not contagious, that I can tell you."

A contraction began and Gwen's gaze roved around the
room, coming to rest on the photos of Maeve's two children.

"And how is Maureen keeping?" Gwen asked.

"More and more of a handful, if you want the truth of it.
Her confirmation is next month and a blessing that'll be. I'm
hoping it settles her down."

Gwen smiled at her friend. "So, the bishop has a magic
wand?"

That made Maeve chuckle. "Point taken. My little girl's
growing up, 'tis all." Then she sighed. "But the two of us are
knocking heads more often than not. Her brother's able to
steady her more than myself and that's the truth. So having
him gone now is an extra penance."

"Can you be opening a window?" A strong contraction made
Gwen gasp but pain was no stranger and she breathed through
it. The cool night breeze from the window felt blissful on her
face. When she could talk again she asked, "And how is Keenan
liking Dublin and the university?"

"Grand," Maeve answered. She stayed by the open window
and lit a cigarette. "He's doing well. Who knew a couple of duf-
fers like myself and my man could have such a brilliant lad, eh?
Mad about books, he is."

"Always . . . was." Another contraction gripped Gwen.

"That's the truth. The priests at the school used to say . . ."
Maeve's voice blurred in Gwen's ears as the contraction didn't
abate but gained strength and purpose.

Maeve threw her cigarette out the window and came to the
bed. "Right. Let's have a look at you. This isn't the first baby
born at the Leeside and God willing it won't be the last."

An hour later Gwen held her newborn son. She was cursed no more by her two miscarriages.

"He's a grand little one," Maeve assured her. "You did well, Gwen. Quick as a wink, compared with my Keenan. Like birthing a cart horse, that was . . ."

Gwen listened only dimly to Maeve's chatter. She looked at her son, red and wrinkled, his head topped with a wisp of apricot-colored fuzz. *This is the blessing of my life. This and the road under my feet and the road that's always just beyond. That's my turf, that is. And he'll come to love it as I do. That he will, my little Turf.*

She was seized with a fierce gratitude for her son, for her dear friend Maeve, and for this place, this haven which she had grown to love over the years—as much as she could love any fixed abode. A special, private place to rest, to bask in rare acceptance, and to share the warmth of true friendship. Even among her own people, Gwen knew she was considered too fanatical about the old ways, too private, and too proud. But she didn't care. Her community was her quiet, steady man, and the birds in the trees at dawn and dusk. Her sense of place was a union between herself and the ribbon of road that led to just what was over the next rise. And now she would share the glory and grit of it all with her boy.

"Maeve, don't be telling anyone about this," she said suddenly. "About my baby being born here, eh? It's best that way, so."

Her friend looked surprised but answered readily, "I'll not then, if you don't want me to."

Relieved, Gwen nodded. "I don't want our people knowing. Some of them don't hold with mixing with settled folks. They wouldn't understand us coming here to this place." She looked at her son. "Anyway, 'tis no one's business."

"No one will be hearing it from me."

"You're a treasure, Maeve Doyle, do you know that?"

Maeve snorted. "I do not. Close your eyes, now. The little one's asleep and you should have a kip yourself."

Gwen did as she was told. She was comforted by the warm, sweet bundle tucked between her shoulder and breast, and the quiet sounds of Maeve moving about the room. Just as Gwen grew sleepy Maeve's voice breached her drowsiness. "You and your man are welcome to bide here for a time, to rest up and get used to the child."

Gwen shook her head slowly, eyes closed. "Ah, bless you for that but we'll be off in a day or so. We need to be getting him home—and the road is home."

Maeve went down to the bar for some brandy and to tell Gwen's husband that all was well and he had a son. He said little but Maeve saw the relief and quiet happiness in his face. They shared a slug of brandy, toasting the new life with a Gaelic blessing. Then he stretched out on the old oak settle for a sleep.

Maeve dozed that night in a chair by the bedside, occasion- ally checking on the new mother and child. A few times she went into the bathroom when she felt a coughing fit coming on so as not to disturb them.

So far she'd kept the news of her lung cancer to herself. Looking in the mirror now she wondered if she could unbur- den herself to Gwen. Keeping the secret was eating her up as much as the killer inside her. Gwen was safe; she was wise and strong and loyal. Maeve hadn't found a way to tell her own chil- dren yet; the thought of that was infinitely more painful than the disease itself. Not used to shirking difficult things, she had begun to wonder if that made her a coward. But Keenan was blossoming in Dublin, finally given the chance to be immersed in the book learning of literature and history that he'd always loved. Her chest fluttered with pride whenever she thought of him. And Maureen would soon turn thirteen, on the threshold of young womanhood. Already Maeve saw signs of a deep restlessness and knew that her daughter's fearless and generous nature wouldn't be contained within the Leeside. In her darker moments Maeve couldn't shake off a foreboding that Maureen's irrepressible spirit might lead her down an ominous path. She would just have to trust that the close bond between Kee and Maureen—though different from each other as chalk and cheese—would hold strong if she herself . . . if she were gone.

Two days later Galway Gwen's little family was ready to roll away from the Leeside in their yellow-and-blue barrel caravan. Her husband waited patiently and expressionless on the high front seat behind the raggedly black-and-gray pony while the two women shared a prolonged farewell inside. Having just heard her friend's distressing news, Gwen's heart ached even as she promised to keep the secret of the illness.

"I'll not tell a soul. But you're having treatments, ya?"

"Oh, aye. I'll be around for a goodly time yet but sharing this with another living soul has helped," Maeve said, trying to sound hearty.

But as they looked into each other's eyes both felt a thrill of fear. Surely they would see each other again?

Little Turf started fussing and Maeve took him from Gwen's arms. "Time you were off with your mam and da," she said to him.

Gwen laid a hand on her friend's arm. "God bless you, Maeve Doyle. And your family. Remember that I'll be thinking of you every day." She kissed Maeve on the cheek and Maeve smiled at her.

"I'll remember, so I will. And keep reminding God about that blessing."

Out of the pub they came, Gwen's arm around Maeve's waist.

"He's a darling," Maeve said. "But I don't envy you traveling with a baby. Won't you have a time of it?"

"Not at all," Gwen answered with warm pride. "Born to the life, he is. A freeborn man of the traveling people. Help me settle him in his special place."

Behind the high seat was a wooden compartment with a built-in basket. Cleverly constructed, it was padded and hinged so that it swayed gently with the caravan's movement. Maeve complimented Gwen's husband: "You made a grand job of that." He nodded his thanks.

After the overflowing of grateful tears, Gwen gave her friend one last hug and whispered, " 'Tis a blessed place, this. And you at the heart of it. Take this as thanks." She handed Maeve a soft wool shawl, the color of Connemara gentians. Maeve tried to refuse but it was little enough in Gwen's eyes as a token for her friend's kindness and perpetual welcome.

After the caravan disappeared from sight Maeve wrapped herself in the shawl, savoring its warmth as she coughed heavily in the chilly March air. She went back into the pub and sat down until the spasm ended. When she felt well enough she went upstairs to clean her bedroom, setting everything to rights. She must launder all the sheets, blankets, and towels as well, removing all traces of the travelers' visit before her daughter came home. As promised, Maeve intended to tell no one.

As she worked Maeve said a short prayer to the Blessed Mother and Saint Christopher to watch over Gwen and her son. Traveling was a fierce, hard life but it was in Gwen's blood. Maeve herself hailed from Cork City and every day missed its bustling streets and pulsating crowds. But love had brought her here to the west, to a remote country pub in an untamed valley of rough beauty. The yearning in Maeve's heart for city life had never abated. It was just part of her, like her thick black hair and crooked smile. Over the years, especially since the death of her husband, Maeve's yearning had become knitted into the inertia of her life, not to be followed or acted upon. She was bound here by love and loyalty, and not the first or last woman to be so. Maeve lit a cigarette in her bedroom, looking out the window at the distant Clifden road. She reflected that if the women in Ireland were all to follow their hearts—well, the earth would crack open. Maybe that was why she feared that Kee's steadying hand wouldn't be able to keep Maureen from following the yearning of her untamed heart.

Maeve went slowly downstairs; she was tired but it was time to open up for customers. She missed her friend already. She'd just have to be content believing that she'd see Gwen and her family again in September, their usual visiting time. But before the autumn equinox Maeve Doyle was dead and buried under the turf in Saint Brendan's churchyard.

. . .

Almost three years to the day of his mother's death, Keenan Doyle yelled up the pub stairs, losing patience with his younger sister.

"Maureen! For the love of God, will ya get yourself down the stairs and out the door!"

His sixteen-year-old sister answered back without a beat. "I'm practically parked at my desk. Keep your hair on." Clattering down the stairs, she was quelled not a whit by her brother's glare. As she stood on the second-to-last step they were eye to eye, since Kee was a Celtic giant and Maureen slight and quick as a thrush, dark-haired and elfin. "See? You can stop your blethering. I'm off." She jumped the last steps to the floor.

Kee felt his anger melt away, as it always did with Maureen. "You'll turn me gray—or Sister Mary Sebastian will. She's a terror when she lectures me about you."

"She can lecture her head off, for all I care. She's just an old penguin!"

"Hey, now." Kee was shocked in spite of himself. "Be respectful, for Christ's sake."

Maureen giggled. "God, you're funny sometimes. And I'm only joking." She looked at him sidewise, a teasing glance. "The sisters are grand, so they are! You're just silly to be scared. Everyone knows penguins are nice as pie." She waddled to the door and Kee couldn't keep himself from laughing. Just as she opened the door, she said casually, "I'm going to the pictures after school and then to a party at Tommy's. I won't be late." The door closed behind her with deceptive gentleness.

Kee lunged for it and followed her out into the yard. Already astride her bike, she was pedaling away furiously.

"Ya will not!" he thundered after her. "You'll come home straightaway after school! I mean it, now!"

Maureen did a half turn and skidded to a stop, partway down the drive. Calmly, almost expressionless, she responded, "You're not Da or Mam. I'm not needing you to tell me what to do or to take care of me. I'm grown up, now that I'm sixteen. I'll be going my own way, so I will."

He watched, stunned, as his sister rode out of sight.

After standing very still for a few minutes while he tried to absorb what just happened, Kee pulled himself together and went inside. He did the needed maintenance mindlessly, cleaning the tap lines and setting up new kegs of Smithwick's and Harp. Then he poured himself the day's first whiskey, went outside, and threw the drink back with practiced ease. Over the last three years he'd battled the lure of alcohol as a panacea against the dreary pub routine and his struggles with Maureen's rebellious spirit. He was losing most of the skirmishes but his losses seemed to matter less and less. He knew Maureen wasn't destined to stay at home much longer and he wouldn't have the strength of will to try to keep her at the Leeside. More and more when he tried to act the role of parent she'd dismissed him with amusement or irritation. But never with such a declaration like this morning. As soon as she left school she'd be off like an arrow from a bow, taking her maddening, teasing ways and carefree light and laughter with her.

Looking out at the lough, he saw that the water was low just now, low and still, with reeds and clumps of grasses breaching the silver surface. It reminded him of a mirror aged with damp. Kee turned toward the Leeside, built more than three hundred years ago of gray stone. He reflected that it was a scene out of time; a coach-and-four would look as natural on the gravel drive as his Ford pickup. Growing up here he had loved the timelessness of it; he'd loved the wildness of the valley, the security of the ancient building that looked like it had sprung from the stony ground. It had all seemed so . . . right.

Now time was broken—he felt it passing him by even as it continued to stand still. Having to leave the university to come home to care for Maureen and run the pub had twisted his relationship with this place. His love for it now was tempered with the burden of responsibility. The unrelenting weight of these stone walls would no longer be kept tolerable by his sister's presence, by the motivation that he was working toward her future as well as his own. *The whole world keeps on turning while you just try to hold your own life together.*

When Kee left Trinity College he'd been taking a class in poetry that changed the way he saw himself and the world. It nearly broke him to pull away from all of that richness, that wealth of words and depth of awareness. Now, looking at his empty glass, a snippet of Thomas MacDonagh came to him:

Though they say that a sot like myself is curst—
I was sober a while, but I'll drink and be wise
For I fear I should die in the end of thirst.

Kee went back into the pub and poured himself the next of many of the day's whiskeys.

· · ·

The sound of the phone ringing awakened Kee from the kind of dead sleep that only hard labor or alcohol can induce. In his case it was both. He was sorely tempted to let the phone ring itself out, but the caller might be Maureen. She'd been living in the North for a few years, God help her, and rang up only when she needed money. Maureen was more of a worry than ever but he still adored her and missed her. She was all the family he had left.

Kee groaned as he pulled his six-and-a-half-foot-tall body off the sitting-room sofa, which was as far as he'd gotten when attempting to go to bed after locking up. He glanced at his new digital clock, glowing red in the darkness: 3:36 a.m. A devil's hour. He groped his way through the swinging door into the pub, to the wall phone hanging behind the bar.

"Hello?" he said grumpily into the receiver, then was immediately put on his guard as the line crackled and he heard police sirens in the background. He didn't even feel himself slip to the icy stone floor as a strange girl's voice apologized for waking him before she broke down crying and told him that Maureen was dead.

"It was a bomb. A fecking IRA bomb," the girl choked out.

"It . . . it blew them apart. Oh, God . . . I am so sorry. Jaysus! This is the worst thing I've ever had to do . . ."

Kee closed his eyes against blinding whiteness. He swallowed hard to keep his emotions in check. Not yet. He wouldn't give in to it yet. The girl's wracked voice went on and on. "It was a nightclub. They were after the soldiers; she was going around with them. I fecking warned her over and over but she'd never listen . . ." He could hear more sirens and the soft whimpering of a child in the background. Sweet Maureen! How was it possible? With her easy laughter and rebellious ways that used to drive him to distraction. Gone. In a puff of hate-filled smoke. An invisible fist pressed into his chest, making it difficult to breathe. It was the pain of knowing that an eternal void would haunt his life from this moment forward.

He knew he couldn't listen to this girl's voice or that child's wailing any longer. It was like an echo of his own pain. "I'll come see to things. Thanks . . . thanks for ringing me."

Kee started to get up off the floor to hang up the phone when he heard the young woman cry out, "Wait! For God's sake! What about Susan?"

He put the phone to his ear again, confused. "What are you saying? Who's Susan?"

"Oh, Christ, are you telling me that Maureen never told you she had a kid? I've got her here with me now. You'll come and take her, you will? I can be waiting for you here at the police station in Comagh."

Kee felt light-headed and sat down on the cold stone floor again. "Wait . . . wait a minute . . . Jesus God," he mumbled into the phone.

"Bloody hell, I never thought she hadn't told you. Always saying you were so close, she was."

So close. A sister he had cherished and to whom he had

been both brother and father. A sister that he hadn't seen for almost three years—and only once in the two years before that—because she liked to be free, had gone "in search of herself." So close. And yet she had never told him she'd had a child.

The girl spoke again, coaxingly now. "Ah, Mr. Doyle—you'll take her home with you, ya? I've told the police that there's no one else, you're her only family. I was babysitting tonight for her when . . . when it happened. Christ, I almost decided to go along! But Maureen told me how much she looked up to you. You'll come, won't you? She's a good baby, poor wee thing. Almost two now, she is. Next week is her birthday, I think, or the week after, maybe. I have to get out of here and go to work later. You'll be coming, then?"

"Yes, yes!" Kee snapped. "I'm coming, woman! I'm leaving now."

He hauled his huge body up from the floor and fumbled hanging up the phone. He leaned over the bar and laid his cold, sweaty forehead against the smooth polished wood. *Christ, why didn't she tell me? How could she be keeping something like that from me? I wouldn't have judged her. I wouldn't have.* But even as he thought it, he faltered. What would he really have said or done? *Well, it fecking doesn't matter now.* He had to get to Comagh as soon as he could. He had to go and make arrangements for what was left of Maureen's body. He had to begin the job of raising Maureen's child.

PART ONE

SIOBHAN

CHAPTER 1

Come away, O human child!
To the woods and waters wild
With a faery, hand in hand,
For the world's more full of weeping than you can
understand.

— W. B. YEATS

Siobhan breathed in the cool lough mist, feeling the moistness fill her lungs and seep into her soul. It was her tonic. Sitting on the low stone wall that hugged the lee side of the lough, she was surrounded by the mist. In grammar school, when she had studied Saint Francis and learned how he had referred to other creatures as Brother Otter or Sister Dove, she started to think of the mist as Sister Mist.

The lough shore was Siobhan's favorite of all her special places. It was here that the poems came to her. She felt them emerge from the mist, or rise from the surface of the water, or descend from the surrounding mountains. They nestled in her mind because she welcomed them gently, nurturing and encouraging, so that when she put pen to paper she only had to write down what was already inside her.

But today she felt an unfamiliar longing, not the secure serenity she always associated with this place. It made her uneasy. Siobhan had always been content here, living with Uncle Keenan by the shores of her lough. Why today did she feel as if a strange new dimension had thrust its way into her life? A sense no longer of just living but of waiting. Waiting for something—or someone. Siobhan was wary of strangers.

. . .

For more than three hundred years imperceptible evolution, like water on a stone, had transformed the Leeside from an old coaching inn into a quiet neighborhood pub. In its early days it sheltered travelers between Clifden and Galway, and secretly harbored the occasional smuggler. But the nineteenth-century famine and poverty in the west, followed by the advent of motorized transport, had isolated it from all but the locals, who finally claimed it as their own. So for the people who had known it all their lives, the pub was the same now as it had always been. Siobhan loved that about the Leeside; it was her rock, her island. Uncle Kee had enisled them both upon it.

Siobhan was, at this moment, standing behind the bar, washing the interminable glasses. She looked around, as she often did, silently chanting her self-made mantra: "I love living here. I can't imagine living anywhere else. I love living here. I can't image living anywhere else. I love living here . . ." Each rendition was another granite pebble in her wall of isolation, another layer of protection.

Siobhan knew that oddness was the cornerstone of her identity. She felt strangers smell her apprehension. People who knew her tolerated her introversion, but to many it seemed out of place in someone who worked in a pub. Siobhan tolerated contact with people she knew for the simple reason that they were unavoidable. Her interactions with friends of her uncle or regulars at the pub were mere ripples on the surface of her sea-chasm of isolation. She smiled vaguely at jokes, ignored banter, and often appeared to be of subnormal intelligence with her air of detached, blank pleasantness. She caught the fleeting looks of puzzlement or pity, and was unconcerned by them. Siobhan knew she was peculiar. How could it have been otherwise? She had no mother. For her, this explained everything. How could she be like the other children? *She had no mother.* For that matter, she had no father either, only Uncle Kee. She'd lived with him since a week before her second birthday, twenty-five years ago.

Siobhan couldn't remember that day. Uncle Kee never talked about it. On her seventh birthday—her "golden birthday," seven on the seventh of April—she'd nerved herself to ask him the question. What she wanted as a gift this year was information.

"Uncle Kee, why did Mamsy die?"

Holding hands, they were standing next to her mother's grave, which was next to her grandparents', in Saint Brendan's churchyard. They visited the graves each year on Siobhan's birthday, early in the morning. Looking down at her, he gave the bare bones of an explanation as to how her mother died, and why she had come to live with him. "Mamsy died in an IRA bombing . . . and also your da. So I came to fetch you to come live here with me."

He squeezed her hand and she regarded him with wide, grave eyes. "Why isn't my da buried here as well?"

Uncle Kee blinked and shifted his gaze to the headstone: HERE LIES MAUREEN NORA DOYLE. BELOVED DAUGHTER, SISTER, AND MOTHER. FLYING WITH THE ANGELS. After a moment or two he cleared his throat and shrugged slightly. "I never knew him, love." He squeezed her hand again and smiled down at her. "So, there you are, then. Any questions?" *Only a thousand.* "Right. Off to school with you."

They turned and began walking toward the school. So that was that. He had explained matters—but not actually answered her question. As she let go of his hand to go inside, he suddenly squatted down.

"One more thing, love. You're seven now and I should be telling you this. I named you Siobhan. Your mamsy and her . . . your da called you Susan. But it didn't suit you at all. Not in my book. So I named you after Auntie Siobhan."

"Susan is an English name," she said.

"Aye."

Siobhan nodded and left him. She understood that Uncle Kee wouldn't want her to have an English name. *Susan.* She puzzled over the word. It sounded vaguely familiar but that was all. It held no value or singular meaning. It didn't sound like a real name, not the name of anyone she would know.

But she had gotten some answers because now she was seven and had been brave enough to ask. The reason she had no mother was because her mum had been killed. *Killed.* Not just died of cancer or in childbirth or something ordinary like that. She'd been killed—and not by getting hit by a bus crossing the road or in a car smash. By a bomb—*an IRA bomb.* Siobhan knew what the IRA was, of course. She always watched the evening news in the pub and read the newspapers. Uncle Kee never censored her reading material. The more she knew about the world outside, he said, the more she would appreciate living at the Leeside. In fact, he often pointed out news stories about young women being killed or hurt. Once he even told her about a former girlfriend of his who'd been murdered in Dublin. "Picked the wrong bastard to fall in love with, she did. Some people wear charm like a second skin and that kind are always trouble, darlin'. Just another reason to give most folks a wide berth."

Soon after her birthday Siobhan started writing MMWK-BAB in tiny letters in her school notebooks, which stood for My Mother Was Killed By A Bomb. Tiny, tiny letters they were, in the margins of all her notebooks. Finally, inevitably, she wrote it on her arm in indelible ink, like a brand. In her neatest printing, as if she were proud of it. But she kept it carefully hidden under the long starched sleeve of her white uniform blouse. After two weeks it was still there; she was careful to wash around it. Then one of the nuns noticed it.

"What's that writing on your arm? Are you cheating, Siobhan?"

No, no, Sister. Just doodling, I am.

Sister Mary Sebastian helped her wash it off in the girl's bathroom with strong yellow soap and righteous scrubbing, until her skin was butcher raw.

Thank you, Sister.

. . .

Siobhan finished drying the last of the glasses; they hung like jewels in their appointed places. She always did her work thoroughly and well, not for her own satisfaction but to ease Uncle Kee's burden and because of Time. Siobhan and Time were kindred spirits. It wound itself slowly around her, never varying its pace in her universe. Time stretched itself, unfolding and expanding, luxuriating in its freedom from its own boundaries. For Siobhan, Time was a friend and, in its turn, Time bestowed itself like a gift on her and never outpaced her, as she saw it do to so many others.

The glasses finished, Siobhan went through the swinging door into the kitchen to prepare the meat pies and sausage rolls for tonight's customers. Because she could daydream, Siobhan preferred cleaning to cooking; the latter demanded her full attention. Once, when she was seventeen, she mortified herself and Uncle Kee by forgetting to add salt and suet to the meat pies—they were inedible. She had never forgotten his pained, humiliated expression, although he had murmured to her that it was all right. She had solemnly vowed never to let it happen again.

The back door banged and she heard Uncle Kee's voice coming from the mudroom.

"Siobhan! What are you doing?"

"I'm cutting the meat for the pies. Why?"

His ruddy face ducked into the doorway, wearing a pleased expression. "Because I've got news, darlin'. We're going to have a guest tomorrow. An overnight guest here at the pub. So we'll have to clean out that extra room."

"A guest?" Siobhan looked at him blankly, her bloodstained hands paused in her work. She felt the familiar tightening in her stomach. A stranger? Staying here at the Leeside?

"Is it someone we know?" Siobhan asked without hope.

Uncle Kee shook his big head. "No, but don't be afraid, now. It'll not be like that other time. It's someone we'll both enjoy meeting. An American professor of Irish studies. He wants to come here to meet me. Sean is sending him down."

"But we don't let rooms," she said tonelessly.

"I know," he said quickly. "But it's only for two nights, and Sean says he's great altogether. He's been staying in Clifden and eating at Sean's restaurant every night for a week. Sean told him about our study of Irish literature and he wants to come. It'll be grand, you'll see."

Siobhan looked at her uncle's flushed face, trying to push down the panic. He didn't get excited very often. Having the man to stay would be all right. She wouldn't mind, she *wouldn't*. It would be all right—no need to have doubts. This professor and Uncle Kee would spend all their time together talking about his greatest hobby, the study of Irish literature. This was an interest she herself shared, especially poetry. She took a deep breath.

"It does sound grand, Uncle Kee. You'll have a brilliant time with the man. Are you knowing anything else about him?" She resumed her slicing carefully, her hands shaking a little. Not everyone was like that other man.

"I'll tell you later at tea. I'll just be clearing the junk out of that room from now until then. Then we can give it a good going-over together, so." He started pulling off his muddy boots.

"Right."

Uncle Kee started up the back stairs and Siobhan heard his head smack against a low beam.

"Ah, goddammit!" she heard him mutter.

Siobhan smiled in spite of herself at his outburst. She thought he must be very excited to forget to watch his head going up the stairs. Keenan Doyle had to be careful coming through the doorways of the Leeside, too, for he wasn't a thread under six foot six and the Leeside was built in the days when he would have been considered a giant. He always seemed to fill any room he was in, and told her many times how his mother lamented that she'd spawned a son who didn't fit the scale of their home. *We should have named you after the giant Finn MacCool*, she'd say. Uncle Kee himself often commented drily that he'd developed quite a thick skull from cracking his head on the low oak beams.

But Siobhan loved his bigness, his protective bulk. She vaguely remembered when she was very small, being awed by his size and amazed by the gentleness of his touch. He acted as if he were afraid of breaking her, wondering at her little-girl fragility. She, in turn, had been circumspect in her physical approach to him, sensing his strength and power. He would never hurt her intentionally, this she knew, but his massive size was daunting and she was shy of it, though not of him. Her mother had been tiny, as Siobhan was, and Siobhan remembered her quicksilver touch, sometimes impatient, tugging her here and there, pulling or pushing on clothes and shoes, snatching Siobhan up to bestow quick hugs and kisses.

As she grew older, Siobhan was less intimidated by Uncle Kee's size and began to delight in his bulk, climbing around on him as if he were a living set of monkey bars. She felt like a feather in his strong hands. She sensed that he loved her small-ness and she was glad she wasn't growing much taller. They were comfortable with each other's sizes. Then as her school years progressed, and Siobhan became prepubescent, she grew reticent about physical play with him after the nuns taught *proper behavior* for young ladies. Strange, mysterious feelings were eluded to with sinister ambiguity. This new physical shyness began her retreat within.

Siobhan brushed a stray wisp of her black hair from her face. She wore it pulled back most of the time to keep it out of her way. Her hair hung almost to her knees and when unte-thered, draped like a cloak around her. She was a tiny, pale woman with grave, clouded eyes and limbs like kindling. Her one friend, Maura Doherty, once told her that for a long time she'd thought Siobhan was a fairy or kelpie who would one day disappear back into her fairy mound to be lost forever. They had laughed at the silliness of it.

Years of helping Uncle Kee in the pub had developed Siob-han's stamina; she was much stronger than she looked. From a very early age she was determined to help him, to do her part, to make his life easier. His grateful smiles were the sun in her world.

After the meat pies had baked, Siobhan escaped outside to sit in one of the old basket chairs. The Leeside was a plain, two-story pub, built of gray stone with a slate roof. It sat within an embrace of hills, at once soft and rugged, at the edge of a dark, narrow lough. The pale sky spread like a domed canopy over it all and sent breezes down to ripple the surface of the water and the surrounding tall grasses in concordant rhythm. The pub wasn't situated in the village of Carnloe itself but was almost two miles down the lough road, which was little more than a cart track. This enhanced its atmosphere of isolation.

Siobhan's heart always lifted, she could feel it physically rise in her breast, whenever she gazed upon her lough. She thought of it as *her* lough. She'd written about it once but never could she bring herself to share her poems. They were part of her essence that she carried deep inside.

> *The lough was narrow, deep and primordial,*
> *An unexpected fragment of sea allowed in by the ancient glacial*
> *   shifting of land. When at long last the earth settled,*
> *The lough was trapped there, surrounded by the ice-sired*
> *   mountains.*
> *But Nature was not so cruel as to separate the lough from its*
> *   mother ocean.*
> *A small river was left as a lifeline,*
> *And now the lough welcomed fresh waters from its companion*
> *   mountains,*
> *Feeding them to its progenitor. And the lough was content.*

She was intimate with all its moods, serene under a quiet sky or battling a tempest. She loved it as she loved Uncle Kee.

The day was monochromic; pearl gray air and water, the

hues of the surrounding hills subdued in acid tones. The earlier mists had coalesced and matured into a cool, steady drizzle, and the atmosphere was muggy, heavy with moist anticipation of things to come.

She could see Blasket, her pony, stilled on his familiar knoll, the only movement coming from his swishing brown tail. A Connemara pony, he was sturdy and sure-footed, serene and secure. He and Siobhan understood each other. Part of that understanding was keeping their distance, since Connemaras liked to roam free. But when Siobhan needed to ride with a primeval urgency, the pony absorbed her emotions and ran like a demon, leaving her spirit soothed. Matching the rhythm of her breathing with his and the pulsing beat of his hooves were her only coupling with freedom. For herself she did not seek it, but an occasional taste of his was frighteningly heady.

As Siobhan sat looking at him, the restlessness invaded her limbs and the urge to ride came upon her. A whistle and clap of hands were all that was needed to bring Blasket to her side. Because of her tiny size she always mounted from the stone wall, and then they were off, the free yet devoted pony and his bareback rider. Siobhan reveled in the sweat-tanged smell of him and the velvet moistness of his hide.

But today she didn't ride as long as she normally would. She had the spare room to prepare. As she turned Blasket toward home, she saw her uncle waving at her from an upper window. Time to get ready for the stranger, she thought. Siobhan didn't want him at the Leeside but for Uncle Kee's sake she'd have to bear it. She would bear anything for Uncle Kee.

After she slid off Blasket's back, he trotted away, full of pent-up energy. As she climbed the back stairs with her bucket and rags she was wishing the man wasn't an American. Her mind, so well trained to lock away unpleasant memories, sprang open suddenly to reveal the leering face of the Alabama tourist who, seven years ago, had lunged at her in the dark hallway. She had been petrified into immobility, neither making a sound nor trying to fight the man off. Only when the man's wife heard him laugh and came out of their room did he stop kissing and fondling her. His apology went unheard over the rushing of blood in Siobhan's ears. Flattening herself against the wall, she had slowly walked backward to her own room, not understanding his wife's accusing stare. She locked her door, placed a chair in front of it, wrapped herself in her duvet, and sat on the floor all night in front of the open window, shivering but not from the cold. Siobhan was unable to block the nauseating memory of the man's hand squeezing and roughly rubbing her breast. No one had ever touched her there before, not even she, herself. No one was ever supposed to.

Siobhan didn't know what to do. But she knew she couldn't tell Uncle Kee. He would kill the man and then be sent to jail. The next morning the couple checked out, three days early. Siobhan couldn't keep any food down that day, and finally told her uncle what had happened. The depth of his rage was biblical; the barstool that the man had sat on was smashed against the stone wall. Uncle Kee tore the bedclothes from the guestroom bed and burned them behind the shed. He canceled all the people who had booked the room for the remainder of the season.

They hadn't had overnight guests since. Until now.

CHAPTER 2

We sat together at one summer's end,
That beautiful mild woman, your close friend,
And you and I, and talked of poetry.

—W. B. YEATS

S iobhan urged her bike down the road toward the
Leeside. She was coming home from babysitting
for Triona, the four-year-old daughter of her
friends Maura and Brendan. She loved taking care of Triona,
but she wished Maura hadn't needed her today. The American
professor was arriving.

Siobhan had listened to her uncle talk about the man and
was now oddly eager to meet him. It was a foreign sensation.
She pictured him as an older, learned man, with white hair and
glasses, someone who had devoted his long life to the study of
her beloved ancient Ireland. She had, over the last twenty-four
hours, become keenly aware that this was a unique opportunity
to talk to someone who had great knowledge of ancient Irish
poetry and folklore, a knowledge even greater than Uncle Kee's.
(Was there disloyalty in that thought?) There were so many
questions she wanted to ask the man. She hoped she would not
feel shy of him.

Siobhan rounded a bend and looked about her. No matter

how occupied her thoughts were along this road, she still gazed with a wonder that familiarity never dimmed. The hues of hills and lough were brilliant today, for the sky prism was full of sun. The golden light spread its translucency like sweet honey, warming every rock pore, seeping into every blade of sea grass, reflecting every gentle swell of water. Siobhan felt the strength of the sun's warmth on her face and arms. Usually she pre-ferred the moon's cool, shadowy glow, but today the sunlight heightened her senses and quickened her pulse. She smelled the heat of it in the skin on her arms and felt her cheeks flush with it. Its shimmer danced into her eyes and brain. Cloud shadows flowed in and out of focus, gentle links between earth and sky.

Siobhan realized with surprise that she was excited. She was excited to meet this man. Despite the warmth on her skin, she shivered. And pedaled harder.

Almost home now, she saw a strange car sitting in the yard. He was here then. She felt an odd fluttering in her stomach. She coasted to a stop by the side of the pub, near the vend-ing machine of candy and crisps that Uncle Kee had installed there a couple of years ago. Their visitor sat comfortably on the lough wall. Siobhan carefully leaned her bike against the side of the building. She wanted to go over to him; she *wanted* to. How strange. She was unused to surprising herself. Then famil-iar caution took hold and she hesitated, her eyes fixed on the man's back and shoulders. Half turning toward the pub, she thought maybe she would wait until Uncle Kee was around, so he could introduce her. Then she saw the man stretch his arms upward and throw his head back, carefree and relaxed. The simple honesty of the gesture reassured her. There was nothing to be afraid of here. Her feet changed direction and she walked over to where he was sitting. He didn't have white hair. As she approached, he turned his head.

Siobhan saw a bony, tall man, with dark unruly hair and

deep-set eyes. His face was kind, she thought, kind and strong, and looked as though it was very familiar with smiling.

"I thought you'd be older," she found herself saying.

He smiled and she liked the look of it.

"I thought you'd be younger," he replied. "I saw you in the distance on your bike and you looked more like a child. You're Siobhan, of course. I'm Tim Ferris."

She looked at him intently, trying to identify what it was about him that made her not afraid. Because she wasn't, not one little bit. Perhaps it was seeing the outline of his facial bones so clearly under his skin, a sculpture of vulnerability.

He looked at her patiently, attentively. She nodded.

"I've always been a bit wee. But I thought you'd be at least older than Uncle Kee—a learned professor and that."

"Well, it's not hard to be learned at something if that's all you've done with your life." After he said it he looked a little confused, as if he had surprised himself. The look calmed her even more, since she could identify with uncertainty.

"Irish poetry, especially the ancients, is an easy thing to be consumed by," she said slowly. She felt strangely compelled to continue, so she did, carefully and thoughtfully. "It's so full of the beauty and passion of life—it's intense. It lays bare the evolution of the human condition. The more you go studying it, the more there is to find. It's like layers. You uncover more and more and the deeper you go the closer you get to your own soul. That's the power of it—and the pain."

Tim Ferris stared at her, his face plainly showing that he was staggered by this speech. Siobhan was a little staggered herself. She had told him how she *felt* about it. She'd never done that before. Not with anyone. The two pairs of eyes locked in amazement and an urgent awareness. They both knew instinctively that they had vaulted across the tributary of polite convention into deeper waters. For Siobhan, the newness of this was heady, making her breath come a little faster.

He spoke first, with a mystified smile. "You know, all my life I've never been able to fully explain, even to myself, why this interest of mine draws me so . . . obsessively. And now you . . . you just *say* it, plainly and exquisitely, in a few short sentences. I'm astonished. Does it affect *you* like that? I suppose it must, or you wouldn't have said it."

Siobhan nodded slowly as she came forward and tentatively placed her hands on the wall next to him. Odd to feel tentative about touching the wall, her wall, but it seemed so very much his in this moment; and perhaps more odd was her being at ease with that. They were now side by side, their size difference an absurdity—a sapling next to a sycamore.

"Ever since I discovered the ancient Irish poetry and mythology," Siobhan said slowly, barely above a whisper, "it was as if I had been hungry for it and not known." Suddenly she flushed with discomfort. Even she, with little social subtlety, knew instinctively that the conversation was too personal, too revealing. She forced herself to speak casually. "Of course, Uncle Kee has devoted a lifetime to studying Celtic folklore and poetry. He's totally brilliant. He used to read to me endlessly from books about legends and folklore. When I was a wee one, I couldn't go to sleep without a story, and once I learned to read I was never without a book. I'd even read under the covers with a flashlight. We're both hooked."

He laughed then and she smiled.

He said, "It is easy to get hooked."

"It is," she replied. There was a pause; she was anxious with embarrassment now.

Then Tim Ferris said, "It's understandable, though, isn't it? After all . . ." He began to quote:

"We are the music-makers
And we are the dreamers of dreams,
Wandering by lone sea-breakers,
    And sitting by desolate streams . . ."

He had chosen one of her favorite poems. Siobhan finished the first verse with him and their voices echoed across the water:

"World-losers and world-foresakers,
On whom the pale moon gleams:
Yet we are the movers and shakers
    Of the world for ever, it seems."

Siobhan refused to look at him then and backed away from the wall, saying, "I'd best go get the tea ready." She left him as suddenly as she'd arrived. Fleeing to the kitchen, she leaned on the table with both hands flat and noticed that they were trembling. How wonderful—how *wonderful* it had been to say the words out loud like that! With him. How tremendously wonderful. She turned her head so she could see him through the window. Her heart lifted as it did when she gazed upon her lough, but that wasn't what she was looking at. Siobhan pressed her hands to her face to steady them and felt the warm tingle of blood in her cheeks. There was so much he must know, so much he could teach her. As she watched, he suddenly hopped down from the stone wall and walked toward the back door. She froze for a moment, then seized the electric kettle and filled it with water.

He came in, almost apologetically. "I hope I'm not in the way. Your uncle said I could use the back door."

She couldn't look at him. "No, that's fine."

"I was enjoying the view but then I felt a little lonely." His voice sounded puzzled.

There was a silence, then Siobhan said a little breathlessly, "You're welcome to stay."

"Stay?" He sounded puzzled again.

"I mean here, in the kitchen, if you've a mind to." She didn't know if she wanted him to stay with her or not. Her hands still trembled slightly as she got the rashers of bacon out of the refrigerator.

"Oh! Well, thanks. I think I will." He sat down in what was usually *her* chair. "This is a wonderful old place. Seventeenth century, isn't it?"

"Yes." This was easier; Siobhan was used to telling people about the history of the Leeside. She recited her little piece. "It was built around 1682. The lough has sea access; there's a bit of a river estuary at the far end that leads into Kilkieran Bay. Lots of smuggling went on back then, so we suspect this place was used for dark dealings. There's a good cellar under this floor where they were probably hiding the goods. But its main use was as a coaching inn."

"I see."

Siobhan glanced at him covertly and saw that he was staring into space, nodding. He spoke, but she wasn't sure he was talking to her. She had the distinct impression that he was simply saying his thoughts out loud.

"This is a remarkable place. There's an uncanny atmosphere—it's at once isolated and yet complete. Rather intriguing. Yes, very intriguing."

Siobhan didn't respond but concentrated on her cooking. It was nice that he felt he could be alone with his thoughts, and yet with her at the same time. She was hungry for his thoughts. She could absorb them into herself without disturbing him. All she wanted at this moment was to hear his voice go on talking. Siobhan carefully turned the rashers in the pan and felt her whole body rejoice as he continued, though he spoke barely above a whisper.

"I had the oddest feeling when I first drove up over the rise and saw this place. I was suddenly seized with the temptation to turn around and drive away. It was as if the scene before me was so perfect that I myself would spoil it by entering. Such a lovely picture of sunlight and water, and the hills and the little stone building. It was the first time in all my travels in Ireland that I felt like I was trespassing. I felt that if I left then, right at that moment, I knew I'd still keep this place forever inside me."

Siobhan did not move, her fork poised over the sizzling pan. Her heart raced at the beauty of his words. Here was someone else who thought the Leeside was perfect, and he had only just seen it for the first time today! A little thrill of fear shot through her as she thought of him driving away and not coming here. She would never have met him. He began to quote the poet Yeats, still in that soft, elusive voice.

"The wind is old and still at play
While I must hurry upon my way,
For I am running to Paradise;
Yet never have I lit on a friend
To take my fancy like the wind
That nobody can buy or bind:
And there the king is but as the beggar."

"Oh, yes!" Siobhan spun around from the stove, her eyes shining. "Yes, that's exactly it!"

Tim Ferris looked up at her and his unfocused eyes sharpened with recognition. He was about to speak when Uncle Kee burst into the kitchen from the pub wearing a big smile.

"Did I hear someone quoting W.B.?"

Neither Tim nor Siobhan answered him for a moment, then Tim visibly shook himself.

"Yes, I was. I was trying to convey what this place suggests to me. I was telling Siobhan that it is quite unique."

Kee nodded. "I couldn't call anywhere else home. Come into the pub for a bit so we can chat. I've only got one customer out there, and he's not my favorite person in the world."

Siobhan said, "It must be Niall."

"It is. Come along, Tim. Siobhan, those rashers are burning, love."

She spun back to the stove, flushing with embarrassment, and quickly lifted the pan off the heat. Her heart beat fast. He understood! Her soul floated free with the wonder of it. Who *was* this man, that he could understand and appreciate her home with such keenness when he had never been here before? And . . . and could he understand . . . her? She could feel the difference in herself when she talked to him. Her shyness with him came and went like swells of the sea, it surged up and she became tongue-tied, but then ebbed away as his conversation pulled her out of herself. She propped open the swinging door that led from the kitchen to the bar so she could listen to the conversation as she made potato cakes.

"Would you be wanting a drink, Tim?" she heard Uncle Kee ask him. "A welcome drink, on the house."

"On the house?" a young man's voice exclaimed, before Tim could answer. That would be Niall. "Since when are you a one for giving drinks away?"

"Shut up, Niall. Professor Ferris is our guest, is all."

"I'd like a drink," Tim said quickly. "What do you have besides Guinness?"

Niall asked with a trace of a sneer, "What's the matter, then? Guinness too strong for you?"

"No, I like it. In fact, it's all I've been drinking for the past five weeks."

Uncle Kee said, "You'll be wanting a change. I've got something I think you'll like. Have you ever had a Murphy's stout?"

"I don't think so."

"Well, you'll have it now."

Niall spoke, again with a sneer. "So, what are you *professor* of?"

"Irish and Celtic studies. I teach college in the States."

"Irish studies, eh? What about this, then?" Niall spoke the next sentence in rather halting Irish: "I'll bet you don't know half of what Doyle here knows about all that."

Siobhan heard the smile in Tim's voice as he replied in Irish, "Probably not. That's why I'm here, to learn what Mr. Doyle has to teach me."

Uncle Kee shouted with laughter. He couldn't abide Niall. He said, "Drink up, Niall, and be on your way. You'll be late for work."

Niall blustered, "How the hell was I supposed to know—"

"You weren't. And it's no surprise to me that you're capable of making an eejit out of yourself in the Irish as well as English."

"Oh, sod off, Doyle."

Siobhan heard Niall bang down his glass and thump out the door.

"Sorry about that, Tim," Uncle Kee said.

"That's okay. It was pretty funny. And you were right about this stout, it's great. Won't you join me?"

"I no longer imbibe, thank you kindly."

"Oh." Tim sounded blank. "Well, a soft drink then?"

"Not at the moment, thanks. You speak the Irish well."

Tim sounded rueful as he said, "It took a long time to learn, I can tell you that. I was lucky enough in grad school to have a prof from Cork. He spoke some Irish, although not very fluently. But when I told him I wanted to really learn the language he sent away for a set of Irish Gaelic language tapes. But learning to speak it and learning to read it were two completely separate undertakings."

Uncle Kee laughed. "It certainly is not the most phonetic of languages."

"No."

"But it's beautiful. I've heard some people say it's too guttural, like German."

"That's not true," Tim protested. "The sounds are much softer, if it's spoken correctly."

"That's what I say," Uncle Kee replied, sounding pleased. "Siobhan!"

She jumped at the sound of her name.

"Siobhan, where's tea, child?"

"It's ready now, if you'll come," she replied, grabbing plates from the cupboard.

The three of them sat around the kitchen table to a meal of potato cakes with greens, bacon, and scones. Siobhan felt much more shy of Tim with her uncle there, and she had a vague idea that it would be best if Uncle Kee didn't sense her interest in the man. The three of them sat in the kitchen, with the door to the pub open so her uncle could watch for customers. Since it was Thursday, he told Tim, there probably wouldn't be anyone but a few regulars coming in tonight.

The talk soon turned to Tim's reason for coming to the Leeside. Siobhan heard his voice grow warm with devotion as he described his curriculum, and what he tried to give his students by way of appreciation for Irish literature, especially the ancient poetry. His hosts asked him questions and gave suggestions, and soon all three were in the midst of the most amazing conversation Siobhan had ever experienced. There was no shyness left in her as she took her place beside the two men in intelligence and scope. Nothing mattered but this shimmering exchange of knowledge, ideas, and interpretations. She could see that there were times when Tim was surprised at the depth of their knowledge, and his reaction added fuel to her zeal.

"There's such a seamless intermingling of what's historically real with the supernatural lore. The two great annals of old Irish romantic writing have their basis in historical fact but are then taken into flights of fairy fantasy—much like *The Iliad* and *The Odyssey*, don't you think?" Siobhan looked eagerly at Tim.

He nodded slowly. "I make that same comparison in my Early Irish Poetry class. The intimate and detailed description of fairy cavalcades, for example. I also try to tie in references to Tolkien's *Hobbit* and C. S. Lewis's Narnia books to help the students identify with, as you say, the seamless mingling of history and fantasy."

Siobhan dismissed Lewis out of hand, but agreed that Tolkien's depth of detail was a valid comparison. "His use of language doesn't compare, of course. The language of that early Irish poetry is so brilliant and glowing." And so the conversation continued, flitting back and forth, impatient, eager, excited, fulfilling.

Uncle Kee had to jump up and serve one or two customers who came in, so there were times when Tim and Siobhan continued the discussion alone. During these intervals Siobhan talked more, almost basking in the rays of Tim's obvious appreciation. She found she could even joke with him, and after making him laugh at a humorous interpretation, she looked at herself in wonder. Was this *her*, Siobhan Doyle, sitting here talking with a stranger and feeling perfectly at ease? The thought made her pause, and when she did, Tim leaned back in his chair and gazed at her. Suddenly she didn't feel at ease any longer, as his expression made her scalp tingle.

"You know," he began, "your input is completely unique, yours and Kee's. Your perspective comes from devotion, not scholarship, unlike so many of my colleagues. You have no agenda, no desire to further your theories at the expense of others. You're so open, so passionate—and incredibly knowledgeable. I'm stunned. It's like finding buried treasure."

Siobhan didn't reply and couldn't return his gaze. Insanely pleased at his words, she wanted to thank him, but the words wouldn't come. The timidity had returned.

Eventually the pub became busy enough that Uncle Kee had to stay behind the bar. He invited Tim to join the group of customers in the pub common room. Siobhan hesitated before entering the public area, as she always did, taking stock of who was present. Regulars all, many she'd known her whole life, and yet she had perpetually hovered in the doorway of their lives. She now slipped into her role of quiet observer, watching Tim's reactions to their little circle of regulars.

"Now then," Uncle Kee began, "this here is Professor Timothy Ferris. A man who enjoys an impressive font of knowledge regarding Irish literature and such. But he also is a man with enough humility and good sense to realize that I might possess wisdom and insight in that direction that he does not."

"What are you saying, then?" asked Katie O'Farrell, sitting at the corner of the bar. "He's come to sit at the feet of the master?" She gave Uncle Kee a teasing look.

"Well, Katie, I wouldn't put it quite that way, but he's interested in what I have to say. Which is more than can be said of certain people around here."

Katie said mischievously, "Well, this is the most I've heard you talk in quite a while, I'll say that. So I'm favorably disposed toward Professor Ferris already."

"Please call me Tim."

Siobhan frowned into the glass she was cleaning at the easy charm in his voice.

Katie got up and sat next to him. Siobhan stiffened. "I'm Katie O'Farrell. It's grand to meet you, Tim."

Siobhan watched as they shook hands, feeling a vague resentment. Katie was an old friend of Uncle Kee's, about his age, a sharp-edged predator with short reddish brown hair. Siobhan had always admitted grudgingly that she was good-looking in a ruddy, outdoors sort of way.

Katie continued: "And since Keenan Francis here didn't think to introduce any of us, allow me."

Uncle Kee gave her a mock scowl. Katie gestured to the thin, fair young man sitting at the bar on Tim's other side.

"That's Brendan Doherty," she said, and the two men greeted each other. "Brendan's our commuter. He lives in Carnloe but drives into Clifden every day. He's an accountant, and he and his wife have a little daughter so lovely it almost makes me wish I had one. How is Triona, Brendan? She had a bit of a cold at her riding lesson this week."

"She's better, thanks," Brendan answered.

"That's grand. Now that couple there in the booth," Katie continued, "are John and Mary Kelleher. They live in Ballynaross, which is about six kilometers east of here. They hail from Boston and, ignoring God and everyone, decided to retire here."

Tim swung around on his barstool and smiled at them. The couple nodded at him cordially. Katie came around the counter behind the bar—which Siobhan always hated—and picked up a knife to slice some ham. Uncle Kee was drawing another pint. Siobhan tried not to glare at Katie, but it was difficult. She saw Tim's eyes on her, questioning. He was about to speak and Siobhan quickly asked him if he'd like another Murphy's stout.

She didn't want to talk about . . . about poetry and such things *here*, in front of everyone. He looked faintly surprised but accepted another stout, getting out his wallet as he spoke.

"Yes, please. But no more on the house. Would you like to join me?"

Siobhan felt Katie's sharp eyes on the two of them. She shook her head, feeling the rising flush in her cheeks. She began to draw Tim's stout at the other end of the bar.

Uncle Kee asked Brendan if he wanted another as the young man drained his glass.

"No, thanks. I'm off home. Siobhan, I'll take five of the meat pies to go. Maura was busy with her dad today. She had to take him to the dentist, so I told her I'd bring home some dinner."

"Right." Siobhan went into the kitchen and Uncle Kee finished drawing Tim's pint. Siobhan heard Katie ask Tim if he was hungry.

"I'm just making myself a ham sandwich," Katie said. "I can make one for you as well." Siobhan tensed, listening for Tim's response.

"I'm not hungry, thanks," he replied easily. "I had a wonderful tea with Kee and Siobhan. That'll hold me for the night, I think."

As Siobhan peered through the doorway she saw Katie's eyes rake his tall, thin frame. "You don't look like you eat enough to keep a bird alive."

Tim smiled. "Oh, I do. I just burn it off. Nervous energy."

Siobhan hurried out of the kitchen carrying a paper bag. "There you are, Brendan. Five pies. Mind, the bottom's hot." Brendan paid the fifteen euro for them and picked up the bag.

Katie asked him, "Why five pies? It's just you and Triona and Maura and her dad, isn't it? That's four. Niall's working tonight."

Brendan flashed a smile. "I eat two." He banged out the door.

Tim asked, "Niall? Is that the Niall who was in here earlier?"

Uncle Kee nodded. "That's Maura's younger brother. Not good for much."

"He lives with them?"

"They all live together in Seamus Curry's house, that's Maura and Niall's da. He's getting on and is a bit poorly, so Maura looks after him. Brendan's okay with the arrangement since they'll get the house when Seamus dies. Then maybe they can throw Niall out on his arse."

"Oh, Niall's not so bad," Katie protested. "He's good with the ponies when I need an extra hand. And that part-time job at the fish-and-chips shop in Ballynaross was all he could find, you know."

Uncle Kee responded drily, "Oh, and I know he looked high and low for it. Besides, he's our quality-control expert. He tests all the new barrels of stout to make sure we're up to standard."

Katie chided him. "Will you leave off Niall?"

"Fine, fine. I never took to the lad, that's all."

"You've just never forgiven him for breaking one of your windows when he was twelve."

"That as well."

Katie laughed and pushed against him with her shoulder. Siobhan's stomach turned over as it always did when she saw them touch. "You're hopeless." Katie bit enthusiastically into her enormous ham sandwich. Siobhan hated the way Katie commanded attention, either cheaply, by flirting, or intensely, through her eternal awareness of others. She could see that Tim was curious about Katie.

Sure enough, Tim now asked her, "What do you do for a living around here? You're much too young to be retired, like the Kellehers."

She smiled at him and glanced at Uncle Kee. "Thanks for the compliment. There aren't many going around here. I breed and show ponies, Connemara ponies. I have a place just outside Ballynaross."

"That sounds great. How big is your operation?"

"My operation, is it? That makes it sound very grand. I have twenty-eight right now, twelve of my own and sixteen boarders. Next week is the big show—the Connemara Pony Show in Clifden. It draws buyers from all over the world. I hope to sell quite a few . . . and maybe pick up two or three as well. That reminds me. Siobhan, you'll be coming over on Tuesday and Wednesday to give me a hand, you will?"

As always with Katie it was less of a question than an assumption. Siobhan nodded. She'd go. She always did, for the sake of the ponies.

Katie continued casually: "I don't suppose you want to enter yourself and Blasket in any of the classes? Tomorrow's the deadline so I can still get you in."

Siobhan shook her head without looking at Katie. Tim glanced at her.

"No." Katie sighed theatrically. "I didn't think so. Poor Blasket. When I think of the time I put in on that boy . . ." Siobhan bit her lip until it almost bled.

"Blasket is a pony?" Tim asked, looking at both women.

"He is," Katie replied. "He's Siobhan's. A brilliant animal, but she doesn't like showing him off."

Tim said easily, "Well, some people don't enjoy the competitive aspect of that kind of thing."

Siobhan rewarded him with a look of real gratitude.

"Oh, I know that well," Katie replied acidly. "We've been down that road more times than I like to count. Siobhan's a wonderful rider but doesn't like anyone to know it. Competition's a dirty word in this house."

I'm wishing you were a dirty word in this house, Siobhan thought fiercely, banging shut a drawer.

"Now that's not true, woman," Uncle Kee growled. "There's nothing I like better than a good game of darts. And Siobhan and I are always going at it, having matches between ourselves in our own special field of interest, you might call it. You should see us playing Who Wrote That Stanza? Blood is drawn, I can tell you that."

"Oh, that sounds real exciting," Katie drawled. "Hey, why don't we have a competition between you and Siobhan and Tim here? A battle of the ancient Irish scholars. That would be a lark."

"For who?" Uncle Kee asked. Siobhan knew Katie was baiting him.

"Oh, come on now, Kee. It would be brilliant. You'd enjoy it. Don't say you wouldn't because I'd know you were lying."

Uncle Kee smiled at her. Although she could be provoking, Siobhan knew that Katie amused him considerably. "Well, she's right," Uncle Kee said to Tim. "Could you bear it?"

Siobhan's heart beat faster as she looked at him with alarm. This was a terrifying idea.

Tim said good-naturedly, "Sure, I guess so."

She opened her mouth but closed it again as she caught Katie's warning eye. Katie wanted this. Siobhan's resentment flared sickeningly as it always did when Katie dangled her influence over Uncle Kee, like an apple, in front of her. She turned away.

"Good man yourself," Uncle Kee told Tim.

"But what would it be?" Tim asked. "Like a trivia contest?"

Katie nodded enthusiastically. "Absolutely. It'll be great."

Siobhan forced herself to speak. She had to make this unbearable turn of events somehow bearable.

"I don't want to. It should be just Uncle Kee and . . . and Professor Ferris." Everyone looked at her but she struggled on, keeping her eyes on her uncle. "I mean, someone's got to be the . . . the judge and think up the questions and that. I can do that bit."

Uncle Kee nodded approvingly at her. He understood that she'd not want to be the center of attention. "Good idea, love. We're on then. When shall we have this momentous event?"

"Let's do it tomorrow night," Katie suggested firmly. "There'll be more of a crowd then."

"But the pub's always so busy on Fridays," Siobhan said quickly. "Uncle Kee and I won't have time to—"

"Oh, I'll come behind the bar and help. And Maura can, too. I'm sure she and Brendan will want to be here. It won't be much of an evening unless we get a good crowd. We'll talk it up in Ballynaross, won't we, John?"

"We certainly will," John Kelleher replied. "And now, Katie, we have to get going. If you want a ride back with us, we've got to be on our way."

"Right." She drained her glass.

Uncle Kee asked, "You came with the Kellehers? What's the matter with your Rover?"

"It's in the shop. Needed a new muffler. I can't go hauling ponies over to Clifden next week with a vehicle that sounds like that demented motorbike of Niall's. It'd be giving them all nervous breakdowns. See you tomorrow."

It seemed extraordinarily quiet when they had all gone. Siobhan had been looking forward to everyone leaving, but now that they were gone she had nothing to say to Tim. A *scholars' duel*. It was such a stupid thing to do, such a cheapening of everything she loved. How could Tim and Uncle Kee have agreed? Her disappointment in them both was equally intense.

She glanced at her uncle and could see he was looking rather penitent.

"Heaven knows what I've let us in for, Tim. That Katie can talk a cat away from a fish."

"That's because she's a cat herself," Siobhan said with more spirit than she had intended.

Uncle Kee looked displeased. "Now, now. She just likes her bit of fun."

"But at whose expense? It's a foolish thing."

"She means no harm," he said firmly. "She's a very old friend with the privileges of same."

"Privileges, is it?" Siobhan spoke quietly, with a sideways glance at him.

Tim threw himself into the fray. "I really don't mind. It'll be fun. After all, the three of us are the only ones who'll know what fools we'll make of ourselves."

Uncle Kee smiled. "That's true enough. Siobhan, love, you'll come up with some grand questions for us, won't you now?" He was coaxing her, wheedling her into a better humor. Despite herself she smiled.

"I will then," she said, "and I'll make sure that the odds aren't with the house."

"The devil you will! Well, Professor, we can't say fairer than that."

Tim smiled. "I suppose people will be betting on us."

"They will indeed. But it's harmless enough."

"I'm not so sure of that," Siobhan said. "Uncle Kee, you'd better ring Eamon and Liam—they weren't in at all today."

"I will. Thanks for reminding me." He went to the phone hanging on the far wall.

Tim asked her with a smile, "And who are Eamon and Liam?"

She returned his smile shyly. "They're brothers, old farmers in the district. They usually come in every day, unless one of them isn't well. They live alone, so we try to keep an eye on them."

"That's good of you," Tim said.

"Well, they've known Uncle Kee since he was born. They were friends of his parents'."

Tim hesitated, then asked, "Tell me about your parents. How did you come to live here with your uncle? I don't mean to pry, and don't tell me if you'd rather not. But I'm really interested. In both of you," he added a bit hastily.

She managed to answer him. "I don't mind." She was bemused. He was interested in them, in their history, their lives . . . She wasn't shy about her parents' story since everyone here knew it. "My parents were both killed in an IRA bombing when I was two."

Tim's eyes widened, and he was about to speak again when Uncle Kee hung up the phone and came back to them.

"They're all right. Eamon was a bit under the weather today so they stayed home. They hope to be here tomorrow night with bells on."

Tim Ferris stood up. "I think I'd like some fresh air. Siobhan, would you like to come with me while I stretch my legs?"

At his suggestion, her shyness swelled up once more and swallowed her. She fought against it but in vain. She just couldn't go out with him into the gloaming—alone. It would be too intimate, too intense. The night was her space, always experienced alone. Sitting in the kitchen with him was one thing, but this was entirely different. The lump of terrified ice in her stomach would not thaw, not even in the warmth of Tim's easy smile.

"No." It came out in a whisper. "No, thanks. I've things to see to."

A quick glance at Uncle Kee revealed that he was frowning

slightly, looking at Tim. His voice, so familiar to her, sounded a shade deeper than usual as he said easily, "I'll come with you, Tim. We'll let Siobhan mind the store for a bit. I could use a hand with some kegs in the shed. Would you mind?"

"Sure. Okay."

Did he sound disappointed? Siobhan wondered desperately as she escaped into the kitchen. She wanted so much to make friends with this man. But she didn't know how. Keeping people at a distance was her specialty.

An open cupboard door half caught her attention and she closed it without thinking. But then she slowly opened it again and stared without seeing at the rows of jarred spices. How do people open doors in their lives for other people to step through? With words? What words? She shivered. How chilling it must be to open a door only to have someone pass it by. But how much worse, how infinitely worse, it would be to have someone enter for a time and then go away. Siobhan was comfortable with being ignored. The thought of being acknowledged, and then rejected, was horrific. She shivered again.

Why did the opinion of a total stranger matter so much to her? It never had before. Always she had placed strangers into two categories: those to be feared and those to be ignored. She could not ignore Tim, and didn't want to. But she didn't fear him, either. Was it because he loved what she loved? She *admired* him. Except for Uncle Kee, she couldn't remember admiring anyone in the real world before. Her beloved mythic heroes had captured all her devotion, until now. Siobhan was shocked at how much she wanted to know how Tim perceived her. She recognized herself through the eyes of Uncle Kee, but through the eyes of someone else? Who would she be?

Siobhan railed at her timidity. There was so much she wanted to talk to Tim about. It was never going to happen if she allowed her shyness to dominate her. Before now her self-imposed diffidence with strangers had been born of disinterest. Their presence didn't affect her, it was her choice not to let them in. Now she wanted to let someone in. And much more than examining why, she was concerned whether she should. Why did she need anyone but Uncle Kee to give her life meaning? Was it wrong to feel this way, to want something *more*?

Anxiety came rushing in and she took a deep breath, closing her eyes, using her calm voice. *Now, Siobhan, you can talk to the man on a purely intellectual level. That's all it needs to be. There's nothing wrong with that, nothing frightening. You learned long ago that thinking too much about yourself is dangerous. You know you must travel along the surface of the lough, not explore its depths. The depths lead to drowning.* Siobhan nodded to herself vaguely as she gently shut the cupboard door. *They lead to drowning.*

CHAPTER 3

Love, I shall perfect for you the child
Who diligently potters in my brain . . .

—SEAMUS HEANEY

Siobhan spent Friday morning making pub fare for the evening ahead, her mind racing. She'd had a bad night, restlessly wondering if it would be an "intellectual" decision to show her poetry to Tim. What would he think of it?

She now sat behind the Leeside with a folder of poems on her lap. The weather was misty but the mist had a weakness to it, as though it knew it wouldn't have the strength by noon to withstand the penetrating sun. The day would be warm.

Staring into the glowing air, Siobhan tried to convince herself that all she wanted was Tim's opinion as a teacher and a scholar. Her poems were written in the style of the sixth and seventh centuries, epic poems of heroes and saints, tragic poems of love and poverty, poems of tribute to Ireland's beauty and its sustaining effect on the human spirit. But were they any good? That question had haunted her for years. She had never shown her poems to anyone since she'd left school, not even Uncle Kee. What if she showed them to Tim and he wasn't touched by them? He would be polite, of course, and gracious, because that was the kind of man he was, but when he left he would dismiss them, and her. That was the heart of her dilemma. Secretly she wanted some way, some excuse to stay in touch with him after he'd gone. She didn't want him to disappear from her life. If getting up enough courage to show him her poetry was the only way to accomplish this, she'd just have to push herself to do it.

Last night she ran upstairs to intentionally listen to Uncle Kee and Tim talking out by the shore as the darkness hid them from her view. She shivered as she sat on the floor of her darkened room, below the open window, listening with the alertness of a vigilant animal. She herself was nocturnal but the comfortable dark lost its calm with Tim's presence. Siobhan felt no guilt listening in; she often eavesdropped.

"That's a good night's work," Uncle Kee had remarked. "I thank you for helping me with those loads in the shed. Siobhan is much stronger than she looks but I find I'm not able to lift what I once could. I'm going to be fifty soon and not looking forward to it."

"You're much stronger than I am. You seem very fit to me."

"Oh, aye. I suppose I'm just a bit superstitious about it. My mother died when she was fifty—my father didn't live to see forty-five."

"How did they die?"

"Dad died in a lorry accident. He was a driver for a fish-packing company. And Mum passed away from lung cancer—she smoked like a sack of turf."

"I'm sorry. So Siobhan never knew her parents or her grandparents at all."

Siobhan had held her breath in the pause that followed. Then Tim continued: "What happened to her parents? I hope you don't mind my asking. Were they really killed in a bomb attack? How terrible."

Uncle Kee's voice sounded a trifle gruff. "Aye, t'was terrible."

Still Siobhan dared not breathe. Would he keep on? Would he talk about it, that shadowy dark night? Her breath came out in a gasp as she heard her uncle's voice continue, heavy with resignation. She covered her mouth with her hand.

"My sister, Maureen, left home when she was sixteen. Both our parents were dead by the time she was thirteen. I had to come back from Trinity College to take care of her and run the pub. We'd always been close, she and I, but I had to start being a parent instead of a brother to her. That caused problems. Jesus, I was hardly an adult myself. A free spirit she was, a lover of life. Mum worried about her something chronic. After Maureen left school she started helping me in the pub full time, but she tired of it. Soon after her seventeenth birthday she went to Belfast with a girlfriend, and over the years I saw her only a couple of times." He paused, as if remembering.

Tim said, "That must have been hard."

Uncle Kee's voice was hard to hear. Still with her hand over her mouth, Siobhan had to strain to catch it, pressing her head against the windowsill until her forehead ached.

"It was. I missed her something terrible. She was always one of those people who are the life and soul of a place, you know? But Maureen wanted adventure and excitement. And she got it." His voice sounded like a bitter wind.

"Where was she killed?"

"A nightclub in Comagh. The IRA hit it because it was a British army hangout."

"I'm sorry," Tim had said again. "And Siobhan's father was killed that night, too?"

"That's right," Uncle Kee answered shortly. "He was a Brit—a solider." Then, evidently feeling he had said too much, he forced a laugh. "How did we get on to talking about all this? It's water under the bridge now. Ancient history. I must be more tired than I thought to jabber on like this. Time for bed, I'm thinking. Let's go in."

Siobhan had sat wrapped in bewildered wonder. Never would she have dreamed that Uncle Kee would talk about the past like that, with a stranger, as he never had with her. About her mother and her . . . father. She had never known before that her father had been a British soldier. A momentous revelation— she felt bewildered that Uncle Kee had finally talked to some- one about it, and that the someone wasn't herself. Her heart constricted with the pain of that and also with the new history about her mother.

Sitting behind the pub now she shivered, even as the sun broke through the remaining shreds of defeated mist. What had made him talk about her parents? The story made her heart ache in a strange, soaring way that was difficult to bear. The ache spread out along her bones into her arms and hands, then her legs took the pain and made her thighs tremble. Frightened now, she suddenly wanted to be in the lough, to feel its familiar cold wetness.

Siobhan stood up stiffly and walked straight into the water without any hesitation. She knew where to enter, when the water would come past her ankles, her calves, her knees. She had no memory of being afraid of the water. The lough had been part of her family from early on. As a young child its clean freshness had seemed a miracle; it dispelled the vague recollec- tion of sour smells and the gritty feel of her skin from her days with her mother. The expanse of water before her young eyes went on forever. She didn't mind that it was cold, for it wasn't the inescapable cold of too few clothes and rooms without

KATHLEEN ANNE KENNEY · 52

heat. This cold was glorious, a celebration, full of tingling energy. A rebirth.

Soon Siobhan stopped walking and sat down on the sandy bottom, tucking her knees beneath her chin, an absurd little figure, but eerily at home among the swaying reeds that pulsed against her neck and trapped her hair.

She closed her eyes. Why had it been so long since any poems had come to her? This unsettled inner stirring did not invite the words inside, it tossed them into a flurry of senseless sounds. The words ran away, eluded her, which was frustrating and confusing. They had never frustrated her before. They were, aside from Uncle Kee and the Leeside, her greatest treasure.

Sunlight poured down over Siobhan's blue-black hair, which absorbed and spread the energy into her scalp and down her neck. The water was exquisitely cold all around her but her head was filling with heat. Her cheeks and lips burned with it. Eyes still closed, she imagined tiny blue flames dancing along her hair, silent, secular, sensual.

The heat overcame her and, unable to stop herself, Siobhan plunged her head under the water, and in the next moment stood up, gasping. Rarely did she put her face in the lough, as that was an intimacy she did not seek. Dripping, she pulled herself back to shore and sank into the basket chair, itself intensely warmed by the sun's rays. She could not escape the heat unless she went inside. She should go inside. But inexplicably she still sat, feeling the warmth creep into her again. Was that heat within her chest caused by the penetrating rays of the sun, or something else entirely?

"Siobhan!"

Hearing Tim's voice sent the warm confusion coursing throughout her body. She looked up at Tim coming toward her, unable to reply.

"You certainly know the sunny spot," he said, as he sank fluidly to the ground next to her, surprisingly so for one so tall. His eyes crinkled in the bright light as he gazed out at the scene before them. "Do you always go swimming in your clothes?"

Siobhan swallowed twice before she could answer. "Well, I got so warm." He'd think she was really thick, sitting here in dripping-wet clothes.

"I envy you your spontaneity. When one is too warm, and has a beautiful lough at one's doorstep, going into the water is the natural action to take. The sun is certainly unusually intense today, for an Irish sun."

He didn't think it was strange at all, she thought with relief.

"Have you finished your baking?" he asked her.

"Yes, I'm done."

"I'm glad. I had a wonderful walk this morning; I went into Carnloe. It's a lovely little village, so tiny. I had a chance to show off my Irish to the lady in the shop." He laughed slightly.

Siobhan tried to relax and told herself to speak to him. *Ask him something about him you want to know.* So she asked him, "Why did you want to learn it—Irish, I mean?"

He shrugged slightly. "It seemed vital, I guess. Vital to my understanding of everything I was trying to study. Vital to getting the true flavor, the nuances, the subtle allusions. All of that. I'm glad I did it. It helped me get closer, when I couldn't come here myself."

All she wanted was for him to go on talking, so again she lost her shyness and asked him, "Why couldn't you come here? I thought you'd been here often."

He glanced up briefly, with a warm smile, and shook his head. "It was a long time before I could afford to come. I first visited with my parents when I was eighteen. We stayed for three weeks and it was then I decided to change my chosen course of study at college from prelaw to Irish studies. I've never regretted it. But my parents didn't have a lot of money, so I had to work while I was in school. Then after I got my master's degree I was foolish enough to get married."

Siobhan sat very still. "Married?"

Tim nodded. The woman he had married, he told Siobhan, was a drama teacher at the local high school who shared his passion for Beckett and Wilde. But she spent money to an extent he hadn't known was possible. She kept him in debt, a thing he abhorred, throughout their marriage and when she became bored with him and left, Tim felt nothing but relief. Now he could begin to save. Only now could he truly immerse himself in the ancient knowledge that was his passion. Poetry, mythology, folklore, and history—all were grist for his obsessive mill.

Tim paused and looked up at Siobhan, a question in his eyes. He spoke lightly. "You're not really interested in all this semi-ancient history of mine, are you?"

She nodded and said simply, from the heart, "Please tell me more."

He took a deep breath and closed his eyes briefly, then opened them and met her gaze resolutely.

"Then I'll tell you something I haven't told anyone else. I haven't even put it into words to myself yet. I'm feeling . . . Something is happening to my passion for ancient Irish literature. It's sort of veering off course with my experiences of not just the dead-and-gone Ireland but the present-day Ireland." He gestured expansively. "All of it, the villages and towns, Dublin, the incredibly beautiful hills and shorelines of today's Ireland are all so very much alive, so vibrant. I'm enjoying the pubs as much as visiting the ancient tombs and abbeys, and studying the manuscripts in the libraries. It never occurred to me that the ancient poetry and legends are part of what makes the people and the heritage what it is today—it seems strange but I honestly never thought about how it's all interconnected and that you can't really understand the . . . sensibilities of the past without knowing the present. How's that for scholarly blasphemy?" He laughed slightly. "I mean, if my reason for coming really isn't to do research into the ancients . . . what am I doing here . . ." Tim's voice trailed off and he stared out at the lough.

Siobhan didn't try to respond to his question. Even she, with her disconnection from people, knew that he was asking a question all humans had within their souls.

. . .

It was almost ten o'clock that evening and the Leeside reveled in its raucous crowd. There was live music playing; Brendan Doherty had brought his guitar and Katie O'Farrell had persuaded her head stableman to come and bring his fiddle. Siobhan listened to them playing and thought they were doing a grand job, considering they didn't play together very often. Of course, most people were only casual listeners, preferring instead to visit with neighbors or acquaintances they didn't get to see regularly. So the pub was also filled with the muffled roar of simultaneous conversations.

Siobhan dreaded the contest ahead and was silently brooding on last night's overheard conversation. But for Uncle Kee's sake she'd try to get into the spirit of the evening.

"Great craic tonight, isn't it, Uncle Kee?"

He laughed happily. "Oh, aye, the jokes and stories are flowing free, so they are."

"Too bad your pints aren't," quipped someone in the crowd.

"They might not be free," he shot back, "but flowing fast they are, with all the lovely assistants I'm blessed with tonight."

They'd been very busy for the last two hours, and Katie, as well as Brendan's wife, Maura, were helping behind the bar.

Maura was her only childhood friend, and Siobhan smiled at her now with pride. Maura was a stunning redhead, and looked as if she had never done a day's work in her life. But Siobhan knew her efficiency at the taps, as well as the capable yet gentle manner in which she cared for her elderly, frail father, now settled in a special chair Uncle Kee had brought out for him. Maura and Brendan's little girl was with them as well, a child almost too beautiful to be real. There were many willing neighbors to watch over Triona and the elderly Seamus while Brendan and Maura helped the Leeside to have a good night. The two ancient farmers, Eamon and Liam Kelly, came in and sat at the table with their old friend Seamus. They looked with bemused wrinkled faces at the enchanting Triona, who, for the most part, sat and colored with crayons in a large coloring book, when she wasn't on her feet dancing to the beat of her father's music.

Another person Siobhan noticed in the crowd was Father Keith O'Grady, the one priest of the neighborhood. He handled the duties of the two churches, St. Brendan's in Carnloe and the bigger St. Mary's in Ballynaross, with as little effort as possible. A man in his late sixties, Father O'Grady didn't make a secret of the fact that his dominant characteristic was laziness. He performed a daily Mass in Ballynaross and one Mass in Carnloe every Sunday, and little else. He tried to have regularly scheduled confessions, but often failed to show up. Since few people took advantage of this sacrament, however, it didn't matter.

The priest usually frequented the big pub in Ballynaross, but once a week or so he stopped in at the Leeside to keep in touch with his Carnloe parishioners. Father O'Grady preferred the Ballynaross pub since that publican was more likely to forgive his drink bill, which Kee Doyle certainly was not. He'd never

absolved Father O, as he called the priest, simply for being a
priest. Fresh in his mind and not forgiven were the vicious
clouts he received from priestly hands as a schoolboy. Not to
mention the hypocrisy of forgiving the same group of wor-
shippers for the same sins over and over again. And Kee still
remembered his fear of the clerical retribution that had threat-
ened to descend on Maureen for her "bold" behavior. But it
was Siobhan's unspoken opinion that Father O'Grady at least
attempted to serve his parishioners. He was a good listener,
because he said he found listening so much easier than talking
and pontificating never helped anyone. Siobhan remembered
him saying once that if you let them talk long enough, people
usually managed to figure their way out of their own problems.
And the women of the parishes quite liked him. He was nice-
looking, in an Anthony Hopkins kind of way, always very neat
and clean, and smelled of cologne, which was more than could
be said of many of their menfolk. And nary a breath of scandal
about him, which was a small miracle. He was a good man, if
an idle one.

Siobhan decided, for reasons she refused to examine, to
have her hair down tonight, not in her usual braid. Fronds of
black silky hair hung almost to her knees, sweeping gracefully
around her small body with each movement. She observed the
scene before her with more indulgence than she usually felt
when the pub was full. The atmosphere was alive with good-
will and wit. She knew that Uncle Kee enjoyed watching the
faces and listening to the banter. Although he often appeared
taciturn, he was in his element tonight and she was happy for
him. But the happiness leapt back and forth among a cluster
of other emotions, each elbowing for attention in the pit of
her stomach. Nervousness about the upcoming competition,
annoyance at Katie's bossiness and low-cut red blouse, thrilling

shocks of excitement whenever her eyes captured Tim's looking at her, and dismay at the realization that her familiar detachment seemed to have deserted her. Tim's expression flustered her anew each time their eyes met, and her varied emotions played across her face like a silent movie.

Siobhan saw that Niall Curry, Maura's brother, was jealously noticing Tim's interest in her. Niall had had a boyish crush on Siobhan for a long time, and now it was just habit. He walked boldly up to Tim and fixed him with a challenging stare.

"You're a college professor, eh?"

"That's right."

"Right. Well, to my mind, that doesn't sound like a real job." Niall had raised his voice slightly, glancing at Siobhan.

"Not a real job? What do you mean?" Tim asked.

"Well, it's not a real man's job, is it? Not putting in an honest day's hard labor, like some of us."

Uncle Kee snorted loudly and remarked, "We'd love to hear you expound on that subject, Niall, but we're not quite sure who this honest laborer might be that you're referring to. Someone from around here, is it?"

Niall gave him a dirty look.

"I'm only asking," her uncle continued innocently. "I wasn't aware that bending the elbow constituted—what was it?—an 'honest day's hard labor.'"

Niall left them and Tim laughed. "You really don't like that kid, do you?"

"Silly little sod."

Tim asked Siobhan, "What's your opinion of that young man?"

"He's harmless enough," she answered softly.

Uncle Kee chided her. "Ach, he's been in love with you for years, darlin'. That's why you're easy on him."

Siobhan felt herself flushing and found herself saying the first thing that came into her head. "I hope tonight goes well." Katie overheard this and declared, "We should get started." Siobhan's nervousness lurched to the foreground of her being. Her stomach swam and she stepped back to lean against the kitchen doorjamb, her hands clasped tightly behind her. She listened to Katie's raised voice, sternly telling people to slow down their eating and drinking so the bartenders could take a break.

Uncle Kee protested mildly. "The more they buy, the more money I make, in case you've forgotten, love."

But everyone quickly settled down and the attention focused on the upcoming challenge. Siobhan closed her eyes briefly and willed her stomach to quiet down. She opened them again, reached for her notes, and found Tim looking at her with real sympathy.

He said to her in a low voice, "I'm nervous, too. I'll just have to pretend I'm in class." Siobhan looked up into his face.

"Do you do that sometimes? Pretend things, to make things easier?"

"Who doesn't?" he answered, and smiled. It was reassuring and her jitteriness subsided a little.

Katie's loud voice cut through their conversation.

"We did a grand job of talking up tonight. This had better be good. There are even a few tourists here, I think. Maybe you've finally been discovered."

"God forbid." Uncle Kee feigned a shudder.

"You're hopeless," Katie told him. She then hoisted herself up easily onto the bar and clapped her hands. "Right! Listen up, everyone! Quiet down now. You're all going to learn something and it won't be any too soon. Are you two gents ready? You'd best sit in the musician's chairs by the window."

Uncle Kee and Tim self-consciously walked over and sat down. They smiled somewhat sheepishly at each other. Katie said to Siobhan, "Where are you going to stand? Do you have the questions ready?"

"They're ready," Siobhan replied quietly. "I'll stay here behind the bar. They'll be able to hear me."

"*I* can barely hear you," Katie scoffed, and jumped down from the bar. "At least stand up here so people can see you. Go on!"

Oh, why do Katie's bossing ways bother me so? Siobhan asked herself, as she did as she was told. Her face flushed again, this time with embarrassment, and she hoped people would attribute it to her clambering onto the bar. She felt nervous and exposed standing on the bar, and thought how odd everyone looked as she stared down at the tops of their heads. She was so used to looking up at people; this was an unfamiliar point of reference.

Katie gave Uncle Kee a firm nod and he obediently launched into his speech.

"Good evening to you all. It's grand that you're here, having a good time and spending your money. Especially that last." This got a laugh. "I hope you've all got your bets placed by now. We're going to have a little contest, Tim and I are. By the way, this is Professor Tim Ferris who's over here from Minnesota to reap the benefit of my extensive expertise in the field of Irish literature."

There were shouts of derision at this and someone yelled, "Less talk, more action!"

Then another person called out, "What does the winner get? What's the stakes?"

Uncle Kee and Tim looked at each other blankly. They hadn't thought of any prize. They both shrugged and Katie commented, "What about half the taking on the bets?" But this met with loud boos and a chorus of refusals.

Uncle Kee made a calming gesture with his hands.

"Now, now. Tim and I are competing for the pure pleasure of it—to cover ourselves in glory. That's enough for us, right Tim?"

Tim nodded gamely and it looked to Siobhan like he wished he was elsewhere.

"What about a kiss from Katie?" a raucous voice yelled. "That could be the prize!"

There was a swelling chorus of agreement. Siobhan's fingers froze in their nervous shuffling of her note cards. There were more shouts from the crowd.

"Aye, and a good prize that'd be!"

"She doesn't have to stop there, neither—that'd be up to her!"

"That'll light a fire under 'em!"

There were several other more ribald comments, and Katie shouted out, "Oh, shut up, you sods! Fine, fine. We'll do that, to satisfy your savage instincts." She sounded reluctant but her teasing eyes were sparkling at Uncle Kee and he gave her a wink. Tim just looked embarrassed. Siobhan's instinct was to flee the building, but she was trapped by the surrounding humanity, and by her promise to Uncle Kee.

He now said, "Let's get started, Siobhan love. You all agree Siobhan will be the judge of the contest? What she says goes for the answers! No googling by you lot."

The crowd murmured its consent, and Siobhan swallowed and nodded. She consciously willed her brain to fog over and told herself the only way to get through this was to go numb. Fortunately she could always do that when needed.

"I've got twenty-one questions here," she began in a clear, toneless voice. "I made up an uneven number of questions in case there's a tie. Whoever calls out the answer first gets a point. If it seems you both said it at the same time I'll be asking for more information about the answer. All right?"

Uncle Kee and Tim nodded.

"Question number one. What was the name of the land-owner who owned the young Saint Patrick as a slave?"

Before she could quite finish the question, Uncle Kee called out, "Miliucc!" Tim nodded ruefully and Siobhan said, "Correct." There was a smattering of applause, and Siobhan quickly continued, also feeling a small thrill of pride in her uncle.

"Question number two. Which mythological poem tells the tale of a supernatural being with a mysterious sickness that can only be cured by the love of a fairy girl he saw in a dream?"

Tim said quickly, " 'The Dream of Oengus.' "

Siobhan met his eyes, smiled and nodded.

"But that's the theme in a lot of poems," Uncle Kee protested, " 'Echtra Conli,' 'Serglige Con Culainn'—"

"No," Siobhan replied, surprising herself with the firmness of her tone. "In all those poems the lover is a human man, not a supernatural one."

He smacked his thigh and grinned. "You got me there," he remarked.

"Wow, you're tough, Siobhan," came a voice from the crowd.

"Question number three. Who said, and in what context, 'To every cow her calf, to every book its copy'?"

Uncle Kee hesitated and Tim answered, "King Diarmait—after Saint Columcille secretly tried to copy a book of the king's that he coveted. When the king found out, he gave his permission for the book to be copied—probably history's first copyright case."

"Very good," his opponent congratulated him.

And so the contest went on, with Siobhan's questions

becoming more and more difficult. Each time Tim or Uncle Kee managed to find the answer—she was never able to stump them both. The three of them were caught up in the familiar magic of the myths and poetry, and Siobhan, underneath her shell, felt an unfamiliar sense of control, even power. Uncle Kee and Tim awaited her questions and her judgments with deference. And palpable, even to Siobhan as she tried to pretend the room wasn't full of people, was the appreciation and attention of the crowd. The two competitors had captured the imagination of the spectators.

When there was only one question left, the score was tied ten to ten. Siobhan looked at her last question, and she realized she must have subconsciously wanted Tim to win. The question was about a fairly obscure epic poem the two of them had just talked about the evening before. But now, if Tim won, the prize was . . . Her detachment evaporated in a flash fire and she had a sudden, vivid, Technicolor vision of Katie kissing Tim. For a horrible moment she thought she might pass out. She knew that Katie and Uncle Kee had kissed before—more than kissed. Siobhan didn't want Katie to kiss either of the contestants, but if she had to pick, it would most certainly be Uncle Kee.

Appalled at the violence of her emotions, and feeling defiant and guilty at the same time, Siobhan quickly thought up a different question. "What—what saint had a vision of his soul leaving his body and being shown both heaven and hell?"

"Saint Fursey!" Uncle Kee exclaimed.

Siobhan caught Tim's eye, hesitated, then nodded. "That's right."

A cheer went up and Tim shook hands with her uncle and complimented him. He sat back in his chair as the winner was led off to the bar in triumph. Siobhan found Tim's face in the crowd and there she saw rueful awareness at what she had just done. She lowered her eyes, scrambled down from the bar, and disappeared into the kitchen. Uncle Kee's last answer was wrong. Tim knew it and Siobhan knew it. Saint Fursey had a vision of his soul leaving his body, it was true, but it was not taken to heaven and hell; rather the forces of good and evil in the guise of angels and demons fought over it. The angels were, of course, victorious. Unlike in the current battle over her own soul.

Siobhan's stomach was fluttering with panic. She knew that Tim knew she'd made him lose on purpose. He would be angry with her, and he had a right to be. Her mind was flooded with panic and shame that he might guess the reason—that she didn't want him to kiss Katie. But why should she *care* if Tim kissed Katie? On the surface, Siobhan. *Stay on the surface . . .*

The kitchen door burst open and her uncle, beaming, swept her into a hug, a rare demonstration of affection. She smiled wanly.

"Congratulations, Uncle Kee."

PART TWO

SIOBHAN AND TIM

PART TWO

SIOBHAN AND TIM

CHAPTER 4

Shy thoughts and grave wide eyes and hands
That wander as they list—
The twilight turns to darker blue
With lights of amethyst.

—JAMES JOYCE

The night was just about over. The entire crowd partied until closing time, and Kee decided to drive the two old farmers, Eamon and Liam, home in their ramshackle truck as they were both a little worse for wear. Katie followed behind in her Rover so she could bring Kee back to the Leeside. In Siobhan's opinion, this was taking much longer than necessary. Before her reluctant eyes, and the appreciative eye of the attentive crowd, Katie and Kee had made a great show out of the winner's kiss, with him bending her back in true dashing style. Siobhan worried that the reason they were delayed getting back was because Katie had upped the prize to the next level.

Maura and Brendan stayed to help clean up. Seamus dozed in his chair with his feet up, while Triona was tucked up on the sitting-room sofa. Siobhan avoided Tim; he tried talking to her a couple of times but shame choked her. She'd done a terrible thing, making Tim lose the contest for her own selfish reasons.

And she had deceived everyone, including Uncle Kee. Everyone but Tim. Strange that the person truly wronged by her was also the only one who knew the truth. She felt the heaviness of it in the air between them, a barrier of blame. She managed to send him off to clean tables on the far side of the room.

For Tim's part, if Siobhan had only known, he felt nothing but sympathy for her. His assumption was that her desire to have her uncle win was too tempting, especially in front of the crowd of friends and neighbors. He, too, was aware that only the two of them knew what had happened. Her humiliation was palpable, and his only concern was to clear up the misunderstanding between them.

"Quite an evening," Maura remarked as she came up to him, wet rag in hand.

"It sure was." Tim smiled at her. "I had a great time."

"It'll probably pass into local legend, with many embellishments along the way."

He laughed and then, as Siobhan went into the kitchen, Maura asked, "What do you think of Siobhan and Kee?"

Something in the tone of her voice told him it wasn't a casual question. Tim straightened up, pausing in his cleaning.

"I think they're both amazing," he replied simply. "Absolutely amazing. I could talk to them forever."

"They really know their stuff, don't they?"

"They know it so well I was toying with the idea of asking them to come over to my university for a series of lectures."

Maura looked taken aback by this. She began, "I don't think that's—"

"Oh, I'm not going to, don't worry. I think Kee might enjoy it but not Siobhan. It's not something she'd be comfortable doing. And I'm assuming Kee wouldn't come without her, so . . ."

"You assume correctly. He couldn't and wouldn't."

There was a pause, then Tim said, "You know them well." His voice held an unconscious hint of envy.

Maura smiled. "I've been friends with Siobhan since we were five and met at school. My favorite stories had always been those about fairies and kelpies and sprites, and, I thought, here one was! For the longest time I was convinced she was only temporarily in human form, and would be disappearing back into her fairy mound one day."

"I've gotten that feeling, too," Tim admitted.

"I'm not surprised. But she's real. Just in her own world. Unfortunately. She was so full of stories as a child, always full of stories. Even by the age of eight or nine she was an expert in ancient tales and legends. When she was telling one of those it was the only time she really came alive, came out of herself. It's almost the same today." Maura's voice was a little sad.

It was a relief to Tim that someone else, someone who knew her so well, also saw Siobhan as being too secluded.

"Has she *never* been away from here?" he asked.

"Oh, sure. Keenan has taken her on a few day trips, to Iona, Wexford, and such. Always, of course, to visit the ancient stones and ring forts and dolmens and that. I remember once our family was going on holiday to Scotland for a week, and I was desperate for Siobhan to come along. My da said it would be all right. Siobhan didn't even really want to come but I was determined to make her. We were both about ten, I think. I got up my courage to ask Kee. He said no."

"Do you think he's still overprotective of her?"

Maura hesitated and Tim felt he'd gotten too personal. Maura studied his face for a moment before she answered.

"Yes. Although he doesn't have to be. She's an expert at it herself."

Tim stared at the closed kitchen door and found himself asking the next question before he could stop himself.

"Hasn't there ever been any man in her life? I mean, Siobhan is really lovely. She must meet men all the time here in the pub. There must be some who were . . . are attracted."

He looked over at Maura and found her regarding him with attention.

"Attracted?" Maura replied, with a wry smile. "You mean, besides Niall? Oh, absolutely, any amount of them. But it isn't that they don't get any encouragement. There's just no recognition on her part that anything is happening. It's no wonder she has such passion for her Irish studies, it's the only passion she's ever experienced." Maura looked Tim in the eye. "She has little experience with men."

Just then, they were interrupted by Brendan.

"What's all this sitting down on the job?" he chided his wife good-naturedly. "It's almost three o'clock, love."

"Oh, God, you're right." Maura stood up.

"You go on home," Tim told them. "Siobhan and I will finish up."

Maura gave him a knowing smile and agreed. "I'll get Triona. Brendan, wake up Da, will you?"

Brendan said, "Where the hell are Kee and Katie, I'd like to know? They've left us with all the clearing up to do."

"Where do you think they are?" his wife replied drily. She left them and went through to the kitchen.

Tim asked Brendan, "Are Kee and Katie . . . do they . . ."

"They are and they do," Brendan answered. "Katie would love to get Kee to the altar but he's able to keep her at arm's length most of the time. Once in a while, though, they have a bit of fun. Friends with privileges, right? They're adults."

He walked over to his sleeping father-in-law and awakened him gently. "Come on, Seamus. It's time to go. That's right, steady now. Let me give you a hand."

Siobhan came through the swinging kitchen door carrying Triona in her arms. Tim watched her and Maura go out, followed by Brendan supporting the frail, sleepy Seamus. Tim felt, at that moment, infinitely grateful that Siobhan had these good friends who cared about what happened to her. He was surprised at how glad he felt about that. He also felt a quiet anger toward Kee for creating out of Siobhan a kind of half ghost, a female shadow of himself to ensure that he would always have someone of his own. Then Tim reproached himself. The man had had to make the best of a very difficult situation. Living here alone with her bachelor uncle in such an isolated place, it was probably a wonder that she wasn't more removed from reality than she was.

It was a few minutes before Siobhan came back inside. Tim turned around and they faced each other across the room.

Siobhan spoke in a rush. "I'm sorry about the contest. It was wrong of me—"

Tim interrupted. "Don't even say it, Siobhan. It doesn't matter, don't you know that? I completely understand that you'd want Kee to win, especially in front of everybody. I think it's great. He was really pleased. That's what counts."

A relieved, happy smile lit her face. Tim had to force himself to ignore his own surge of delight at the sight of it.

"Let's go out into the fresh air," he suggested impulsively.

She lowered her eyes, nodded, and opened the door. The two of them stepped out into an Irish night of shifting clouds, light and shadow, the elemental smell of earth, and cool, moist air that blessed the skin. He felt his entire body and spirit become buoyant with the beauty of it.

Siobhan led the way to a path that wound around the lough shore. Tim found her extraordinarily peaceful to be with. Although this was one of the most romantic settings he had ever been in with a woman, the woman he was with was as far removed from a romantic liaison as he could imagine. She was appealing and lovely but in a curiously intangible way. It was like being with a . . . a fairy. Perhaps she was a fairy, he thought wryly, despite what Maura had said, one of the little people. Her approach to him was completely sexless, an attitude that he found at once endearing and disturbing. He did not have extensive experience with women, certainly, but she was unique in his sphere.

Still she did not speak. The endless summer gloaming surrounded them and there was no sense of time in the air. Tim decided to make the first opening.

"I've never stayed anywhere in Ireland that was right out in the countryside before. Always in a town or village. It's more than peaceful, almost ethereal. And very satisfying."

Siobhan nodded. "There is no other place."

He found this remark disquieting. Was she really content to be so isolated? He hesitated but decided to leave it. He said, "This lough is beautiful. Does it have a name?"

"Lough Carnloe." She paused, then continued haltingly. "It's so wonderful, and I know very rare, to live in a place that doesn't leave you wanting more."

"It is rare," he agreed quietly. "It's also rare to discover a place like that."

Again the shy smile he was learning to wait for. "I suppose so," she said softly.

Choosing his words carefully, Tim continued: "Perhaps it can mean even more to discover a place that you believe is what you've been searching for, after not having had it in your life."

Siobhan looked troubled at this. "But your home is such a big part of who you are; it shapes a person."

"It does that, certainly. But not always in positive ways. Home can be a negative as well as a positive force."

The troubled look deepened. "Oh, I'm knowing that well. Was your home an . . . unhappy place?" She stopped walking, and her large eyes stared up at him. The baldness of the question emphasized her childlike approach to him. He smiled down at her.

"No, not at all," he answered. "But there wasn't . . . completeness. I wanted more."

"And now?"

"Now?"

Still her gaze held his.

"Are you wanting more?"

Looking into her innocent eyes was making him slightly giddy and he willed his head to turn away. Maura's words echoed in his head: *She has little experience with men.*

"Yes, I suppose so. Contentment can turn into complacency." His voice felt slightly rough and he cleared his throat.

They continued along the path, their feet softly disturbing the moist earth. Otherwise there was no sound, no other movement around them. The night was as still as a painting of itself.

Tim slid a glance at his companion and saw that she was deep in thought. He waited, hoping she would share what she was thinking. Finally her soft voice broke the silence.

"Is there a chance that someone could never be finding the place they're supposed to find? Or maybe actually be there but not be knowing it for what it is?"

He could hear the underlying anxiety in her tone, and could only answer honestly.

"Yes, that could happen. And does for some people."

"But that's a terrible thing."

"Yes."

He saw her raise her head and look around. "I came here to Uncle Kee when I was two, so I've been here most of my life. All of my life, really. I'm not remembering much of my mother or anything before coming here. Uncle Kee is brilliant."

"You're happy here."

She nodded. "Very happy. This place, and Uncle Kee, have given me so much."

"And it's still enough for you?"

"Oh, yes," she replied with faint surprise. "I can't imagine being anywhere else."

Her attitude saddened him. Surely there was something wrong here, that this lovely young woman was satisfied to be isolated here, studying the past. Wasn't she missing out on Life, with a capital L? But who was he to judge? He, too, had pulled the narrow focus of his own life too tightly around himself, like a protective blanket. He was no expert on widening one's horizons.

And yet he was driven by curiosity to ask, "Haven't you ever wanted anything more? With your abilities you might become a leading scholar in Irish literature. I guess I feel pretty strongly that people have to use and develop their talents. It's just . . . I'm so impressed with you. I suppose it's the teacher in me." He was apprehensive now, as she stood pale and still before him.

"It's okay," she almost whispered, after a quick intake of breath. "Thanks for minding. Only Katie has ever, well, pushed me to do things, urged me to want more. She always said I had such a talent for riding, so she did her best to make me become a rider and jumper on the Connemara pony circuit. Katie's been the only person who has sort of been impatient with me for not . . . wanting more out of life." Siobhan looked away from him for a moment, then spoke slowly. "Something Uncle Kee doesn't know—no one knows. I failed my Leaving Certificate exams at sixteen so I could stay here, you see."

Tim was moved that she had confessed this to him, although disappointed that she had made such a decision for herself. What a choice to make alone at such a young age.

Siobhan looked at him then. "You probably think it a foolish thing. But it was right for me."

Tim took a deep breath and smiled at her. "Well, I'm no one to judge. And it's true that a person can educate oneself. You and Kee certainly seem to have done that."

Siobhan nodded happily, and suddenly Tim felt that at this moment there was a strong affinity between them. She seemed so relaxed, so open. He searched for something to say, to divert his strong desire to reach out and touch her lovely face. Shoving his hands into his pockets, he looked up into the translucent sky.

He said quietly, "It's such a lovely night. Do you know A.E.'s poem—silly question, of course you do—that begins:

"When the breath of twilight blows to flame the misty skies,
All its vaporous sapphire, violet glow and silver gleam,
With their magic flood me through the gateway of the eyes;
I am one with twilight's dream."

"Oh, yes," Siobhan breathed.

Suddenly Tim heard a shuffling sound and looked beyond her. Startled, he said bluntly, "There's a horse behind you."

The animal had come out of the gloaming and, intent on their conversation, he had only just noticed it. Siobhan turned her head. "That's Blasket."

She whistled softly and the pony came up to nuzzle her shoulder. He was rakish-looking, with an unruly shock of dark hair hanging over his forehead. As far as Tim could make out in the half-light, the pony was light-colored with darker spots.

He stood sturdily, without grace, as Siobhan rubbed his forehead and told him regretfully that she had no treats with her at the moment.

"I don't see any fences around here," Tim said. "Does he just roam free?"

"Oh, yes. It's what they're used to. He'll not go far. He knows where home is."

Here's another creature content to stay by the Leeside, Tim thought wryly. "What about in bad weather? Do you have someplace to put him?"

"Uncle Kee built him a lean-to on the side of the hill where he can go if he's a mind. But Connemaras are pretty hardy. A bit of weather doesn't bother them. He's a brilliant animal—but he'd hate all that primping and training and traveling about all over on the riding circuit. He likes being free." She stroked the pony's neck and quoted:

"He has an eye like any hawk, a neck like any swan,
A foot light as the stag's, the while his back is scarce a span;
Kind Nature has so formed him, he is everything that's good—
Aye, everything a man could wish in bottom, bone and blood."

Tim watched her lay her head on the pony's neck. He asked lightly, "Is he everything a woman could wish, too?"

Siobhan ducked her head shyly. "Oh, yes. He . . . he is. At least . . . yes, of course."

There was an awkward pause and then Tim asked, "What is that poem? I don't know it."

She replied, seeming relieved, "It's an old highwayman song, from around 1828 or so. 'The Trotting Horse.' And so you are," she finished, giving Blasket a friendly slap on his side. He ambled away and they continued walking.

"You really are amazingly well versed," Tim said. "I don't think I could stump you if I tried."

"I didn't stump *you* much tonight."

Tim laughed. "Kee really enjoyed himself."

"I know. At first it seemed like a sort of . . . cheapening of it, I suppose, for want of a better word. Uncle Kee and I keep all this pretty much to ourselves. We don't go talking about it much. Not too many people are interested in it."

"As opposed to us, who are completely obsessed. It seems like Middle Irish is his specialty. He was brilliant tonight."

Siobhan's eyes shone. "Wasn't he? Just brilliant. But I prefer the Mythological Cycle, the heroic and epic poetry. God-warriors and saints, the visionaries. It sings and soars. It takes you up to exultant heights and plunges you down into the lowest depths of hell . . ."

Tim walked quietly beside her and listened, for her mind was off like an arrow from a bow. How fascinating she was! One minute filled with the simple naïveté of a child and the next speaking with such passionate eloquence that more than just his scholar's imagination was exhilarated.

She talked on and on, expressive, enthusiastic, empowered. This was her element, he realized. This was the one thing in her life that she believed gave her a unique identity. Was she a shade too fanatical about it? Perhaps. But her insight was incredible. She, and no doubt Kee as well, could go up against any Irish scholar of his acquaintance. He began to toy again with the idea of bringing them over to his university to give a series of lectures. He would love for his students, and his colleagues, to hear these two people, to benefit from their unique knowledge and fervor. But could Siobhan be pried away from her precious Leeside? And would she be capable of speaking this eloquently and passionately in front of a group of strangers, out of her element? It seemed impossible. *You can't take a kelpie from its cove.*

They turned and headed back toward the pub. With Siobhan still talking, the two of them now returned to the lough wall and sat on it. They sat side by side, looking at the dark water and darker hills, and Siobhan's voice finally ran down. The sky held no more clouds and through the remaining shreds of mist, Tim had never seen so many stars. There was a silence between the two of them. Tim knew now what people meant when they talked about feeling like they were the only ones left in the world. He felt like that, in this moment, that he and Siobhan were alone in the world. But the earlier sense of affinity eluded him now. Sitting here on the wall, Tim had an odd feeling that Siobhan had forgotten he was there, that she had withdrawn from him.

She said faintly, as if to herself, "There is hardly enough room on the cloak of night for all my stars to be hung upon it."

Tim looked at her curiously. "I'm not familiar with that poem."

"No," she whispered, and then he tangibly sensed her drift away. Her body was there beside him but her mind and spirit were elsewhere.

Was she far away, he wondered? No, not far away, but in a world deep within herself. Who was he to try and enter the inner world of this strange and provocative woman? But, God, how desperately he wanted to. If she'd been another kind of woman he might have been emboldened to press his advantage in the dark, to speak soft Gaelic under the stars. But if she were another kind of woman, he wouldn't want her. It washed over him in a terrifying wave then, how much he wanted her.

"Siobhan?" He spoke her name tentatively. Getting no response, he slowly got up off the wall and walked toward the pub. He turned around once, as he got to the corner of the building, half expecting to see that she had disappeared, returned to her enchanted form as fairy or water sprite, he thought eerily. But she was there, sitting motionless, and looking as much a part of the landscape as the sky full of stars—and just as far away.

CHAPTER 5

The blood-dimmed tide is loosed, and everywhere
The ceremony of innocence is drowned . . .

—W. B. YEATS

Tim sat down at the bar and realized he was shaking. Who was this woman? Why did she fascinate him so? Was it just their shared passion for his beloved obsession? Or was it more? He thought vaguely that he should probably go to bed; he felt intensely weary. It was very late and he was leaving tomorrow. Leaving. The thought seemed, of its own free will, to refuse to register in his brain. He didn't know how long he sat on the barstool, staring into space, before he heard the sound of a car outside. Kee was back.

He burst through the door.

"Still up, Professor? Doing a bit of crying in your beer, I'll not doubt!"

Tim looked at him carefully. Was he drunk? No, just pleased with himself. Tim thought about what Brendan had said about Kee and Katie. Well, it looked like Kee had had more than one success tonight.

"A hell of a night, wasn't it?" Kee asked him with a smile, dropping heavily into a chair.

"It was. I enjoyed it enormously."

"As did I, Tim, as did I. Where's Siobhan?"

"Outside, getting some fresh air."

Kee nodded, then frowned slightly. "When did the others leave?"

In his tiredness, Tim was tempted to laugh out loud at Kee's obvious suspicions. He could see that Kee wasn't happy he and Siobhan had been alone at the Leeside. As if he were any kind of a threat.

He sat down across from Kee at the table. "A while ago," he replied, looking at his host somewhat sardonically. "Siobhan took me on a walk and introduced me to Blasket."

Kee smiled then, and rubbed his eyes. "Did she now? God, I'm tired. Siobhan's not upset about tonight, is she?"

Tim shook his head. "No, she knows you had a great time. That's all she cares about, you know that. She's devoted to you, that's quite obvious."

Kee looked at him; Tim hadn't been able to keep a note of envy out of his voice.

"Aye, she is."

At that moment Tim cursed convention; he wanted so much to just ask how it felt like that, to have someone—to have *Siobhan*—believe you were the most wonderful person on earth.

He settled for stating obliquely, "It must be great to have her here with you. I mean, family's important," he added lamely.

Kee's eyes narrowed and Tim felt himself being measured. He met Kee's gaze honestly. "You two just seem to have a really wonderful relationship."

There was a long pause, then Kee sighed, his exuberance ebbing away. He shook his head.

"We do, and that's still amazing to me," he said. The eyes of the two men met. Then Kee looked beyond Tim and spoke in a reminiscent voice. "The only little girl I'd ever really known was

Maureen. She was five years younger than me. But I was know-ing next to nothing about children. Siobhan was as different from Maureen as it was possible to be. Maureen embraced life, Siobhan didn't trust it. I found out they'd been having a fairly miserable hand-to-mouth existence, the two of them. That was hard for me—I wish I'd known. And, of course, the trauma of losing her mother and going to live with a complete stranger—me—was enough to give her all sorts of 'abandonment issues,' as the doctor explained to me years ago. It was touch and go with her for the first few days. Now I know what hell is . . ." Kee paused, the tired look on his face deepening into weariness.

They both heard a sound behind them, a penetrating intake of breath into a tight chest. Siobhan came slowly into the room from the kitchen. She looked at her uncle, the skin of her face ghostly, stretched over delicate bone. With her gaze never leaving his face, she walked to the table and sat down next to him. She whispered to him in Irish, "Tell me. Tell me about when I first came here. About all of it."

Kee's face also drained of color, a strange sight on him, a man with so ruddy a complexion. He looked terrified, as if confronting long-buried demons, or of saying the wrong thing. Tim sat immobile, mesmerized by how these two people would handle this delicate, critical moment in their lives.

Slowly Siobhan reached out and laid a tiny hand on her uncle's massive arm. Her touch seemed to melt him and he expelled a long-held breath. Looking down at the table, he nodded and began speaking in a low, resigned voice.

" 'I thought of her as the wishing tree that died, And saw it lifted, root and branch, to heaven . . .' That stanza of Heaney is the per-fect epitaph for Maureen. Such a bright light, always search-ing, always yearning . . . I wanted so much for her. For both of us." He sighed. "I wanted to be a teacher. That's the degree I was going to take at Trinity. Having to come home and take over the pub was a bloody big blow. I remember when I was a kid, we sold a few groceries here as well. That was the one big change I made when Mum died. I didn't come down from university to be a bloody grocer. A publican, now that at least has some time-honored tradition behind it. I was master in my own domain. I think I would have liked that part of teaching."

Kee paused and began to sweat, suddenly desperate for a drink of whiskey. It had been a very long time since that urge had crashed in on him. Swallowing hard, he took a deep breath and looked at Siobhan. Her dear face was anxious yet somehow encouraging . . . and hopeful. She needed him to do this.

He asked if he could have a drink of water. Tim got up swiftly, poured a large glassful at the bar, and brought it over to the table. He set it down and, realizing he had no right to be here, said, "I'll leave you now. Good night." They barely noticed him. Tim went into the darkened kitchen, hesitated for a moment, then quietly left the door ajar. Ignoring his conscience, he sat down and listened as Kee took Siobhan down a dark tunnel of twenty-five years to the night of her mother's death.

. . .

"A phone call in the night can change everything. You're faced with the fact that your life will always be a little emptier. It's a strange reality—exhausting and vague—like trying to wrap your mind around some complex scientific theory. You know it to be true but you can't understand how it could be true." He looked up and his eyes came into focus on her face. "That call told me two things: that Maureen had been killed and that you existed. Not one but two things that would change my life forever. One for the worse and one for the better." He smiled tiredly at her and took another sip. Siobhan's whole being was focused on what would come next.

"That drive to Comagh was a surreal nightmare. There had been two bombings that night, one at the barracks in Antrim and the one in Comagh. Security and tensions were sky-high. I was stopped at a border crossing near Armagh and searched and questioned by three British soldiers. Fecking bastards. I had to tell them everything about myself, and what I was doing there at five o'clock in the morning. I've got a dead sister and a baby to bring home with me, I said. When they let me go on, I made them give me a letter of permission. I wasn't wanting to be delayed by some damned road patrol . . . that might well be out for blood."

When he reached Comagh, he told her, the town had been completely cordoned off. He had to wait again until the checkpoint-police rang the Royal Ulster Constabulary station. They made him leave his car on the edge of town and gave him a ride to the station in a police vehicle. Civilian cars were not allowed on the streets that morning.

"I remember asking the sergeant if I could see the nightclub. He drove me past rows and rows of council houses; I got this horrible claustrophobic feeling. I just couldn't imagine living in one of these small industrial towns, hemmed in by the sameness. I was thinking, Why couldn't Maureen have stayed at home with me? But she was . . . well, if she'd been doing that, she wouldn't have been Maureen." He sighed heavily. "Maureen never settled."

Siobhan thought how strange it was that she and her mother could be so different; that the woman who gave birth to her and whose blood flowed through her had wanted to leave the Leeside behind, had wanted such a different life than she herself wanted.

Kee rubbed his eyes. "I'll never, as long as I live, be forgetting the sight of that nightclub—or what was left of it. The torn walls, charred and gaping, all black and dripping with water. There must have been a million shards of glass lying on the road. That blood-spattered road. And the smell . . . nauseating. The stench of incinerated life. It was so obscene. If Maureen had been in there, Jesus! What could possibly be left of her? I thought I was going to be sick, but I wouldn't give that RUC bastard the satisfaction, that was for damned sure.

"And then, when I got to the police station, there you were. I swear to God, my heart . . ." Here his voice faltered and Siobhan's tiny hands tightened on his arm. She'd never seen him overcome by any emotion save anger. She was frightened, but determined not to show it.

Kee cleared his throat and took another drink of water. He shook his head slightly and smiled again. "My heart actually twisted in my chest when I saw you. You were just the mirror image of Maureen." His gaze rested on her face then, and she knew he was seeing not her but the two-year-old her. "Your thin, pale face and black hair, and those huge dark eyes—orphan's eyes, they were. As if you already knew."

"Did they know anything about my da?"

Kee shook his head. "They said nothing about him. All the men killed . . . I found out later that he was a British soldier. That was hard. Bloody damn hard. To know that she—that Maureen had been going around with the Brits. The occupiers. I didn't know how she could. It hurt me a lot to know that."

He patted her hands absentmindedly; he seemed still deep in the past, his face reflecting the pain of that dark time.

"But I had a niece to see to. And you wouldn't come to me. You were so scared, so bloody scared. This tarted-up little friend of Maureen's had been taking care of you, and the police had to pry you out of her arms kicking and screaming for 'Mamsy.' I just wanted the floor to swallow me. I was thinking, Jesus God, what am I going to do? You were so bloody terrified and miserable. I knew I had to make it right somehow, say the right things, do the right things. And I had no idea how. None."

Siobhan whispered, "But you did. You did say and do the right things."

Still his mind didn't surface back to the present.

"This female RUC officer helped," he continued in a surprised tone. "She got you settled in my car somehow. Maybe by that time you were too exhausted to care. You just stared at me, clutching your dirty yellow blanket and sucking on the two middle fingers of your hand, like Maureen used to. We drove off into a . . . a gray void. We started out with nothing in common but shared grief. But I'd learned to live without Maureen in my life. Who better to teach you how to do it? We both loved her, and now she was gone."

Kee came back to her then, looking at her with present-day eyes. She sensed he was inclined to stop, but she wanted more.

"And when I got here, what happened then? Did I love it?"

She saw him hesitate, and then he replied too briskly. "You did, then. It was grand." He made a move as if to stand up, but she held him there, her tiny hands tightening on his arm.

"Tell me." Her gaze was steady.

He sighed. "Oh, Siobhan. If you're wanting to know, it was hell on earth. Those first few days. The crying, the fear, the helplessness. It was agony knowing that I was no comfort to you. Who was I to you? Some hulking stranger that had taken you away from everything familiar. But I couldn't fail—I knew that wasn't an option. One thing that happened was I stopped my drinking. I'd been well on the way of becoming an alcoholic when you appeared, love. And I knew for your sake that I wouldn't go back to it, ever. You know, people drink for a lot of reasons but they stop drinking for only one. Something or someone else becomes more important."

Siobhan was saddened by the fact that he had had such a hard time with her when she'd first arrived at the Leeside. Why couldn't she remember that fear, that unhappiness, if it had been so intense?

She asked, "How long did it take before I, well, settled in?"

He smiled at her, and she was glad to see that smile. "It happened all at once. I'd been having the feeling that you and I were isolated from the whole world, underwater like, and only when you accepted me could we surface and begin to breathe again.

"It was on the afternoon of the third day. You hadn't spoken a word since you'd arrived. You were napping upstairs and I'd placed a photograph next to you on the bed of Maureen and me, taken on her confirmation day. I was going to show it to you when you woke up. But then I fell asleep in a chair next to the bed. I opened my eyes some time later and saw you looking at the picture. You studied my face and then looked back at the picture. You did that a couple of times. I remember I sat very still, like you do when you're not wanting a wild animal to run off. And slowly you climbed off the bed and brought the photograph over to me. You pointed at Maureen in the picture, and said, 'Mamsy.' I nodded, and then you pointed to me in the picture. I nodded again, and said, 'Uncle Kee.' Then you climbed right into my lap and settled there like a contented little cat. I wrapped my arms around you and that was that. We were a family. It seemed like a bloody miracle."

They sat quietly, Kee's huge hand resting on top of Siobhan's tiny one. They were alone in the universe just then, two people fused in the marrow story of their relationship. Only they belonged to it, only they could at this moment fully realize its depth—its connective impact. For Siobhan, just knowing the truth was an enormous relief, with the persistent, decades-old cloud of concealment burned away by the knowing of it. Her heart swelled with the joy of that knowledge, the incredible power of it. To know—to finally *know*. Reality had never before held such magnitude for her.

There was no turning back now for either of them, and neither wanted to let go of the other. Words were unnecessary. Their hands rested upon each other, not moving, the warmth of their skin melting away years of silence and unanswered questions. Even Time itself could not have told how long they sat without moving. Then Siobhan slowly lowered her head until it rested on her uncle's chest, eventually falling asleep, and Kee was overcome by the powerful release of the story's telling, and the fierce tenderness only a parent can feel for a child. He wept.

CHAPTER 6

Lone and forgotten
Through a long sleeping,
In the heart of an age,
A child woke weeping.

—A.E. (GEORGE W. RUSSELL)

The next morning Siobhan came down to the kitchen very early. She needed to get breakfast ready, for Tim planned an early start to make his flight at Shannon Airport. Her heart was light as she got out pans and food. Last night's revelations made her feel as if a huge window had opened in her mind. Now there was light and clarity where there had been a dim labyrinth.

Thinking about it now, tiny snapshot memories emerged, memories that she had never understood and had been frightened of, and thus had suppressed for most of her life. A cluttered dank room with a soiled smell that was comforting only because it was familiar; the soft sound of a woman's low laugh and the harsh sound of a man's loud one; the feeling of being bone-tired as she was hurried along a crowded street, surrounded by a frightening forest of unfriendly legs. Then a limbo, a leaving of familiar arms for foreign ones, but being too overcome with exhaustion to care; a deep ache in the pit of her stomach as she longed to hear a voice that was silent, to feel the touch of fingers that had disappeared, to savor snuggling into a shoulder that had left her. Confusion. Fear. Then large lighted rooms full of streaming sunshine, warm fires, the smell of wholesome cooking and clean clothes. The massive figure of her uncle walking quietly around her, emanating an adult patience that was unknown to her. And finally, the shining revelation that a new shoulder can be even more restful and secure than the old one. All pieces of a puzzle that she had been leery of even trying to put together now fell into place with the certainty of a sunrise.

All of it made her feel strangely brave and strong, emboldened in her decision that before Tim left this morning she would show him her poems.

Both men, when they came down for breakfast, were a little subdued. Uncle Kee ate quickly, talking about some shopping he needed to do in Ballynaross. Siobhan felt guiltily glad of this; it would be easier to give her poems to Tim and talk about them without Uncle Kee around. She needed to think about when, or if, she would share her poems with her uncle. It was different from sharing them with Tim. Siobhan didn't quite know why, she just knew that it was.

The door banged behind Uncle Kee after he said his quick goodbyes, and Siobhan took a deep breath.

"I've something to show you," she said, without looking at Tim. Before he could reply, she rose and ran up the stairs. The pages were where she had put them, folded in a book about Queen Maeve. Quickly she went back downstairs, and he looked up expectantly.

"I thought you might be wanting to see these," she said a little breathlessly and handed the sheets to him. He smiled as he took them and started reading. The smile disappeared after a few seconds, replaced by an expression that Siobhan could only describe to herself as spellbound. Her heart beat hard against her ribs as she watched him. He had actually gone a little pale. Slowly he stood up, still reading.

"Where did you get these?" he demanded, as he read. "They're incredible. I've never seen these before. What was your source? Can you tell me?"

For a moment or two Siobhan didn't understand what Tim was asking. What did he mean, *where did she get them?* Then she realized her name wasn't on the poems. He didn't know she had written them. He thought—Siobhan's whole body tingled with the wonder of it—he thought they were real ancient poetry! She was about to exclaim that they were hers, that *she* had written them, when something in his face stopped her. He was fascinated with them, yes, enthralled with the thought that these were previously undiscovered ancient poems. Would he be as interested if he knew they were only her attempts at emulating her beloved ancient verses? Would he? Of course not. *Of course not.* His interest was as a scholar, in their historical and cultural significance.

Her spirits, so high a moment before, plummeted to the depths and she turned away from him. Tim was too busy reading to notice she hadn't answered him yet, but not for long. Siobhan knew he'd want answers and would pursue them with a true scholar's zeal. What was she going to do? He'd be so disappointed. What could she say? What *could* she say? Could she . . . could she . . . An idea came to her, a shameful idea but one that might, just might, bind him to her for a while, at least, until she could figure out what to do. If Tim thought she knew where there was a previously undiscovered source of ancient Irish poetry, he'd have to keep in touch with her. He'd *want* to. And then they could still exchange ideas and thoughts with each other. They could . . . be friends.

All this raced through her mind like fire through a parched glade. She jumped when she heard Tim's voice behind her.

"Siobhan? Come on, you've got to tell me. These poems are classic examples of early Irish epic poetry, probably twelfth century. They're perfect; beautiful, full of mysticism. I've never seen or heard of either one. You'll tell me where you got them, won't you? Isn't that why you showed them to me?"

Slowly she turned around, met his eyes, and nodded. "I . . . there's a book."

"A book?" Tim's voice was sharp with excitement. "What book? Where?"

"There's a woman, an old woman. The book belongs to her."

"But who is she? When can I see her?"

"You can't," she said quickly. "I mean, you're leaving."

"Siobhan, you have to tell me where she is. I have to contact her."

"That's not possible. She . . . she lives on Inishmaan, one of the Aran Islands."

"But she has a phone?"

"No, no phone."

"Hell! Well, what's her address? I can't believe I have to leave! What lousy timing. I'll have to write to her—"

"Tim," Siobhan interrupted him a little desperately. "Tim, this woman . . . she's old, really old, and . . . and kind of deaf. And she doesn't like strangers. I can . . . go and talk to her for you, if you'd like."

"Of course! Yes, you must, Siobhan. Please, it's important. Siobhan, you've seen this book yourself?"

She nodded.

"That's where you got these poems? You copied them out of the book?"

"Yes. Yes, I . . . I wanted to see if I could translate them. The book is written in ancient Irish."

"It is? My God, this is amazing. This could be one of the most important discoveries in ancient Irish literature of the last hundred years."

A voice screamed in her brain: *Tell him the truth, you fool! Stop this, it's going way too far. It's going to get out of hand.* But what Tim did next chased all thought of caution away. He took both her hands in his and looked gravely down into her pale face. It was their first touch and left her weak to the bone. His eyes were shining.

"Siobhan, you have to help me. I'm going to need you to be my contact with this woman. Will you do that for me?" She nodded, unable to speak. His hands were warm and firm around hers and his eyes were looking at her so intently she could hardly believe he didn't see the lie within her. "As someone who studies Irish literature, you yourself must realize that this book could be an important discovery. You'll need to ask her if she'll let me see it, study it. Maybe she'd sell it? Well, never mind, one thing at a time. You'll go and see her, and call me. I'll give you my cell number."

"And there's e-mail, as well," Siobhan said suddenly. Talking on the phone to him might be too intense.

"Of course." Tim laughed unsteadily. "Great." He was still holding her hands, and she was unable to look away from his eyes, bright now with excitement. "God, I wish I didn't have to go."

He didn't want to leave the Leeside. Siobhan searched his face then, surprised at her own hunger to learn if his words held a deeper meaning. Tim seemed to hesitate, then dropped her hands abruptly. Instantly they felt cold to her.

He said, as if to himself, "I don't want to blow this." There was a pause and he looked at her with a rueful smile. "Well, I guess it's time I got my stuff."

He ran up the stairs and she stood still, wondering if he'd

wanted to say something more, but thought better of it. She'd never know. And now he was leaving. But a link had been forged, and she'd have to be content with that beginning.

She went through the motions of cleaning up the table, listening to Tim moving around upstairs. His words echoed in her head: *I don't want to blow this.* She picked up his coffee cup and stared down into it. Slowly she ran her finger along the rim, stopping where she knew his mouth had been.

"Siobhan? I've got to get going."

The cup fell and smashed on the stone floor. She spun around to face him.

"I'm sorry—I startled you." He looked at the broken cup. "My fault. Can I help clean it up?" He started to put down his bag.

"No," she heard her voice answering. "I'll sort it."

He seemed to hesitate. "Are you sure?"

"You need to be off. It's a long drive."

"Well, okay. Don't cut yourself."

"I'll be careful."

They stood there for a moment. Then Tim nodded. "Good, good. Well, I guess I'll . . ."

"I'll walk you out to the car," she said quickly. She had the vague idea that it would be easier to say goodbye to him outside. She led the way through the bar and opened the front door. There were low clouds blowing in, some obscuring the tops of the surrounding hills, hiding from view their familiar shapes. Siobhan shivered.

"Yes, it's a chilly morning," Tim said. He threw his bag into the passenger seat, then turned to face her. "Oh, hey," he said suddenly, "we need to exchange e-mail addresses."

He opened his wallet and drew out two business cards. "Here's my card from school. Write your e-mail down on the back of this one." He pulled a pen from his bag and handed it to her.

She wrote quickly and gave him the card back. She watched as he stowed it carefully away in his wallet. "Great. You'll be hearing from me soon, believe me."

Even that promise couldn't check the misery that suddenly swamped her. There was no controlling this emotion, this horrible, choking, abandoned feeling. She couldn't speak, couldn't look at him. For the love of God, what was wrong with her?

Then she felt his fingertips touch her arm, a drop of warmth from a few inches of eloquent skin that went straight to her heart. The touch was brief but there was reassurance there, and she was able to raise her eyes to his.

"You're cold," he said, and his face looked very serious. "Go back inside."

"I'm all right," she managed to say.

He nodded then, and looked uncertain about something. She thought for a brief moment he leaned toward her but just as quickly he backed away.

"Well, goodbye," he said, as he walked around to the driver's side of the car. "Thank you for a wonderful visit." His tone was strangely stilted. He opened the car door, hesitated, and said again, "Goodbye, Siobhan." This time he looked directly at her.

"Goodbye." It was almost a whisper.

He got in quickly, and the car threw up gravel as it spurted away down the lane. Siobhan stood hunched against the cold, silky strands of her black hair fluttering around her. Just as the car was about to disappear, a fitful breeze lifted her hair in a dusky swirl to wave him on his way.

CHAPTER 7

Each wave, that we danc'd on at morning, ebbs from us,
And leaves us, at eve, on the bleak shore alone.

—THOMAS MOORE

Tim's flight home was agony. Thinking back to the night before, when he had secretly shared the story of Siobhan and Kee, he felt so humbled and so alone. With a beginning like that it was no wonder that these two people had forged a universe of their own, out of that most basic element of need. Almost everyone else they knew was totally excluded from it. How could he hope to be let inside?

To keep his mind from going around and around about Siobhan, he told himself to concentrate on the ancient book that Siobhan had possibly discovered. If authentic, it could be a very important discovery; it could be the making of his career. But most important to him was the thought of the unknown poems; learning them, translating them, trying to ascertain their authenticity, authorship, and essence. It would be a defining experience for him as a scholar.

But his mind would not be completely diverted from thoughts of Siobhan. He ruminated on the fact that she had never told anyone, not even her uncle, about the book, that she had betrayed the old woman's confidence for *him*. In going over the scene in his mind she seemed like such a child, a child saying, "Look what I brought you. Please be my friend." As if he could help himself.

He waited two endless days before e-mailing Siobhan, asking if she had contacted the old woman yet. She sent a message back saying she hadn't been able to find a day she could get to the ferry, and hopefully in a few more days she'd be able to go for a visit. She said she would contact him as soon as she had some news. He'd have to be content with that, but it was difficult to wait.

Again and again he read the two poems Siobhan had given him. They were like a lifeline. Both were extraordinary; the first one was a reflective work about the ancient land of Tír Na n'Og, or the Land of Youth, being replaced, after the advent of Christianity in Ireland, with the belief in heaven as the reward beyond life. It was both an expression of regret at the loss of the old folklore and a celebration of the newly embraced faith; a most unusual work. The second poem was about Saint Patrick. It dealt with his character as a man, a quiet, spiritual man with great inner strength who was driven to righteous wrath only in the face of slavery or human carnage. It was very powerful.

In fact, the poems were so unusual that the more he read them, the more they puzzled him. There were elements in each that seemed to hint at a foundation in Celtic paganism, but then the next stanza would be strongly related to early Christian mythology. They fascinated him.

Tim was extremely frustrated by the fact that he couldn't discuss the poems with anyone. He knew the inadvisability of disclosing, or even hinting at, the possible existence of the book until he had a chance to see it. His belief in Siobhan's story notwithstanding, his scholar's discretion told him this was best.

Dear Siobhan:

I'll try not to be too impatient. I know you'll do what you can. But it's a difficult secret for me to keep, especially since the two poems are so wonderful. Since I can't discuss them with anyone but you, Siobhan, would you mind giving me your impressions of them? I'd love to hear what you think. For instance, in that second stanza in the poem about Saint Patrick, do you think the line about God's anger is a reference to . . .

Thus they began a regular cyber correspondence, writing to each other twice a day. As a week went by, then another, Tim thought briefly that he could e-mail Kee as well. But somehow he never got around to it.

. . .

Siobhan sat in Maura's kitchen, telling the story that Uncle Kee had unfolded that night, the story she'd longed to hear all her life. Maura's eyes grew larger and larger with each new revelation. Her arms full of Triona, who was sleepy with a fever, Maura was riveted.

As she finished the telling, Siobhan exulted, "It's just such a burden gone, knowing it all. Since that night I feel so different, there are no dark corners anymore."

Maura shook her head in wonder. "Jesus, Mary, and Joseph! It's a bloody marvel, it is. Who knew that Kee Doyle could be opening up so? I'm glad for you, love. It's brilliant."

Siobhan sat back in her chair and gave a great sigh. "No more wondering. All of that behind me." She took a sip of tea.

"I can't imagine how much of a relief it must be. Are you remembering any of it?" Maura asked curiously. "Did the story bring back any recollections to you?"

Siobhan thought of the glimpses of past events that had opened in her mind after hearing her uncle's story. "Some," she admitted. "Nothing what you might call real memory—more feelings, like, and sounds and smells." She looked at her friend sadly. "Not nice things, some of them. Disturbing. Scary and confused. But flashes of excitement and fun, as well. The truth of it is it's all a kind of jumble."

"I never did understand how you weren't knowing every second of your history since Adam walked, like me. Like most folks around here. It made you seem so mysterious-like." Maura smiled at her. "You know, Siobhan, when we first became friends I felt almost that I'd invented you. I remember telling Tim that I thought here was a fairy, straight out of my favorite stories, just for me, to be my friend! Sometimes I was that scared you'd disappear into your fairy mound one day. And be gone."

"You thought that?"

"Well, I was just a kid—but as we got older I used to feel guilty about once believing that you weren't, well, real. Seems awful to think of it now."

"It wasn't awful at all. You've been a brilliant friend to me, you know that."

Triona stirred in her mother's arms, her angelic face flamed with feverish scarlet cheeks. Maura looked down at her. "All children look like fairies sometimes, don't they?" Then she looked at Siobhan and said soberly, "It sounds as if life with your mam wasn't fairy-like at all. A bit roughish. Not . . . secure.

I'm sorry for that. But it shows that you were a sturdy little thing, doesn't it? You came through it, and it all worked out right in the end, coming here with your uncle."

This was a new idea to Siobhan, that she might be a strong person . . .

"It did come right in the end, didn't it?" she replied slowly.

"Certainly. At least . . . it's not the end, God willing!" She laughed, then said breezily, "Just think, if Tim Ferris hadn't come to visit none of this might have happened—I mean, it all sort of started with that."

Siobhan flushed a bit. "Maybe so."

Triona started to awaken and fuss. Maura stood up. "I thought he was lovely. Tim, I mean. Are you keeping in touch at all?"

Siobhan nodded. "A bit, we are. With e-mail."

Maura smiled at her. "I'm glad." She left the room, murmuring under her breath, "It's a start."

· · ·

It was one fifteen in the morning and Siobhan had just finished sending Tim her last message for the day. They'd fallen into the habit of corresponding each morning and night at seven o'clock his time and one o'clock hers. It was a schedule that seemed to fit both of them. Siobhan turned off her computer and put her hands to her face. She didn't know how long she could continue the deception. She had told Tim the old woman was ill and wasn't seeing anyone for the time being. Every day she both feared and longed for Tim's messages, parrying his inquiries about the book and at the same time reveling in their discussions of the poems—*her* poems—and many, many more subjects as well. Just last night he had written:

I keep coming back to what you said that day when we first met by the lough wall, about studying ancient Irish poetry. Maybe I am searching for my soul within its depths. My soul has eluded me, I think, thus far in my life. But perhaps I'm secularizing things too much. Do I mean my spirit, rather than my soul? And is it a man's province to be intimate with his soul, or is that realm reserved only for a Higher Power?

Siobhan touched the computer screen gently with the tips of her fingers. She began to wonder if she loved Tim. She had nothing to go by, no personal yardstick to use. Her only knowledge of romantic love was through her beloved poetry. Were those feelings, eloquently expressed by so many writers, what she was experiencing now? The exultation, the yearning, the tenderness—were those what made up love? She didn't trust her own interpretation of her emotions. Maybe what she felt was only a beautiful platonic friendship. There were so many poems and essays about that kind of spiritual kinship. Siobhan simply didn't know. She thought of talking to Maura about it, but kept putting it off. The whole situation sounded insignificant. What could she really say? Tim had come for a couple of days and now they were e-mailing each other regularly. Even Siobhan knew that was pretty tame stuff these days when, and not only in the films and on television, people seemed eager to have sex at the first opportunity.

She knew that Uncle Kee and Katie had sex occasionally, and although it upset her, in many ways it truly puzzled her. Why did they feel they needed that in their lives? Surely they didn't feel the passionate, hopeless love for each other that the ancient poems described. Siobhan knew the mechanics of sex, of course. The nuns had done their duty teaching the bald facts and making the act of love sound like the wife diligently tending to her husband's leaky plumbing. But people obviously enjoyed it. More than enjoyed it. And if one were really in love . . . Siobhan could not even imagine what it would be like doing . . . *that* with Tim. Her whole body shivered involuntarily and quickly turned her mind away from the thought.

And then there was the Lie. The terrible, unfair Lie that she was building their relationship on. How could she put an end to that? Should she perpetrate another lie and tell him the woman had died and the book was lost? Would that finish the thing? Of course not. Tim would search and search for the book. He'd want to question the woman's family and her neighbors, anyone who had known her. Oddly, the woman had become quite real to Siobhan, small and wizened with pale, mistrustful eyes. She knew Tim wouldn't give up easily because a find such as a book like that was too important, not only to him personally but to Irish scholarship. What in the world was she going to do? The only lie in Siobhan's life before this had been the intentional failing of her Leaving Certificate, and she had carried the guilt of that around for ten years now. She had an inbred repulsion toward untruthfulness, which she pictured as an insidious octopus with ever-expanding tentacles. She found she had trouble eating these days and was distracted to the point that Uncle Kee had been impatient with her once or twice.

Siobhan even contemplated going to confession with Father O'Grady, though it had been years since she'd stepped in the church. Only while in school had she attended Mass regularly. Her uncle had been very honest with her: He found Mass boring and pointless, and he'd had too many priests knock his head into walls throughout his childhood to seek their counsel. So until Siobhan had been able to bike into Carnloe

herself, he had taken her to Maura's house every Sunday and
Siobhan had gone to Mass with the Currys. The nuns in school
were aware that her uncle didn't attend Mass, but they never
commented on it. They would have been appalled, however,
if she herself had not gone. That was not to be contemplated.
After all, with an uncle like that, they were the ones responsible for Siobhan's immortal soul and so they had practically
ordered the arrangement with Maura's family. She'd biked
alone into Carnloe from the time she was eight years old.

Siobhan always noticed how prominent God was in Maura's
house; it was hard not to. He was like the Other Family Mem-
ber, a stern relative whom they had taken in to live with them
out of a sense of duty and who made them all bend to His
will and whims. Rarely had Siobhan been invited over to other
girls' houses for birthdays and such, but when she was their
houses were the same, with the prominent painting of Jesus,
the photographs of present and past popes, the statue of Mary.
There was nothing like that at the Leeside. Again, another sign
of being different.

After much asking on her part, Uncle Kee finally unearthed
an old mildew-stained painting of a mournful-looking Jesus
that even he had been too superstitious to throw away. He told
her she could put it up in her room if she wanted. But she was
ashamed of it, and scared that God wouldn't like such an ugly
picture of His Son put on display—it looked like He had acne.
So she kept it in her wardrobe, resting against the side panel
in the dark. She would occasionally place little wildflowers
in front of it, but they saddened quickly in the darkness and
wilted. Siobhan never "outed" her God. He was kept in the
closet.

Siobhan had not been to Mass now for years, since Triona's
baptism. She had not been to confession since she left school

ten years ago. And anyway, what would Father O say? He'd tell her that her sin of lying could only be totally absolved if she righted the wrong and told the truth . . . and said three Our Fathers and ten Hail Marys.

Siobhan got up and went downstairs, letting herself out into a cloudless night. Not very often was the night crystal clear above the Leeside. Mists usually rolled in over the hills from the sea, or the lough itself created a haze from the humidity and cooling evening air. But tonight her world had a knife-edged sharpness to it. A full moon had turned the lough into a fairyland of black and silver—fluid, secret, mysterious. It seemed to not be her friendly, familiar lough at all but some elegant stranger paying an unexpected visit. Finding her intimate landscape so transformed was unsettling. Like looking in the mirror and discovering that the person looking back at you wasn't who you expected to see.

· · ·

"I don't know what the hell is going on with Siobhan these days," Kee said to Katie as they snuggled in her huge bed after an afternoon of enjoyable sex. "Her head's in the clouds all the time."

"How's that different then?" Katie teased.

"Very funny. She's never been as bad as this, and that's the truth. She barely hears me when I talk to her, her head's like a sieve with forgetting things left and right. It's bad."

"Maybe she's in love."

"Is that meant to be funnier still?"

Katie looked at him with raised eyebrows. "Do you think she's forgotten the professor then? He was like a man from a dream to her, you must be seeing that."

"I see nothing of the kind."

Katie snorted. "As usual."

Annoyed, Kee moved slightly away from Katie and put his hands behind his head, looking at the ceiling.

"She enjoyed talking with him, of course. He's a smart man with lots to say about Irish literature. It was a nice change for us to have him. But that's all it was."

She raised herself up on one elbow. "You are the most fecking blind man I have ever met. And that's saying something."

"Hey, now," Kee exclaimed, frowning. "Watch yourself."

Katie laughed derisively. "Oh, is that blasphemy then? Well, sorry if I don't apologize. We've known each other for how long now? I moved here fifteen years ago and you had me to bed within a month."

"That was your doing."

"I don't remember getting much resistance or hearing any complaints from your side of the mattress."

Kee retorted, "Well, what do you expect? At the end of the day I'm a man like any other."

Katie regarded him for a moment. "No," she said with surprising softness. "Not quite like any other."

Her words caused Kee uneasiness. For so long he had been leery of forging any bonds with a woman, and with Katie he was in real danger. Over the years she had been admirably transparent of purpose, with a clarity and honesty that he had found alternately alluring and alarming. Keeping Katie at arm's length emotionally while desiring to bed her had been tricky, but he'd managed it so far. He now realized this was getting harder, her pull was stronger. Maybe because he was getting older or for some other reason that he couldn't face right now.

Resisting a cruel temptation to just roll out of bed without a response, he smiled at her. "Don't be turning my head now with flattery." He kissed her briefly on the lips and then threw back the covers. "I'd best be off. No rest for the wicked and we're both that, eh?"

. . .

An unaccustomed restlessness was driving Tim up the wall. He hadn't even gone through his pages and pages of notes he brought home from his time in Ireland. Usually it was a task he couldn't wait to get to, rereading his translations and commentary and reflections, organizing them, printing out hard copies and filing them in his Ireland filing cabinet. But not this year. It was as if his entire trip had telescoped into those two days at the Leeside, and the two poems given to him by Siobhan were the only fruits of his journey.

On a Friday afternoon in late September Tim was cutting his grass so that the job wouldn't hang over his head for the weekend. He always used his friend Dave's riding mower and bought his own gas for it. Dave, a psychologist, lived up the hill from Tim's small, riverfront cottage. As Tim swung the mower around the curve of lawn he saw Dave's old Jeep stop in the yard and Dave climbed out. Tim finished cutting the swath and then rode over to the edge of the lawn.

"Hi, Tim," Dave greeted him. "Say, I have a conference in Glasgow next month and Becky is thinking of coming with me. She was wondering if you have any information on Scotland."

"The bulk of my Scottish knowledge dates from before the seventh century."

Dave smiled. "That probably wouldn't be much help then."

"I doubt it."

"Well, I told her I'd ask. We might take the boat out on Sunday. Do you want to come along?"

"Maybe. I'll let you know." Tim hesitated, then asked somewhat awkwardly, "Dave, do you think . . . are there people who have been so removed from life, so sheltered, that they wouldn't be able to acclimate themselves to the real world, ever?"

Dave looked at him in surprise, and Tim waited anxiously.

Dave spoke slowly. "Well, yes, there are people like that. But I also believe a lot depends on the individual. If they are basically normal and healthy, and have enough motivation to develop and expand themselves, then, sure, they can jump in and get their feet wet like the rest of us. Often with people like that they've just never been given the chance, or the choice, to come out of whatever cave they're in. But usually they need help. They can't do it alone."

Tim nodded thoughtfully. Dave smiled and slapped his friend on the shoulder. "Someday you'll have to tell me what the hell that was all about. Let us know if you want to go with us on Sunday."

That night Tim wrote an e-mail to Siobhan that hinted at his preoccupation with his visit to the Leeside.

I still haven't organized my notes from the trip. Somehow I just feel in a bit of a fog—distracted. Which can have consequences! I was almost late with an article, and—very unfortunately—the development director buttonholed me in the hall and got me to agree to attend an alumni event. She's a force of nature with steamroller charm. I'm committed now! I seem to have a head full of cotton wool—or maybe Irish wool?? Even my classes haven't fired my imagination. It's as if I'm in limbo. I'm just keeping my head down and doing the work. But sometimes everyone has to do that, right? I think I miss the Leeside . . .

He leaned back in his chair. Everything was on hold, nothing seemed important. Nothing except . . . Siobhan. Why kid himself? Those two times a day when her messages arrived were the current focal point of his existence. He got out of bed every morning with a light heart knowing that her words would be waiting for him. He devoured them eagerly, then went back and read them again and again, more slowly and almost dreamily, imagining her soft voice speaking to him. Then for the rest of the day the sound of her voice would stick in his mind to the exclusion of all else, like the last song someone hears.

Tim deleted the last sentence of his e-mail and clicked Send. He sat staring at his Scenes of Ireland screensaver. The romantic in him, always stronger than the pragmatist, wouldn't allow him to stop thinking of her. Like nothing else he had ever experienced, this girl had started an elemental struggle between his intellect and his emotions. She was such an elfin thing, a fairy without wings or wand. Tim read and brooded on the many ancient poems that warned mortal men of the dangers of fairy charm. *Do bhlaiseas do bhéal, a mhilse na miles! Is do chruas mo chroí ar eagla mo mhillte.* (I kissed thy lips, O sweetness of sweetness! And I hardened my heart for fear of my ruin.) He was at a loss as to how to proceed—or whether to proceed at all. She had bewitched him with her powerful innocence. That innocence, coupled with her passionate love for his own obsession, pulled him like the tides to the moon. And like the moon, she was unattainable. The tide did not pretend it could capture the moon. It adored from afar, reveling in the reflection of its beloved, but always apart.

PART THREE

SIOBHAN AND KEE

PART THREE

SIOBHAN AND KEE

CHAPTER 8

I might . . . eavesdrop on
their hopeless wisdom
as a blow-down of smoke
struggles over the half-door

and mizzling rain
blurs the far end
of the cart track.

—SEAMUS HEANEY

M aura had written an amusing article
about the "scholars' duel" for *The Irish*
Times, which put it on a wire service. A
few London papers picked it up for their Sunday supplements,
and one of the people who read it was a man named John Trotter. He sat in his flat in the Hampstead district and read about
Keenan Doyle and the Leeside. It was a gray, dreary Sunday
morning and John reached up to adjust his reading lamp. He
had to use his left arm because he couldn't raise his right arm
above shoulder level. John had been shot in that shoulder
twenty-seven years ago when he was a British soldier stationed
in Northern Ireland. On cool, wet days, such as this one—all

too common for London—his right shoulder ached just below the scapula. The disability had not mattered in his career as the manager in an auto dealership.

After he adjusted the light he continued reading. Keenan Doyle. The Leeside. John lifted thoughtful eyes from the newspaper. That place sounded familiar, although he hadn't gone into the west. Of course . . . Keenan Doyle. Maureen Doyle—*his* Maureen. This was her brother. He knew the name sounded familiar, it was an unusual one. And the pub—he remembered Maureen telling him her brother owned a pub by that name in the Connemara region. He read part of the article again. There was a niece who lived with him, a twenty-seven-year-old niece . . . Oh, God . . . a twenty-seven-year-old niece . . . It couldn't be . . . It wasn't possible . . . but just maybe . . .

John leaned back in his chair and closed his eyes. Instantly he was transported to that night at the fish-and-chips shop, almost twenty-eight years ago. The girl serving their meal had been flirtatious and adorable. He couldn't stop staring at her. His fellow soldiers ragged on him when he remarked there was no harm in asking her out for a bit of fun. He was engaged to a girl back home in London, but this girl pulled him like a magnet. He and Maureen began a lighthearted affair, full of fun, sex, good times, and plenty of alcohol. John had been miserable during his stint in Northern Ireland. He was scared and not sure what the hell he was supposed to be doing there. He didn't like walking down the street carrying his weapon at the ready and seeing the small children watching him with their big eyes, which grew less innocent by the day. Maureen offered him an escape from all that. She could make a joke out of anything, find fun—or make fun—anywhere. She was sweet, sensual, uncomplicated, and undemanding. When she told him about the baby he felt terrible, but she said not to worry about it. She wouldn't want anything from him: "These things happen, love. That's life. Believe it or not, I don't really mind—but God knows what my brother will say. Anyway, it was worth it. You were lovely."

He knew she wouldn't have an abortion. She was quite religious and went to Mass every Sunday, no matter how late they had been out the night before. A week after she told him about the baby, John was shot in the shoulder during a street melee in Armagh and invalided back to London. He wrote to Maureen once from the hospital, enclosing a few quid, but he didn't hear back from her. The next time he wrote to her the letter came back marked ADDRESSEE MOVED—UNABLE TO FORWARD. By then his wedding plans with Barbara were well under way and he decided he had to put Maureen out of his mind. It was obvious she considered herself done with him. He would just chalk it up to youthful indiscretion. It was a long time, however, before he stopped seeing her face when he turned off his light at night.

Then, two years later, John read about the Comagh bombing in the London papers. He always read the news stories of the Troubles carefully, and in this incident several British soldiers had been killed. The paper listed the names and had photos of all the victims and he saw it: Maureen Doyle, aged twenty. Maureen—dead. Adorable, vibrant Maureen. *Dead.* And the baby . . . what about the baby? *His* baby. He reasoned with himself: Maureen was probably married by now, so the child would have a father, right? But . . . but no, her last name wouldn't still be Doyle, then. So perhaps the baby was . . . John sighed. His wife was expecting their first child within the month. This would be terrific news to hit Barbara with. "By the way, dear, I've got a two-year-old kid from when I was over in Northern Ireland and now the mum's dead. What do you say? Care for another?" *Oh, shit.*

But the news nagged at him and after a couple of days he

phoned the police station in Comagh, explaining that he had been stationed in Northern Ireland a couple of years ago and was an old friend of one of the victims. He thought she had had a child; was there any way he could find out what had happened to the child? The RUC was helpful; they told him that the child was a little girl and she'd gone to live with her uncle, Keenan Doyle. He hung up the phone. He had a daughter. *A daughter.* But there was nothing he could do. She was at least with her uncle and not placed in an orphanage or foster home or anything. She was probably perfectly happy. She was fine. It was impossible to tell Barbara about it now, when they were expecting their first child. He had put Maureen out of his mind; he'd have to put his daughter out of his mind as well.

. . .

John Trotter's disabled shoulder now gave him a twinge as he came out of his reverie. He remembered it all so clearly, and so much had changed since those distant days. He and Barbara were divorced. Their son, Richard, was in his last year at the London School of Economics. John was still the manager of the auto dealership but the younger employees were aggressive and hungry for promotion, making him increasingly uneasy about the future. He lived alone in this flat, which he hated. He missed their little house with its monkey puzzle tree, climbing roses, and patio. But Barbara lived there alone now.

Slowly he got up and went into his bedroom. When he moved out of the house he'd gone through all of his things, deciding what to keep, throw away, or leave behind. He remembered finding the clipping of the article about the bombing and a photograph of Maureen, the only thing he had of her. He'd taken it himself. She was in a group of people, one of two girls and three soldiers in his regiment. He remembered the

day many years ago when Barbara had found it. He told her
that the two girls in the picture were dates of his friends and
that he had kept it as a keepsake of his friends in the regiment.
He looked at the photograph now. Maureen's bubbly spirit
glowed through the passage of time. What a darling she had
been. He wondered if his daughter looked like Maureen. He
wondered . . . He looked up and caught sight of himself in the
mirror above the dresser. *What are you doing?* he asked himself.
*What are you thinking? There would be no point—no point—in trying
to meet this girl. It was all such a long time ago . . . My God, it was a
long time ago, like it had happened in another lifetime, or to a different
person.* John's tired, sad eyes looked back at him from the mirror. *Don't go looking for trouble; it's not worth it. You've learned that
much in life. The fact that you're lonely and bored with life isn't enough
reason to do this.* He opened the drawer again to put Maureen's
picture back. Then he hesitated, closed the drawer, and, picking
up his wallet from the dresser top, slid the picture inside it.

· · ·

It was the time of year when the travelers came. On the fading
last day of September, when the hill greens were subdued and
interwoven with early autumn golds, Siobhan saw the little
group appear out of the soft, muggy mist. Galway Gwen and
her family were annual visitors at the Leeside. From astride
Blasket up on the hill, Siobhan spotted the bright blue van
in the lane, pulling a beige camper. That would be Gwen's
son, Turf, and his wife sitting in the van's front seat. Their
numerous offspring would be riding in the back. Every year
Siobhan looked forward to seeing if another baby had appeared
during the year's interval, or if another was imminent. Turf's
wife, JoJo, cheerfully produced them like an annual crop of
runner beans. The van drove very slowly, and soon the old

yellow-and-blue barrel caravan that Galway Gwen called home came rattling behind it. Her son and his flighty wife might prefer their fancy camper, but she'd stick to her pony-drawn abode that had been built by her late husband's own hands some fifty years ago.

Siobhan rode slowly toward the pub to greet them. These were old friends. Every year they stopped at the Leeside, and every year she and Uncle Kee bought sweaters created on the old woman's needles. Gwen knitted sweaters specifically for them now, for after years of selling to them, she knew their sizes and preferences for color and design.

Occasionally they would buy other things. When Siobhan was confirmed Kee had purchased a handmade necklace of copper and seashells for her, which Turf had made. Siobhan wore it on special occasions. There was a very special occasion approaching: Uncle Kee would be turning fifty in a few weeks. Siobhan hoped Gwen would have something unique that would be the perfect present.

"Hello the house!" she heard Turf yell. He always did that. He had seen it in the film *The Quiet Man* as a youngster and it had tickled him.

"Hello yourself!" she called as she approached.

The van doors opened and a wave of humanity tumbled out. JoJo climbed down with difficulty, as she was heavy with the late stages of pregnancy. But Turf moved like lightning, a quick, redheaded, scruffy fox of a man. Their five children were like drops of quicksilver, darting and fluid, redheaded like their father and, like him, reticent in speech. Ranging in age from eight to eighteen months, they were half wild with the freedom of their lifestyle, but their big shrewd eyes were wise with the knowledge necessary to survive a precarious existence.

Turf left his brood to fend for itself and went to guide his mother's pony into the pub's side yard. Siobhan knew that he liked doing things, keeping busy. He'd told her that anything was better than standing around talking to people. As Siobhan eased Blasket in the direction of the pub, she thought back to the night, twenty years earlier, when Turf had been a boy of thirteen and Uncle Kee caught him stealing a box of crockery from the pub's shed. Even now the thought of it sobered her, for the sight of six-and-a-half feet of her angry uncle bearing down on Turf filled her with awe. One clout from those over-size hands and Turf lay dazed on the ground. She remembered holding her breath as Uncle Kee squatted down and looked Turf in the eye.

"That's to let you know I settle my own scores, such as they are. I don't bother with the Guards. You and your mum, and your da when he was alive, have been coming here ever since I can remember, and are always welcome. You can go the way of those tinkers who want to steal everyone blind or you can keep your honor as a traveling man who wants only the open road and enough to keep his belly full. If it's the last, you'll always be welcome at the Leeside as a friend. If it's the other, there'll be no more stopping around here for you and yours. It's for you to decide, Turf."

He had succeeded in putting the fear of God—and the fear of Kee Doyle—into the boy's heart. Turf had told Siobhan he'd rarely stolen since. He and his family eked out a living collecting dole, selling wares, and scavenging, and Turf was usually able to get some carpentry work in Galway during the winter.

His mother, Galway Gwen, was stoic and steady like a rock—a traveling rock, if such a thing existed. She was most content during their traveling months, and just marked time while they camped on the outskirts of Galway during the cold, gray winter.

Siobhan rode up to Gwen's caravan and dismounted.

"Hello, Gwen. Hello, Turf."

"Good day to you, Siobhan," Gwen answered in her soft, gravelly voice.

Turf said, "Blasket's looking grand."

"Thanks. He's doing well. I see you've got yourself a new cart horse." Siobhan went over to the big skewbald with its shaggy hoofs.

"Aye," replied Gwen. "T'other one got sick and had to be put down. Ten euro it cost me. The bastards wouldn't let Turf do it."

"I didn't want to," Turf said to Siobhan in a low voice.

Gwen continued: "We picked this one up outside of Ballinaboy for not a bad price. He's a good-enough beast."

Siobhan patted the pony on the neck and looked into its placid eye. She didn't bother to ask its name. Gwen never named her animals.

"How does he look to you, Siobhan?" Turf asked diffidently. He had a healthy respect for her feel for horses. In some ways Siobhan had seemed "not all there" to him when he'd been younger. He had been a bit wary then, a bit in awe of the remote young girl. Now, after years of visits had shown him her guileless nature and kind heart, they were friends.

Siobhan deftly looked at the horse's teeth and eyes, then ran her hands down the pony's front legs and withers. She pronounced her judgment: "He'll do fine for you."

The door of the pub opened and Kee stepped outside.

"It's the Galway Gang, is it? You're welcome, as always. JoJo, would you like to take a load off?" She leaned against the side of the camper resignedly while the children clustered around a preening Blasket.

"Go on inside, woman," Kee ordered her. He reached up to

help Gwen descend, though she showed no sign of appreciating it. Siobhan held the door open for JoJo and motioned the children inside as well.

Turf said to his eldest, "Get the buckets, Dan, and give both these animals some water."

"Yes, Da."

Kee showed the young Dan where the outside spigot was and watched the boy deftly carry the buckets of water to the ponies. Galway Gwen stood by impassively as Kee reflected, "Watching Dan reminds me of myself at that age."

She nodded. "Simple things are tradition." Then she surprised Kee by quoting Seamus Heaney: " *'Once a year we gathered in a field of dance platforms and tents where children sang songs they had learned by rote in the old language.'* That one always puts me in mind of Puck Fair."

"Gwen, I'm speechless. You know Seamus Heaney then?"

"I've got to be doing something with my evenings. I can't abide television."

She moved slowly toward the door, coughing slightly, and Kee walked beside her, marveling at the complexity of these people beneath their deceptively primitive surface.

"How was Puck Fair this year?"

"Not bad. Young Dan won a goodly purse in the fishing contest."

"Lots of tourists?"

"More every year," she replied with some disgust. "It's getting so that except for the crowning of the bloody goat there's no much difference about it."

"But more people to sell your wares to."

"That's true enough," she admitted.

Gwen entered the pub and seated herself at a table alone. She sat regally despite her worn pink sweater and baggy flowered skirt. The wind had blown her wild white hair into spiky tufts like a crown upon her head. Gwen always bought a pint when she first arrived "to wash the road out of my teeth." Turf and JoJo had a pint as well, although at times Turf preferred whiskey. Siobhan always treated the children to Cadbury's hot chocolate, heavy on the milk. It was a rare change for them from their usual fare of sugary tea and carbonated soda.

"Isn't this nice, now," JoJo remarked after she drained half her glass in one draw. "You're both looking grand."

"When's the baby coming?" Kee asked her.

"In God's good time, Mr. Doyle. The doctor tells me it'll be around October eighteenth."

"That's my birthday," Kee said. "I'll be seeing fifty this year, and not with delight."

"Well, good luck to you, Mr. Doyle." Turf raised his glass. "Our babe could do no better than to share your day of birth, a fine gentleman like yourself."

"All right, that'll do," Kee said with a wry smile. He opened the cash register and took out a twenty-euro note. He placed it in front of JoJo. "Get something for the child."

Her thanks were profuse as she deftly took up the note and deposited it in her bosom, amply augmented by her pregnancy. After the drinks were disposed of, everyone went outside again so Kee and Siobhan could inspect the available wares. The children scattered like wild birds to burn through some of their energy. Galway Gwen hauled herself up the rickety caravan steps and opened the half door. She removed a large red velvet cloth from a huge old chest that doubled as a table. She opened the chest and lifted out two thick sweaters. She rarely gave Kee and Siobhan a choice anymore, but it didn't matter. They always liked the sweaters she showed them and bought them without hesitation.

"Here you be," the old woman said as she descended the steps. "I thought you might be wanting to see these two," she continued politely, knowing full well that the sweaters were as good as sold.

"They're grand as always." Kee handed them to Siobhan while he pulled out his money.

Siobhan stroked them with pleasure. They were beautiful. Uncle Kee's was a dark rust color and hers a soft heather blue, both knitted in an intricate pattern related to the Aran Island sweaters. As Kee paid for them, a look passed between the two women. Gwen correctly interpreted it as a signal that Siobhan wanted to look at more merchandise without her uncle being present. This was accomplished by Gwen thanking Kee politely and remarking that she wouldn't keep him away from his business any longer.

"Take these inside, Uncle Kee," Siobhan said as she handed him the sweaters. "I'll help JoJo round up the little ones."

Kee disappeared around the corner of the building, and Gwen said, "Right. Now then, missy, come along up and look around."

Gwen's caravan was kept neat, if not very clean. The walls and barrel ceiling were permanently grimed from the smoke of a million campfires mingled with the grease of bacon fat and the moisture of nature and humanity. But because it was so small, everything had its niche. It had always been a fascinating place to Siobhan from the time she'd first climbed the rickety steps at age three. Here was a world unto itself, as was her own world, but this one moved about. It was like being a turtle or a snail. Siobhan wondered what it would be like taking your house with you, out into the strange world, so that no matter where you ended up, you were home. When Siobhan was sixteen, and facing the dilemma of going off to university if she passed her exams, she'd asked Gwen about going out into the world. Did Gwen think that there were some people who were meant to stay in one place all their lives, just as there were people—like the travelers—who were meant to always be moving on? The old woman had considered the matter gravely before answering.

"I believe," she told the girl, "that there are some people who can never travel and some who can never settle. There are people who *think* they want the one and are stuck with t'other. But I do believe that there are a wheen of people who can make the change—if the want is real enough, and big enough. I'm thinking it's fierce hard to be a traveler and become a settled person, harder than the other way round. But maybe that's just my own eyes looking at it. I could never settle." Gwen paused, then went on thoughtfully, watching Siobhan's face. "The women in your own family had to decide about settling or no. Your grandmother—one of the dearest friends of my life—did it, but it went a bit against her nature. It's not that she wanted a free life, for she didn't. But she was a city person at heart, and life here was a mighty adjustment for her. But she did it out of love."

Siobhan's heart beat a little faster; Gwen rarely talked about the past.

"I wish I'd known her."

Gwen sighed. "As do I, lass. The two of you would have been grand friends."

Swallowing hard over the lump in her throat, Siobhan said, "I . . . I'm not remembering my mother much. You knew her. Did she . . . need to be free? Was that her decision about settling?"

"I wasn't knowing her well; she was young when she left. I remember that most times when we were here your mother would fly around like a sprite, always laughing and teasing. She had more energy than a flock of curlews. I'm thinking it wasn't so much a decision as her knowing her own nature. And following it. I think that took some courage."

"It's hard sometimes . . . not to be wondering what might have happened if . . . if she'd come back here, with me."

Gwen reached over and patted the girl's hand, a rare gesture.

"No regrets, child. You don't need that pain in your young life. Just look at the road ahead. It's worked for me."

Siobhan looked now at all the goods that Gwen, Turf, and JoJo had made, collected, bartered, or bargained for over the last year. Jewelry, belts, scarves, hats, tea towels, pots, pans, and tools. There was nothing that struck Siobhan as being quite right, quite nice enough for Uncle Kee's birthday present. She knew Maura would take her into Clifden to shop if she wanted her to, but it would be more special coming from Gwen. She had hoped to find something here. She hesitated, reluctant to not buy anything, wondering if she should just get some small item for herself. Then her gaze fell on a carved mask hanging on the caravan wall. It was about ten inches high, carved from bog oak, and was a faithful rendition of an ancient Celtic statue. It was perfect.

Siobhan said, "That mask. Where did you get it?"

"Oh, some carver at Puck Fair had them. He fancied one of my sweaters and asked to pay with that. I thought it was pretty enough." She coughed hollowly.

"It's grand. Could I . . ."

"It's yours for thirty." She didn't mention the fact that she had demanded two of the masks in payment for the sweater and the second one hung in Turf's camper.

"But is it really for sale? I mean, if you like it . . ."

"I've looked at it for a month. That's enough." Gwen took

the mask down from the wall and handed it to Siobhan without hesitation. Siobhan accepted it gratefully and paid her. She could have bargained Gwen down but that was not their way. Uncle Kee had talked to her about it years ago. "These people have little enough, compared to us, with the dole and all. We can afford to pay what they ask—it's only once a year."

Siobhan lingered and knew that Gwen sensed she wanted to talk about something. Time was nothing to Gwen so she perched on her blackened stool and lit a cigarette. Siobhan felt peaceful and at ease with her, and made no effort to hurry herself into conversation. She'd always felt comfortable with Gwen and Turf; even though their lifestyle was a complete inversion of her own, they were "different"—set apart, a bit peculiar—as she herself was.

"Gwen," Siobhan finally asked, "can you love someone if you don't really know them? And how can you tell if you love them?"

Again, as she had years ago, Galway Gwen considered the matter gravely before answering.

"Those questions are as old as those hills out there, missy. Have you learned nothing from all that old poetry you're always reading? But then, the poets never get it quite right, do they? Because what's true in love for the poet might not be for them that's reading it. Love has as many faces as there are faces on God's earth, that's the way of it. And there's no one trick or rule that'll tell you what you want to know. But I'll tell you what *I* think. If when you're not together there's a little emptiness inside you—not some bloody craziness, mind, but an empty hollow deep down in yourself—then that's a love for a lifetime. That's the way of it, as I see it."

. . .

Siobhan sat down at her computer at 12:45 a.m. to e-mail Tim:

The travelers came today. Gwen, the old stalwart, her son
Turf, his wife JoJo and their children. They come every
September around this time. Sometimes they camp
overnight, although they didn't this year. Remember
the lines from the fourteenth century "The Land of
Cockaigne"?

In Paradise what can you see
But flowers, grass, and greenest tree?
Though joy and pleasure there are good
Ripe fruit's the only kind of food;
There is no hall nor bower nor bench
But water man his thirst to quench.

Every time they visit I think of that—Gwen and her
family experience all those feelings just like our ancestors
did a thousand years ago. I think that means a lot to her;
it unites her freedom with her history. And I love being
connected to the rhythm of their lives. I always look
forward to them coming. Each year we buy sweaters from
Gwen. They are thick and warm and knitted in lovely
colors. One of my favorite things is a soft blue shawl that
my grandmother got from Gwen years ago. I love the feel
of it around my shoulders. I also bought a present for
Uncle Kee. His fiftieth birthday is next month, and Gwen
had a wonderful carved Celtic mask, of the Janus figure on
Boa Island. She is a kind, wise woman. I think she likes the
world to believe she's hard. Maybe she is, in some ways,
but only in things necessary to survive—things in her head,
not in her heart.

Siobhan's own heart beat a little faster as she typed the next paragraph.

I find myself lately wondering more about what it would be like to see some of the world. I've spent my whole life at the Leeside. I see people who go here and there but don't seem happy. I also see people who've taken a good look at the world, and only then have made their decision about where they want to be. Like the Kellehers, or Brendan and Maura, or even Katie. How does a person really know where they are meant to be? Do you think you've seen enough of the world to know where you would be happy?

Or with whom, she finished the thought. She clicked the Send button and her message was cast out into the dark early morning.

CHAPTER 9

> *Although I can see him still—*
> *The freckled man who goes*
> *To a gray place on a hill*
> *In gray Connemara clothes . . .*
>
> —W. B. YEATS

Maura's father died a week after the Galway Gang had come and gone. Seamus Curry was seventy-six and had outlived his wife by almost twenty years. Siobhan thought about Mrs. Curry as she biked into Carnloe to help Maura get ready for the wake. Siobhan had only a few memories of her friend's mother, who died after giving birth to Maura's brother, Niall. She did have a vague recollection of a rich laugh and large, soft bosom and hips. The smell of flour and yeast had hung about her, whereas the smell Siobhan most associated with her own mother was the sweet muskiness of cheap perfume. Siobhan barely remembered Mrs. Curry's death. One day she was there and then she wasn't. It seemed frighteningly simple.

And now Maura's father was dead. This was the first time in Siobhan's adult life that someone within her tiny sphere had died. The idea that she might miss someone who wasn't

KATHLEEN ANNE KENNEY · 128

around anymore was new, although deep within her were the charred embers of the young child's grief for her mother. These had been fanned to a soft aching glow after the night of Uncle Kee's revelations. Now, approaching the Curry house, Siobhan slowed and stopped her bike. For the first time she contemplated walking into that kitchen and not seeing Seamus in his ancient basket chair, going into the sitting room and not smelling the smoke from his old pipe, and not seeing Triona sitting on his lap pretending to follow along as he read to her.

Something caught in her throat and to her horror Siobhan realized it was a sob. She wanted to cry. She pressed her hand over her mouth to hold it in. Oh, God, she thought, so this is grief. How awful it is, how powerful! How did people bear something that made all that was familiar so painful? *Nothing could be worse than this,* she thought, *because everything familiar is our security, is what we hold on to.*

Again the wail rose in her throat and she stood motionless, willing it to go away. She could not, would not give in to it, for if she did it would swallow her up.

"Siobhan! Come in, what are you doing out there?" Maura's voice cut through her emotional turmoil, and she turned panic-stricken eyes toward her friend. She saw Maura's face, concerned and puzzled, coming closer, and felt the touch of her hand.

"Siobhan, what is it?"

Siobhan swallowed hard, swallowed the sob into the pit of her stomach, where it lay like a bitter draught.

"Maura," she whispered, "how can you bear it? How can you?"

Maura's eyes flickered and she took a deep breath.

"Come inside, *now*," Maura said harshly and propelled Siobhan through the door, leaving the bike to clatter to the ground. Closing the door and leaning against it, Maura gave a shuddering sigh and looked at Siobhan accusingly.

"Mother of God, Siobhan, what do you expect me to say? Do you expect me to explain the whole mystery of death and loss and grief to you? I'm having a hard enough time holding it together for Triona and Niall without you draining me dry as well!"

Siobhan could not have been more shocked if Maura had slapped her, but it served the same purpose.

"I'm sorry," she whispered, "I'm sorry."

"Oh, God." Maura closed her eyes. "No, I'm sorry. I didn't mean it, Siobhan. I'm just worn down. I've hardly had time to cry it out myself these last three days."

"Do you want to cry now?"

Maura looked at her, startled, then started to laugh. But the laughter quickly turned to sobs and Maura covered her face with her hands. Some instinct told Siobhan to put her arms around her friend, guide her to the sofa, and sit with her until the shaking stopped. She was full of compassion for Maura, who was so strong, always in control. Not anymore. Only grief could do this, Siobhan thought. Only grief is stronger than the strongest of us.

Later, much later, they talked over tea. Maura even managed to laugh about the old basket chair.

"Triona has informed me that it is *her* chair now. I'm not even to think of getting rid of it, which is a pity. Much as Da loved it, it's a disreputable-looking old thing. I had hopes of throwing it on the harvest bonfire. Ah, well. Having it here still might ease things a bit for Triona."

"How is she doing?"

"Very well, actually. Grandda's in heaven with the angels and she feels if we can't have him here, that's the next best place."

There was silence for a few minutes, then Siobhan said, "As I was biking over, I was remembering when your mum died."

Maura smiled sadly. "I've been thinking about that as well. I was so hurt by it. I thought that God must dislike me very much to take my mother away, or at least didn't care enough about me to keep such a horrible thing from happening."

"I remember when we'd be playing how you'd stop sometimes and bury your head in your arms."

"Poor Siobhan. How helpless you must have felt."

Again there was a silence and then Siobhan leaned forward, a troubled, guilty look on her face.

"I used to be secretly glad about it," she whispered. "It made you more like me, not having a mother. I hated myself for feeling like that."

"Oh, Siobhan." Wearily Maura shook her head and sighed. "How secretive you've always been, how ready to accept the burden of thinking badly about yourself. It really must stop, you know. Please try. Promise me you'll try."

Siobhan nodded, eyes downcast. "I will try. I don't like feeling that way, so I will try, Maura."

"Good." Maura smiled and patted her hand.

Siobhan lifted her head and looked around. "The house feels different. A stuffiness, like there's too much air cooped up inside . . . like it misses Seamus breathing its air. Do you feel that?"

Maura shuddered slightly. "Jesus, Siobhan, I don't know. I suppose I do, but I don't have your poetic soul. I just wish I could get one more hug and tell him I love him." She visibly shook herself and stood up.

"This isn't helping us get ready for tomorrow, is it? Let's get busy."

Later when Siobhan biked home there was little comfort for

her in the familiar beloved scene. This would have frightened her if not for Maura, who had explained that this intense grief might be overwhelming now but would be diluted by time. They must give in to what they were feeling now, or it would prove more painful to purge themselves of it later. If they pushed the fresh grief from them, it would leave a dull sheen behind, coloring the everyday in shades of gray that no amount of tardy tears would wash away.

Since the night of revelations, as Siobhan thought of it, she and Uncle Kee were trying to talk more about, well, everything. There had been too much silence, too much traveling on the path of least resistance. The steps they were now taking were on a more difficult path, slower going and unfamiliar to both, with a far more varied landscape and infinitely more satisfying.

Siobhan went into the pub and straight over to where Kee was cleaning the taps. She laid her head briefly on his shoulder, and he touched her face with his fingers.

"Ah, love. A bit roughish, was it? How's Maura taking it?"

"She cried a lot today. I think it made her feel better."

"I'm sure it did."

"She said it's all right to feel so awful now, that we should give in to it."

"Well, she's right about that. When the wound is fresh, that's the time to feel the pain."

Siobhan sighed and spoke softly in Irish, "It seems very cruel, the strength of grief, the power it has over us."

Kee looked into her face. He spoke slowly, "It may seem cruel, yes, but to feel it and give in to it is a strength, you know. People are afraid of grief, afraid of the reality it gives the passing. They see it as a bottomless pit but that's wrong. It's more of a . . . a bloodletting, I suppose. Something we must go through to get beyond, to get better."

"Did you grieve for my mother?"

His head moved slightly back from her at the question, and his eyes left her face, fixing on the window beyond.

"Not as I should have, not as I needed to. I didn't have time." He gave her a quick smile. "I had a little child to make welcome, remember?"

It occurred to her that, like Maura, Uncle Kee had lost his mother and father as well. Could she ask him about it?

"Uncle Kee, do you remember when your father died?"

The question seemed to disturb him, and he frowned. "Of course. Most people would be remembering a thing like that."

"Can you talk about it?"

"Well, I can but I'd rather not."

"Oh." She didn't press him, but continued thoughtfully: "It's a wee bit strange that you and I, and Maura, have all lost our parents, isn't it? Mothers and fathers all. I never think about my father anymore, but I used to."

She felt him tense, and he looked away. Was she hurting his feelings? But she was in the mood to talk, a new circumstance for her. She was determined that they should talk about things more. "I'm sorry, Uncle Kee—but isn't it natural that I would wonder about him?"

"I suppose."

"That night, when you went to Comagh to bring me home, did you—"

"Siobhan." He cut her off, looking troubled. "Siobhan, some things . . . It can't all come at once," he said carefully.

She understood. Important things were worth waiting for.

Siobhan moved to safer ground. "Why were Maura's parents so much older?"

He smiled, clearly relieved at the change in subject. "I've wondered why you've never asked me that. Seamus was a fisherman, as you know. Never really interested in women. He was almost fifty when he married Maura's mother. She herself was over forty, a spinster who'd come to Carnloe to visit a friend. They were two lonely people who just decided that they were each other's last chance."

"Even though Seamus was older, she died first?"

"Aye, she died giving birth to Niall, a fairly worthless product. She was forty-nine at the time and not in good health, I remember. It was too much for her."

"So they weren't married very long."

"No, only eight years or so."

"But it was important that they did get married," Siobhan persisted, "important that they found each other."

Kee looked into her earnest face. "Yes, love, I'd say it was very important."

"It was the loneliness that made them do something about it, made them want to change things."

"Aye, it was the loneliness," Kee repeated softly, almost to himself. "It was the loneliness."

Siobhan nodded and went into the kitchen to cook for the evening customers.

Later she sent a long e-mail to Tim about Seamus's life history and death, and her talk with Maura. Tim wrote back, filled with compassion.

Maura and Kee are very wise. The reality of emotion is easy to run away from, especially when there's pain involved. I've done it myself. I certainly closed myself off from people after my divorce. It just seemed easier, and I felt that I probably wasn't too great to be around anyway. I went into a sort of cold forensic analysis of it all, which helped me somewhat, but in the end I just had to chalk it up to we didn't care about each other anymore. The end of a marriage is a strange thing. You become almost more aware of the density of a relationship after it's over.

Please tell Maura how sorry I am about her father. It's hard when people you've known all your life start to leave you. Those are the ones that help tether us in the universe, I think. And death can illuminate missed chances, which adds to the sadness.

You asked me if I had seen enough of the world to know where I would be happy. I'm not sure we can attain happiness from a place outside ourselves, and I'm still searching for that one. I love Ireland, yes, but I may be asking too much of it to bring me contentment. I don't know. Surely we should believe that people are more important than places?

. . .

Seamus Curry's funeral had an unreal, theatrical feeling for Siobhan: the church packed with familiar people, looking strange in their best clothes; the incense with its cloying, artificially sweet smell; and the words of the service sounding like lines in a play that one shouldn't examine too closely so as to not discover they have no significance. To Siobhan it seemed that the function of those prayers was to wash over people, numbing them, so that their ears merged the words into soothing noise. The responses by the congregation seemed to ebb and flow with an empty endless rhythm. She knew, however, that most of the people around her did receive comfort from this and felt, surprisingly, a tiny hollowness inside herself where this comfort could not be found.

Afterward everyone crowded into the Curry house for whiskey, beer, tea, and cake. Siobhan helped by keeping an eye on Triona, and followed her when she suddenly pushed her way through the crowded kitchen and out the back door. The little figure in the dark blue dress, red curls flying, sailed through the gate at the end of the garden. Not bothering to call after her, Siobhan followed, keeping her in view. She saw Triona head for the tiny quay where a few fishing boats lay stranded by low tide. The little girl stopped at a derelict iron bench, the place where, in fine weather, her grandfather had sat watching the boats and men do what he had done for so many years. Triona scrambled up onto it and lay faceup, shiny pink nose and shiny black shoes pointing to the sky. Rigid and unforgiving, she stared at the mixture of white clouds, whirling seabirds, and windy sky swirling above her head.

Siobhan came up and sank to the ground beside the bench. Neither of them said anything for a time, then Triona spoke in a tight little voice.

"So, that's where he is, up there, in heaven? That's right, isn't it?"

Siobhan nodded. "That's right," she answered with conviction. After all, she didn't *know* it wasn't true.

"I'm not sure heaven is all clouds and that. Grandda would be very bored if that's all there was."

"Maybe heaven is a different place for different people, you know, what everyone would be wanting."

Triona nodded sharply. "I like that. I think that's right. I'm sure Grandda's heaven has lots of water and a boat just for him."

"That's nice."

There was silence for a few minutes. Then Triona sighed heavily.

"Those people are all so silly. I wish they'd go."

"They'll go soon."

"Can we stay here until they do?"

"Yes."

Siobhan got up and sat on the bench, lifting Triona's head so that it could rest on her lap. Triona closed her eyes and Siobhan looked down at her angelic face, as she had many times before. Now there was a difference, however. Siobhan felt fierce, protective stirrings, a primal need to make Triona's pain go away. She also felt the helpless frustration of realizing that she could not. *So this is how Maura and Brendan feel*, she thought, *how Uncle Kee feels about me.* A tenderness of such intensity it weakened the knees yet gave birth to a granite resolve. That the strands of love could have such power seemed a wondrous and mysterious thing to Siobhan, a revelation of emotional fulfillment on a cosmic level. Would she feel this way about a child of her own? But she would never have a child, she knew that, had always known that. The tears that she would not shed at the funeral came now. What would it take for her to grow up? She just wanted to grow up.

"Siobhan! Triona!" It was Brendan calling them. "You two all right?" He glanced at Siobhan's wet face, then addressed his daughter.

"Come along, love, Auntie Nora is leaving and she wants to say goodbye." He scooped her up in his arms.

"Is everyone gone?" she asked with a frown.

"Just about."

"I want to see Niall."

Brendan glanced at Siobhan. "He went off for a bit with his friends, darlin'. You'll see him later on."

He walked quickly back to the house, Siobhan trailing behind as she wiped her tears away. As they came in through the back door they heard raised voices.

"I can't believe you're not giving the boy the boot!" It was Uncle Kee. "Now that your da's gone, get him out of the place so you and your man and wee one can have some privacy."

Maura's voice sounded exasperated. "You know nothing about it, so keep your advice to yourself, if you please. He's family! Or don't you understand that concept, Kee Doyle?"

Siobhan hadn't seen Maura with her eyes flashing with anger and her hands on her hips since her friend had flown to Siobhan's defense in grammar school.

"He's important to this household! I love him, he's my brother. And Triona loves him. I'll not have her life disrupted even more by heaving Niall out of the house before Da's cold in his grave." She caught sight of Triona in Brendan's arms.

"Oh, Lord. Come here, love."

Brendan put her down and Triona ran to her mother with a disapproving look at Kee, who she usually adored. Maura took a deep breath.

"I'm sorry, Kee, but I'll not have you poking a paternal nose in our business now that Da's gone. Brendan and I know what we want, we know what's right, don't we, Brendan?"

Her husband looked Kee in the eye. "Thanks for weighing in with your opinion, Kee, but Maura and I have things the way we want them. Triona, give Auntie Nora a kiss goodbye."

Siobhan and Kee walked back to the Leeside, Kee muttering under his breath and Siobhan preoccupied with thoughts about Tim's last e-mail. People should be more important than places, but what if the two were so intertwined it was impossible to separate them?

She came out of her reverie long enough to interrupt her uncle's diatribe almost impatiently. "There's no point in going on about it, Uncle Kee. Maura and Brendan are right—they're knowing what's best for them. You'll need to respect that."

Her uncle stopped in his tracks, and she looked at him, surprised. He gazed at her with a curious expression, as if caught off guard by an unfamiliar scent.

CHAPTER 10

I met the Love-Talker one eve in the glen,
He was handsomer than any of our handsome young men,
His eyes were blacker than the sloe, his voice sweeter far
Than the crooning of old Kevin's pipes beyond in Coolnagar.

—ETHNA CARBERY

Siobhan was at Katie's farm, helping her ready three of the ponies she had sold at the Connemara Pony Show. All three were being collected today by their new owners.

They had just finished loading one, a placid animal sold to a family with two small children. The boy and girl had been excited, dancing around and yelling, and even Katie's irritated gaze failed to quell them. The pony stood stoic and oblivious of the racket, cropping grass and looking bored. Siobhan hoped he would be all right with this family, but then chided herself. Katie was careful about whom she sold to, and the parents seemed to be caring, reasonable people. They were just letting the kids work off some steam before the long drive home.

When the family left, Katie, Siobhan, and Katie's head groom, Mike, prepared the other two horses for their departure. A mare and a gelding had been bought by a Waterford businessman who would be arriving soon.

"Make sure you put the blue halter on Eppie," Katie instructed Siobhan, who nodded. She was a little sad to see Eppie being sold. Eppie was the youngest half sister to Blasket; she was the last foal out of Blasket's mother who had had four offspring before dying a year ago. Siobhan herself had named the foal Epona, after the ancient Celtic goddess most associated with horse symbolism. Katie had quickly given her the nickname Eppie, which had disappointed Siobhan but not surprised her.

Halter in place, Siobhan checked Eppie's hooves then stood stroking the mare's forehead as she watched Katie and Mike deal with the more spirited younger horse.

"Does this buyer have any other horses?" she asked Katie suddenly.

"No," Katie replied without looking up, "these are the first of his own. He grew up with them, though, and now he's just bought a big place so he's getting started with these two."

"Do these two get along all right? Have you pastured them together?"

Katie glanced over at Siobhan then, eyes slightly narrowed. "Of course. Did you think I wouldn't be doing that, knowing that they're going away together? Have some sense."

"I was just wondering," Siobhan replied, a trifle sullenly.

"I know Eppie's a favorite of yours, Siobhan," Katie continued briskly, "but she's the prettiest two-year-old I've got and I knew she'd sell well, which she did. I am running a business here."

At that moment a large black SUV towing a trailer came bumping into the farmyard. It stopped and a thirty-something man jumped out, looking at his cell phone. He was, Siobhan noticed with an unfamiliar shock, the handsomest man she'd ever seen.

"Good morning!" he called over to Katie.

"Hello," Katie answered, then said in a soft aside, "God, this guy's gorgeous. About ten years too young for me though, damn it. Although I could always try my luck." Siobhan gave her a startled look. "I'm only joking, for God's sake, Siobhan. I think," she added, as the man came up to them.

"Nice to see you again, Katie."

"Welcome to Hilldale Farm, Patrick. This is Siobhan Doyle, a friend who helps out sometimes. Siobhan, this is Patrick Kelly."

The man held out his hand and after a slight hesitation, Siobhan offered hers.

"It's grand to meet you, Siobhan." His voice was like a low, warm harp and held an underlying note within that was unfamiliar.

"Hello."

Katie took Patrick's arm. "Well, here are your new babies. Did you get your barn finished?"

"Just. I had to chivy them along quite a bit but the walls are up and the floor is done. They're coming out next week to do the electrical."

"I remember you telling me about it. Sounds like a nice setup."

Siobhan watched them walk away, chatting. Eppie nudged her shoulder, looking for attention and possibly reassurance. As she stroked the animal she was hoping this Patrick would be *kind*; she was wary of his polished businessman air. Patrick and Katie stopped near the gelding and Siobhan saw Patrick casually but deliberately turn so he was facing her. Then he looked at her with a slight smile, an odd confident smile, as his eyes carelessly took her in head to toe and back again. Then he turned his head back toward the gelding to listen to Katie's instructions.

Siobhan stood very still, her hand paused in its petting.

What had just happened? Then a phrase, something she had overheard at the Leeside from a couple of women, came into her mind: "He was absolutely undressing me with his eyes, the randy bastard." *Undressing me with his eyes.* The phrase had caught her attention because Siobhan hadn't known what it meant, not then, but she did now. Her body tingled with an unwelcome warmth and she led Eppie farther away, turning her back on Katie and Patrick.

Her mind tossed in confusion. In one way she was disgusted and frightened by the look she had received, but in another way it caused a strange excitement. Did he think she was pretty, then? *Was* she attractive to men? She was so used to ignoring the male customers she served at the pub that their looks or flirtatious comments had never had any meaning; to her they were no different than remarks about the latest rugby game. Now she could see that those looks, those words had meaning, a personal meaning, directed toward *her*, because the men had thought she was attractive. She looked at Patrick Kelly again. Suddenly she realized that *she* found *him* attractive. He was handsome and romantic-looking. She knew that a few weeks ago such a thought would never have occurred to her. Something had changed in her.

Her skin was covered in goose bumps and she shivered. Siobhan wrapped her arms around Eppie's warm, moist neck. Did some of Tim's looks, some of his words, hold a deeper meaning that she'd missed? With sudden insight, Siobhan realized that if those intimate signals are sent toward an oblivious recipient, they die a death that is not without some pain for their host. She didn't want to cause Tim pain, she didn't want to hurt anyone.

"Siobhan! Are you sleeping, girl?" Katie was upon her. "I've been screeching at you for five minutes. I supposed you're daydreaming. A great one for the daydreaming, this girl," she remarked to Patrick Kelly.

"Oh, that's not such a bad thing," Patrick said in his mellow voice, as again the intimate smile played on his lips.

"Well, come on, it's time to load Eppie," Katie said impatiently.

Siobhan took hold of the pony's halter and hung back as Katie and Patrick started off toward his trailer. But Patrick paused and waited for her, stepping around so he was on Eppie's other side.

"Katie tells me you named this mare."

"Yes. Her real name is Epona, not Eppie."

"Epona. Oh, yes, the Celtic goddess of plenty and fertility."

Siobhan looked at him, surprised. "You know Celtic mythology?"

"Some. There are some wonderful stories, aren't there? Katie says it's quite a passion with you."

His use of the word "passion" bothered her; he had given it an odd little emphasis.

She merely nodded.

"There's quite a bit of intensity in those old myths," he remarked in a musing tone that sounded faked even to Siobhan's untrained ear. "A lot of wars and magic spells and fiery emotions—romantic desires. Quite fascinating, really."

Siobhan walked faster, her skin infused with heat.

Amid the concentration and commotion of loading the ponies, first Eppie and then the gelding, Siobhan managed to escape to the farmhouse right after the trailer doors were closed. She did not want to talk to Patrick Kelly again nor catch any more looks from those assuming eyes.

She sat in Katie's huge kitchen, breathing irregularly. An unwelcome, almost grotesque question formed itself in her mind: Was her obsession with ancient poetry, poetry celebrating intense passions, a result of a sexual blindness? Hard on the heels of that came other questions. Did she find Tim attractive in a sexual way? Did the thought of being in his arms create an image too profoundly disturbing to bear? Oh, God. Siobhan closed her eyes. Yes, yes, and yes. She took a gasping breath, she felt herself drowning in an emotional tempest. *The surface. Stay on the surface.* Siobhan stood up, trembling, and pressed her hands to her head, almost physically pushing the thought of Tim as a lover out of her mind. She didn't need that in her life, she *didn't*. Only the yearning for it gave it reality. And that, she told herself, she would not do.

On the ride home Katie was in a mood and began asking questions about her impressions of Patrick.

"What did you think of the man, then? Even you couldn't fail to notice a man as bold as that one!"

Siobhan didn't respond. She refused to be baited. Katie tried to provoke a response. "Oh, come on, Siobhan. If you tell me what you thought of him, I'll tell you what he said about you."

Siobhan told herself that she had no curiosity about what Patrick Kelly might have said about her, or anything else.

Katie was exasperated. "God, you're stubborn! You and your uncle are sure enough cut from the same cloth. Can't you say *something*? So that I know you're fecking breathing over there?"

A moment passed, then Siobhan muttered, "He'd just better be good to Eppie, that's all I'm saying."

"He will be," Katie said sharply. "I vet my buyers, Siobhan Doyle, you know that." She paused and then announced, "And by God, you are dead from the neck *down* if a man with that face and body doesn't cause some kind of a stir in you."

Siobhan seethed with disgust toward Katie, and with

self-loathing. Because Katie was right—she had noticed Patrick Kelly. As a woman notices a man.

"I didn't like the man," she declared in a shrill tone, "so all his boldness was wasted on me!"

Katie glanced over at her with raised eyebrows. "Well, well. There are embers burning somewhere. He was interested in *you*. When I was telling him about your giving Eppie her proper name, he pumped me about your interest in Irish mythology. Did he talk to you about it?" Siobhan nodded and Katie gave a snort. "I suppose you're writing the man off because he was ignorant."

Siobhan shrugged. "He knew who Epona was, not that I'm caring."

"He did not! I told him."

Siobhan looked over at Katie with an annoyed frown. She asked, in spite of herself, "Well, why would he say he did, then?"

Katie rolled her eyes. "Oh, for God's sake, Siobhan, the bastard was flirting with you! Just bullshitting! That's how the game is played."

"It's not a game," Siobhan retorted resentfully.

"Well, not to the uninitiated," Katie commented with an annoying smile.

"And why should *you* be looking at a man like that?" Siobhan said with accusation. "I thought you and Uncle Kee—" She stopped herself in horror. The very last thing she wanted was to let Katie think that she assumed they were a couple. Her stomach turned at Katie's gratified smile.

"Well," Katie remarked smugly, "Kee's knowing better than anyone that *I'm* not dead from the neck down."

The rest of the drive was accomplished in palpable silence.

. . .

Kee stretched to reach the far corner of the pub window he was washing. This was usually Siobhan's job but she was up at Katie's farm lending a hand. Katie had sold eight ponies at the Connemara Pony Show—the best she'd ever done, and Kee was proud of her.

As Kee wiped the glass with his smelly rag full of vinegar and water—why bother to buy expensive, fancy cleaners?—he thought about Katie. They had made love again a few days ago—twice in one month, which before now had never happened. Their average was about five or six times a year. And this last time had been at his provocation, not hers, also a first. Was he becoming more fond of her? Or just randier? No, it wasn't that. He was thinking about Katie a lot these days, whereas before he had thought of her only rarely when not actually with her. Their relationship had always had an immediacy to it, driven by Katie's healthy sexuality. It was true that from their first meeting there had been friendship between them and they often had platonic interaction. But more and more when Katie "gave him the eye" his attraction to her erupted with disturbing force. He knew in his heart that the danger of him falling in love with her was real.

Kee had never consciously ruled out marriage; rather he had made an intuitive assumption that marriage was not for him. At first there was Maureen and the pub, big responsibilities he felt were better shouldered alone. Then there was Siobhan; he hadn't wanted anyone else "fiddling" with her. And all through that time there'd been the constant struggle of his alcoholism. When Siobhan got older he felt his independent nature was too ingrained, too much a fundamental part of who he was, to allow another adult into his closed circle. But now that *he* was older, and starting to yearn for the companionship of a real partner, there was still Siobhan. At twenty-seven she was still with him and little better equipped to deal with life away from the Leeside than when she first arrived. Sometimes he betrayed himself by reflecting that he had kept Siobhan far too sheltered, had created for her such a calm harbor that she was incapable of ever sailing away from it. But then he became defensive against such disloyal thoughts. She was a niece—a daughter in all but name—to be proud of. If he had created a soul too gentle for this world, was it his fault? Or the fault of the world for being the kind of place where the kindhearted were damned as fools and gentleness was confused with weakness? Maybe Siobhan had never really lived, as Katie never tired of telling him, but at least she had never suffered either.

His thoughts were interrupted by the beep of a car horn. He looked around to see Katie's Rover bouncing into the yard. It stopped and Siobhan climbed out, thanking Katie for the ride. But Katie was getting out, too, and one look at her told him something had aroused her sexual appetite.

"Well," she began teasingly, "that's a sight I never thought I'd see, Keenan Doyle washing windows. It's a side of you I never suspected."

The wave of longing that the sight of her created actually frightened him. He looked away and only smiled slightly, shaking his head. He sensed Katie's surprise at his silence.

Siobhan said, "Uncle Kee, you're soaking wet. That shirt's going to reek of vinegar."

"I'd best change, then. Nice to see you, Katie." He disappeared inside. Siobhan picked up the bucket, followed her uncle into the pub, and shut the door. A minute later she wondered why Katie was still standing in the yard; Siobhan could see her out the window, just standing and staring. Well, it was no business of hers. She dismissed Katie from her mind and went about her work.

Katie still stood outside alone, because she felt as if a mile-high wall had just appeared between her and the Leeside. That's it, then, she thought dully. She had revived her hopes during the last couple of weeks; Kee had been much more approachable—and *approaching*—than she could ever remember. He'd shared thoughts and worries with her, they'd had walks and talks that were new in their relationship. But the reason for today's quick exit was obvious. He regretted it. *That's it, then,* she thought hopelessly.

Frustrated and hurt, she wrenched open her car door and climbed in. As she drove away she lectured herself, as she had so many times before, that she had to forget about Keenan Doyle. But the hopeless tears that clouded her eyes told her she never would.

. . .

The door closed with a tired click behind John Trotter as he dragged himself home. It had been a long day. He met his new boss, an energetic young woman barely older than his own son, clearly determined to establish herself as a force to be reckoned with. John knew with certainty that facing her every day would be exhausting, and that she clearly considered him "past it." Maybe he was. He felt a hundred years old right at this minute.

Another disappointment had been his son canceling a lunch date for today that they'd arranged several weeks ago. "Too much reading" to get ready for a test at the end of the week had been his excuse. His son had inhaled Barbara's competitive attitude toward everything in life, and the task at hand was always more important than people. After twenty-five years of that attitude John thought he should be used to it by now, but the disillusionment was always a shock.

John lowered himself into his familiar chair with relief, and decided to order Chinese takeaway instead of cooking tonight. He took out his wallet to check how much cash he had, and called to place the order. Then, as he had many times in the last few weeks, he pulled out Maureen's picture to look at it. He'd gotten into the habit of clipping the picture next to his computer at work in the morning and then taking it with him at night. He held it in his hand as he turned on the television and let the images skim over his brain. After a time an advertisement for dog food captured his interest. Today the cleaning lady at work had told him she'd soon be a grandmother, and the ad on the TV showed a comely child romping with a collie on an improbably green lawn, a "this is England" idealized image. John watched the glossy animal gambol in the sunshine.

John turned his attention to the child, a redheaded boy about five years old, laughing and rolling around. He didn't consciously think about the child, he just watched and felt the joy and innocence that the ad's director had intended him to feel. After the ad was over, John looked at Maureen's picture for a long while. Then he found himself getting up and walking to his computer, where he went online and bought an Aer Lingus ticket to Shannon.

CHAPTER II

> *Though leaves are many, the root is one;*
> *Through all the lying days of my youth*
> *I swayed my leaves and flowers in the sun;*
> *Now I may wither into the truth.*
>
> —W. B. YEATS

It was the middle of October and Keenan Doyle was turning fifty in a few days. Siobhan painstakingly planned a party at Sean Cahill's restaurant in Clifden. The Leeside would be closed for the evening, which wouldn't be a problem since most of the locals were attending the party. Sean and Bettina, his wife, had wanted it to be a surprise party, but Siobhan saw the futility in that and told Kee about the planned festivities. He feigned annoyance to mask his pleasure, which didn't fool her for a moment, and promised to act suitably surprised when, instead of a quiet dinner with Siobhan, he would be confronted by a roomful of his friends and neighbors.

"And can you tell me who'll be there?" he asked Siobhan.

She replied, "I don't think it's too much to ask that at least the guest list be a surprise, though I doubt if most of the faces will cause a shock."

He hesitated, then inquired casually, "Have you asked Katie to come, then?"

Siobhan looked at her uncle gravely. Katie had been noticeably absent from their lives lately. "Of course I have, and no, I don't know if she's coming."

Kee nodded and left the room. He had no idea why Katie had been avoiding him the last few weeks. It wasn't a contrived absence from the pub, some stupid stunt to make him miss her or get him thinking about her. He'd have smelled that. For some reason she didn't want to be around him. It was the suspicion that he might have hurt her—*could* she be hurt?—that was bothering him, and bothering him a lot if the truth be told. And he was surprised at how much he missed her, how much he longed for her.

Impulsively he decided right then to go out to her farm. He drove almost recklessly, at one point overtaking a truck stacked with building supplies, and his van bounced into the yard near Katie's large stone barn. Kee was rewarded with the sight of her standing next to a youngster and his mother, and holding a pony by its halter. As he was about to call out, he saw her quickly climb onto the convenient animal and whisk it away down one of the riding trails. Kee froze as he was about to climb out of the van. Had she seen him? He thought she had, but he couldn't be sure. He caught the interested gaze of the young mother as she herded her son toward their vehicle. Quickly he shut his door. Fine, he thought. It was only a neighborly visit, after all. It's not like he needed to see her. Kee started the van's engine and didn't notice that his drive home took twice as long.

The next morning Siobhan wanted to scrub down the pub's stone floor, so she and Kee carried the tables, chairs, and stools out into the yard. It was a mild, sunny day and Siobhan kept the front door propped open as she moved methodically with her bucket and brush across the flagstones. Each was just a little different in size, shape, and color, and she knew them all. She knew the spots that were worn smooth as polished marble, the textured patterns full of hidden color within the gray, and the tiny pitted pockets where the water pooled. It was a job that was very calming; Siobhan's mind was tired from her endless ruminations about Tim, Uncle Kee and Katie, Seamus's death, and a hundred other thoughts.

Outside Kee repaired some of the furniture that was more the worse for wear than the rest. Niall Curry was fond of rocking back and forth on the barstools, which wreaked havoc on the leg joints, a habit for which Kee never tired of rebuking him.

After a while Siobhan heard her uncle call out, "Uh-oh, here's someone coming. We might have to be serving them out here."

They would definitely have to get served out there, Siobhan thought. She was finishing this floor if the visitor was Queen Maeve herself.

There was a short silence and then he exclaimed, "My God, it's Gwen and Turf."

Instantly Siobhan's stomach tightened. Something was wrong. She stood up and walked outside. Turf helped Gwen out of the passenger seat of a very battered old station wagon. Dan, Turf's eldest child, was standing by the car, looking around with bright eyes.

Gwen's sick, Siobhan thought with alarm. Her friend's face was drawn and pinched, the resignation settled into it making it almost a stranger's face.

"This is a surprise," Kee said to Gwen. "Is everything all right? You're not looking quite the thing, Gwen, if you don't mind my saying so."

Gwen didn't answer; the effort of getting out of the car had captured her breath.

Turf looked at his mother, and answered for her. "Mum's been sick, coughing and that. We've been in Clifden for a time, letting her rest."

Kee took Gwen's other arm as he said, "I'm sorry to hear that. Come inside, now. Siobhan, put some chairs back—"

Gwen shook her head impatiently. "I'll sit outside."

Turf looked at her sideways, a little nervously. "Mum, it's a bit cool out here. Remember the nurses were saying that you—"

"Outside."

The two men exchanged glances and settled her in a chair at a table.

Kee asked, "Are you wanting a pint?"

"Tea, if it's not too much trouble." Gwen lifted her gaze to Siobhan, who hadn't spoken yet. She nodded slowly, reading the older woman's look.

"Right. It's no trouble."

Quickly she got tea ready for them all, finding some chocolate biscuits for Dan. The one thing she wanted was to get Gwen to herself. Gwen wanted to talk to her.

Siobhan carried the large tray outside.

"Good news," her uncle said. "It's just a touch of pneumonia. With rest and medicine she'll be great. Right, Gwen?"

"Aye. Thanks for this, Siobhan." Gwen raised the large blue cup to her lips and closed her eyes as she took the first sip.

Turf said, "Mum was just wanting a day out, so I borrowed a friend's car and, well . . . we just came." He seemed a trifle doubtful.

"That's grand," Kee said stoutly. "We're always glad to see you, Turf, you know that."

Young Dan had taken two biscuits from the package Siobhan offered him and now began prancing around.

"Can I, Da? Can I go up the hill to find Blasket?"

"Aye, go on with you," Turf answered his son with affection.

"Why don't you all three go?" Siobhan suggested boldly. "I'll sit here with Gwen." She looked at Gwen, who nodded and added her agreement.

"That's right, you go on. We women want to have a wee chat."

Siobhan said brightly, "You can take your tea with you."

Kee looked surprised but Turf immediately agreed. "Let's be off, then." He picked up his mug of tea and strode away quickly.

"Come away, Mr. Doyle," Dan urged with excitement. "We'll pretend we're stalking fairies!" He ran past his father toward the hill.

Kee laughed and shrugged. "Right. Stalking fairies it is, then."

The two women watched as the men slowly began the trek up the hill path, following the joyful boy. Gwen said with rare gentleness, "Dan'll not be forgetting this day."

"I'm glad you brought him," Siobhan said, and watched Gwen take another sip of tea as if it were some restorative elixir. Siobhan's heart beat a little faster as she asked, "How are you really, now?" She already knew the answer.

Gwen fixed her gaze on the hill. "It's TB I've got, child. I'm dying."

It hurt to have the words spoken out loud. Siobhan heard them with a harshness that wasn't present in the speaking of them. Sympathy seemed out of place here, so she said nothing.

There was silence for a few moments, and then Gwen said matter-of-factly, "I've known for some time. No one's knowing except you, and the folks at the clinic. Not even Turf." She looked at Siobhan then. "You're not minding me telling you?"

Siobhan could only shake her head. She didn't need to state the obvious to Gwen, that she was touched and humbled to be her choice of confidante.

Gwen continued thoughtfully: "I needed to come here. I needed to be seeing the Leeside one more time. It's a special sort of place, I'm thinking. Being sure of a real welcome is a grand thing, and we were always finding that here. Maybe the only place we did. There's a freedom in that."

"I'm glad," Siobhan murmured.

"There are other reasons. I needed to be telling someone about this, to have one other body know. You came to mind. I needed to say the words out loud, to get used to them."

In spite of herself, Siobhan needed to ask, "Why me?"

"Because your granny told me when she was dying. Right here, at the Leeside. She told only me about the cancer—she trusted me with it. Never would I have been thinking that would be the last time we saw each other. But that trust meant the world to me. So, here I am, doing the same with you." Gwen smiled wryly then and leaned forward. "And you're the only woman I'm knowing who isn't silly. You keep yourself to yourself and I respect that. You're not full of jabber. And I knew you'd care," Gwen added, almost as an afterthought.

"Oh." Siobhan poured out more tea, her throat thickening.

"There's a fearsome strength in most women," Gwen went on. "You've got that strength, too, missy, never doubt that you do." She gave a disgusted click of her tongue. "Turf had to go and marry one of the silliest creatures on God's green earth. We've never seen eye to eye on much of anything."

"When . . . when will you be telling Turf?"

Gwen set her jaw. "I'll not be telling him. He'll find out soon enough from the doctor. It's better for him to be hearing it from someone else—and better for me."

Siobhan swallowed hard. She felt compelled to offer, "Do you . . . would you like me to—"

"No, missy." Gwen looked at her with surprised gratitude. "I thank you, but no. The truth will keep." She paused and then said, "But 'tis good of you. Seems to me that women are like rivers that never run dry. And we must be a wellspring for each other."

After that the two women sat quietly together, united in understanding and a sense of kinship. Siobhan thought about what Gwen had said about needing to confide in another woman. It made her feel like an adult of equal standing and Siobhan treasured that feeling, and the confidence it gave her. There truly was an affinity between them because of their sex, she reflected; some mystical bond between women that compelled them to share burdens and joys, and the bearing of life itself. Siobhan had never felt part of that before; she knew instinctively that she should cultivate it, crave it, and that if she did her life would be immeasurably enriched.

They sat there for a long time. At one point, after Gwen had had a coughing spell, Siobhan asked Gwen if she was cold.

"No."

Eventually the men returned, striding through the tall hill grasses in single file.

Gwen asked, "Why do men seem to walk the hills like they need to conquer them? They're always proving something," she added obscurely.

Even young Dan's energy had flagged and the goodbyes were not prolonged. Gwen didn't even reach out to touch Siobhan but Siobhan didn't expect it. Too soon did the ramshackle car disappear over the rise. It was almost as if she had imagined the visit, Siobhan thought. She wondered if she would ever see Gwen again.

Siobhan jumped at the sound of her uncle's voice.

"Did you and Gwen have a good chat, then?"

"Oh, yes."

"She's really not looking well. Let's hope she gets better before the winter sets in."

Siobhan nodded as she gathered the dirty dishes onto the tray.

Kee mused, "It felt strange to be seeing them, didn't it, not at their time? Almost turns the calendar on its ear—they've always been so regular over the years."

"I know." Siobhan started inside.

"Siobhan? Is everything really okay?"

She answered him over her shoulder. "Everything's grand."

Strange that lying for someone else was so much easier.

. . .

In that night's e-mail, Siobhan told Tim about Gwen's visit, without telling him about the TB. But her tone was sober, and she made it clear that her old friend wasn't doing very well. After reading it over, she wanted to lighten things up a bit before she sent it.

One bright spot in the past month. Because of Maura's article on the scholars' duel, Uncle Kee is more of a local celebrity than ever. It hasn't hurt business at the pub either! Most amazing of all, the London wire services picked up the story and he got a phone call from a professor of Irish studies at King's College asking if he'd like to come and give a talk on ancient Irish literature! Wasn't it brilliant?? Uncle Kee declined, but I can tell he felt a great sense of triumph at being asked.

Ever since the day she'd met Patrick Kelly at Katie's farm, Siobhan had felt sorely tempted to ask Tim about his failed marriage. She longed to know why he had fallen in love with his wife. Did he miss anything about her? Did he miss being married? But tonight she clicked Send without taking that leap into more delicate waters.

They still communicated daily, a vital correspondence to each. She tried hard to give her e-mails a friendly tone, nothing more. But it wasn't easy. A hundred personal questions and reflections slipped through her fingers into the keyboard, about things she couldn't resist wanting to hear his thoughts on. Added to that was her guilt about the book deception, which was expanding exponentially. Whenever Tim mentioned the book and his excitement about its potential, she felt trapped. She was running out of things to say about it. In the past few days she had been forced by her own desperation to e-mail Tim another poem.

I saw the woman again and asked about you seeing the book. I explained who you were. She is reluctant and said she'd think about it. She let me copy one more poem, which I've sent in an attachment. I hope you like it.
    Uncle Kee's fiftieth birthday party is tomorrow. Sean Cahill is having the party at his restaurant. And Sean is having that article of Maura's laminated and framed as a present. Isn't that brilliant?

. . .

Tim thought this last poem she'd sent him was quite the most wonderful of the three. It was a passionate ballad about a woman's virginity being the only possession that is truly hers alone. It was full of traditional virginal imagery of blooming roses and rushes by a stream, full of verse that shimmered with emotion. It was achingly beautiful. Tim longed to show it to someone but, of course, he could not. He longed to return to the Leeside to see Siobhan and hear her voice talking about this wonderful poetry.

He couldn't understand why Siobhan had said she hoped he

liked it. Of course he liked it—he loved it. Her attitude toward the poems was oddly tentative. It was true that there were confusing elements in the poems. But his approach was less scholarly and more emotional. Because it was Siobhan that had revealed them.

Their correspondence was growing progressively more personal, more confiding, more intimate. Was it likely that his heart would beat faster and his face grow warm as he read her e-mails if his interest in her was purely scholarly? Some of her questions and messages were so provocative and endearing that he longed to have her sitting right here, in this kitchen, so he could listen to the music of her voice and look into those incredible eyes. But the more Siobhan opened herself up, the more he realized just how naïve and disassociated she was from the modern world. He struggled, therefore, to keep his e-mails more reserved than he wanted to. But it wasn't easy and more and more often he failed. He resisted phoning her because he was afraid that the sound of her voice would defeat his resolve. He e-mailed Siobhan back.

Tell Kee Happy Birthday from me. I'm sure it will be a great party—wish I could be there! It seems to be a year of fiftieths. My parents are having their fiftieth wedding anniversary on New Year's Day. I'm helping some relatives plan the party. Otherwise I might have come during the holidays to see you. I miss you and would love to discuss this last poem face-to-face. It has such beautiful imagery and the verse flows so gloriously. Please let me know your thoughts on it. I still think often of that night we walked by the lough and had such a wonderful talk.

He hesitated in his typing. Was he getting too . . . romantic? Then he remembered what Maura had said about men and

Siobhan. *It isn't that they don't get any encouragement. There's just no recognition on her part that anything is happening. She has had little experience with men.* No, it was okay; Siobhan would only think he was being friendly, nothing more. And that's all I am being, he told himself firmly, as he clicked the Send button.

· · ·

The food at Sean's restaurant was the best Siobhan had ever tasted. Every time she went there the food was the highlight for her. Sean and Bettina were very kind to her, although she didn't feel she knew them very well or they her. She realized now, as she sat looking at them, that the fault was hers. After all, Sean had known her since she had first come to live with Uncle Kee. Siobhan remembered going to Sean and Bettina's wedding when she was about seven or eight. Bettina was comfortable, plump, and serene. She took in her stride the huge demands of running a busy restaurant and was indulgent when more than half the work fell on her shoulders. Her husband was the more gregarious of the two and the customers liked Sean to visit with them; he was part of the draw of the place. Bettina preferred her kitchen duties to socializing. But her heart had gone out to Siobhan when she had met the wee girl and most of Siobhan's cooking skills were learned at Bettina's hands. But cooking was the only plane on which they met. The inert pale girl had not melted in the warmth of Bettina's friendship. Siobhan, more self-aware of how others perceived her, regretted that now. She wanted to stop being shy of people. But how did one go about doing that?

Katie was here tonight. Siobhan was glad for Uncle Kee's sake; she knew how much he had wanted her to come. In fact, Katie was sitting next to him. Siobhan noticed her uncle maneuver that arrangement with a subtlety she hadn't known he possessed. She watched them for a few moments, almost in wonder, as her uncle's big rugged face lit up when Katie smiled at him. They seemed less flirtatious tonight, more . . . genuine than she had ever seen them. Suddenly Siobhan looked away, not wanting to see any more. She wondered forlornly if that small ache in the back of her heart was a yearning for Tim. Was it the emptiness Gwen had spoken of? Or was it the sting of unease about Katie getting closer to Uncle Kee? She toyed with her food, the fresh dilled salmon having lost its appeal for her.

Across the table Katie felt light-headed and not totally in control, a rare experience for her. She had decided to come to Kee's birthday party simply because she'd known her absence would cause comment. Never had she dreamed that Kee would be so glad to see her, so . . . attentive. It threw her off-balance, which didn't happen very often. Could it be happening at last? Was Kee beginning to look at her as more than just a close friend—who was also good for a shag once in a while? It was impossible to keep her soaring hopes under control when he was sitting six inches away and looking at her with those deep-set gray eyes. If he was really ready to take the relationship "to the next level," well, she always thought she'd be prepared, know how to handle it. Good God, she'd dreamed of it often enough. But she felt only a schoolgirl giddiness, most unlike her usual calculating composure. Ever since she had first seen him behind the bar so many years ago she had longed for him, and she was the least romantic of women. The truth was that if this huge beautiful man whom she had wanted for so long actually started to return her feelings, she knew his love would change her fundamentally. For how could she go from being an essentially unhappy person in her very core to being joyfully fulfilled and not be utterly transformed?

"Katie . . . are you listening to me?"

She looked into Kee's eyes, which reflected his uncertainty at her apparent inattention. Katie laid her hand over his, a warm, firm gesture of connection, not coquetry.

"I always hear everything you say."

His face softened and his own fingers closed over hers. Their absorption in each other made them oblivious of the intense interest they were causing among the other guests.

Bettina was sitting across from Siobhan and noticed the girl picking at her food. Siobhan was, as usual, quiet tonight but the loss of appetite was new. Bettina correctly guessed the cause was Kee and Katie's behavior. As it always had in the past, Bettina's heart was stirred by Siobhan. The major sorrow in her own life was that she and Sean had been unable to have children. A bad bout of the mumps when he was a teenager had rendered Sean sterile. Bettina had recognized within herself strong maternal feelings that she had learned to rein in over the years. She was successful in doing this most of the time, although the young restaurant staff benefited from her mothering instincts. But there was something elemental in Siobhan's unspoken needs that never failed to bring out a maternal rush of feelings. That the girl had never responded to her had been a source of frustration when Siobhan was younger; now it was just a lingering regret.

Anticipating that her overture would be gently rebuffed, as had happened so often before, Bettina leaned forward.

"How have things been for you lately, Siobhan? Everything all right at the pub these days?"

Siobhan raised her eyes and Bettina was moved to see real distress in them. Then their expression changed to one of questioning uncertainty. Bettina held her breath. Was it possible she wouldn't get the standard "things are grand" response?

Siobhan, for her part, heard Bettina's question and looked up to meet her gaze. There was genuine concern in those warm hazel eyes, genuine caring, genuine interest.

Siobhan felt as if she were seeing Bettina, *really* seeing her, for the first time. This nice, comfortable woman might understand . . . might listen. Should she respond? Instantly she was transported back to sitting with Gwen that day outside the pub, reflecting on the affinity of women. Bettina knew Siobhan was troubled; Siobhan could feel her concern, like an invisible touch of the hand. Even if there wasn't agreement or understanding, the desire and will to listen was the real gift women gave each other. And few could make it easier than Bettina, who had cared about her since childhood.

Siobhan took a deep breath and said, "Things are . . . a wee bit complicated just now, I'd have to say."

Bettina regarded her with bright eyes and nodded. She merely said, "I was thinking they might be."

Siobhan struggled on. "I'm . . . I'm not very used to thinking about things, you see. Serious things."

Again Bettina nodded. "I know. It can feel like your mind's going around in circles, so it can."

"Aye, that's it," Siobhan said eagerly. There *was* understanding here. "It's so confusing, so hard to sort things out."

"I know. That's why it can help to talk with someone."

Siobhan did want to talk. She felt an almost overwhelming urge to do so. She glanced down the table at Katie and her uncle, then looked back at Bettina.

Pushing back her chair, Bettina raised her voice slightly. "If you're wanting to see the new deep fryer, love, come away into the kitchen."

Siobhan immediately stood up and followed her hostess through the kitchen doorway. Each of them leaned against a counter and when Siobhan didn't speak right away, Bettina reached out and covered Siobhan's hand with her own.

She asked gently, "Is it Kee and Katie that's bothering you?"

"It is," Siobhan admitted. "That and other things. But why?

Why should I mind so? If being with her makes him happy, that's what should matter. I can see that but shouldn't I be able to feel it as well?"

"Maybe. But as my mother used to say, 'It's not a should world.' We don't always do or say or feel what we should. We'd all be wearing wings if that were true. And be much more boring into the bargain."

"But why do you think I'm minding so much?" Siobhan persisted. She wanted some answers.

"Well, you don't like Katie, for starters. I'm not crazy about her either, although she's showing a side of herself tonight that's surprising to me. Katie's a man's woman—and that has lots of meanings but basically what I mean by it is that she's more comfortable with men, that they fulfill her emotional needs better than other women do."

"Isn't that lonely?" Siobhan was again thinking of her time with Gwen.

Bettina regarded her with interest. "Yes, I should imagine it is—at least, sometimes. But we're talking about you. Am I wrong to assume you just don't like Katie?"

"No, you're not wrong, but it's a shameful thing to admit."

"Is it? We can't like everyone, Siobhan, although I'll say in this case, since she's someone who's important to Kee, it's a problem."

"How can I change the way I feel about her?" Siobhan asked bluntly.

Bettina laughed. "Well, that's a tough one, darlin'. I might be asking the same, since Kee is one of our closest friends." Bettina paused and shrugged. "Maybe it's just a habit we've fallen into, not liking her. It never hurts to try to see someone with new eyes, to let go of old baggage. And since it means a lot to Kee, well, it's worth a go."

Siobhan nodded. It meant a lot to Uncle Kee. She would try.

Bettina continued, more slowly this time. "But even if Katie was your favorite female in the whole world . . . well, it would still be understandable that you'd be upset about Kee showing a . . . a serious interest in someone else."

"A serious interest," Siobhan repeated. The words had a strange foreboding sound.

"The two of you have been all in all to each other, love. I'm not saying it was inevitable, mind, but the possibility was always there that he'd fall in love some day."

Siobhan raised sober eyes to Bettina's face. "Do you think they're in love, then?"

Bettina nodded. "I do."

Siobhan didn't feel surprise or dismay or even jealousy. She only knew that the concept of Uncle Kee truly in love was a vast reality she needed time to get her mind around.

Bettina was regarding her with compassion. She smiled. "It goes both ways, you know. You're a young and lovely woman, Siobhan. There's a special man out there looking for you and when he finds you, it'll be Kee coming to terms with that."

Siobhan blushed, and Bettina raised her eyebrows.

"Goodness, child—is there someone?"

But Siobhan felt drained; she wasn't up to beginning a new conversation about her feelings for Tim. She was grateful to Bettina for her insight about Katie and Uncle Kee, and said so.

"You're more than welcome, Siobhan. Thank *you* for talking to me. It wasn't so bad, was it? Let's try it again sometime."

Siobhan gave her the shy smile her friends treasured. Just then the kitchen door opened and Sean came in with an armload of dirty dishes.

"We're starting to clear in there, my lovelies. Lend a hand, eh?"

"Right," Bettina said briskly and she and Siobhan headed into the dining room.

Sean followed them out and asked Siobhan, "So what do you think of our new deep fryer? Cost me an arm and a leg, that did."

For a moment Siobhan looked at him blankly, and then she caught Bettina's amused look.

"Oh, it's grand," she answered quickly. "It's grand altogether." Bettina winked at her.

Sean made his way to where Katie and Kee were seated, and started to clear away more dishes. Katie was speaking to Brendan on her other side, so Sean took the opportunity to lean down and whisper jokingly into Kee's ear, "What in God's name is happening tonight between you and Katie? Are you going to be putting up the banns?"

To his astonishment his friend turned to him with a face alight with happiness and said, "Damned if I know, Sean. But she's bloody great, isn't she?"

Sean looked at Kee in wonder. "She is that, my friend, she is that." He walked off toward the kitchen, bemused at the idea of Kee Doyle in love at last.

. . .

Two hours later everyone was getting ready to leave. Kee and Katie offered to stay behind to help clean up. Siobhan started to protest, saying that she should do it, it was her and Sean's party for Uncle Kee and he shouldn't be cleaning up after . . .

She stopped as Maura quietly came up to her and murmured, "Don't you see they want to do it? They want to stay behind together." Siobhan looked at Maura and saw the truth in what she was saying. Maura raised her voice and announced, "If you two are willing to take on the job we'll not stop you. It'll keep Kee from getting a swelled head after all the lovely bullshit we've heaped on it tonight. We'll take Siobhan home."

Siobhan went up to Bettina. "I loved the leek casserole you served tonight. Can you share the recipe?"

Bettina smiled happily. "I can. The cheese sauce can be a wee bit temperamental. Would you like me to come by the Leeside later this week and we can make it together?"

"That would be grand."

. . .

Siobhan, Maura, and Brendan drove home on the dark roads, Brendan driving quickly and with ease, for he traveled this route every day of his working life. Siobhan sat silently in the back. Maura was trying to decide if she should broach the subject of Kee and Katie, who were obviously in the throes of advancing their relationship. Kee's attentiveness to Katie tonight had surprised Maura, but it had also pleased her. Their preoccupation with each other was a new development and to Maura it had seemed sincere. But how was Siobhan feeling about it? Maura was certain Siobhan would not welcome a deeper relationship between Katie and her uncle but decided to wait on bringing it up now. She'd wait until she was alone with Siobhan and after her introspective friend had had time to get used to the idea.

"There's a car parked in the yard," Brendan remarked as the Leeside came into view. The light was on over the pub door and they could see a lone figure leaning against a sedan.

"Well, the sign says the pub's closed," Maura said. "He can't come in tonight for a drink and that's flat. He'll have to go into Ballynaross."

"He doesn't look like someone wanting a drink. He would've driven away when he found the pub locked. He looks more like he's waiting for someone."

"Maybe he's a salesman," Siobhan suggested, "wanting to talk to Uncle Kee."

"At close to midnight?" Maura was skeptical. "Maybe he had car trouble, or is lost." For some reason she felt a trifle uneasy about the slightly built, well-dressed man who approached Brendan's car as it came to a stop. Brendan opened his door.

"Mr. Doyle?" The man looked questioningly at Brendan through fashionable designer-frame glasses.

"No, I'm not Doyle," Brendan responded as he opened his door. "But this is his niece, Miss Doyle."

Siobhan climbed out of the backseat and the man stood looking at her with what Maura thought was a very odd expression. She stepped out, and asked sharply, "Do you have business with Mr. Doyle? Because it's very late. The pub's closed tonight, as you can see by the sign on the door."

"Yes, I saw that," the man replied. He was English. "I've only been waiting here about half an hour. I . . . I wanted to speak to Mr. Doyle . . . and to Miss Doyle."

"What about?" Brendan asked easily. He could see that Maura didn't trust the man but he seemed harmless enough.

The man hesitated, then said, "I read an article in the London paper about this place."

Siobhan asked eagerly, "The article by Maura? This is her. You read that in the London papers?"

He smiled at her. "Yes, that's the one. And . . . you're Siobhan, I'll guess."

She nodded. "Uncle Kee should be here soon. It's late but do you want to come in and wait for him?"

Maura looked to heaven for guidance. Was the girl daft? She despaired of her, she really did. Besides, from what Maura saw at the party tonight, she doubted very much that Kee would be home soon. She tried to catch Siobhan's eye to telegraph to her that asking the man inside when she was alone was not the thing to do.

"It's pretty late for that, don't you think, Siobhan?" Maura asked pointedly. She spoke to the visitor. "Where are you staying tonight, Mr. . . . ?"

John answered slowly. "Trotter. John Trotter." He looked at Siobhan as he said his name, almost as if expecting her to recognize it. But she had no reaction. Maura suddenly had butterflies in her stomach; this quiet, well-mannered man was alarming.

John Trotter continued: "I don't have a place to stay, I'm afraid. I just came over from London today."

"Are you a journalist?" Brendan asked.

"No." There was an awkward pause, and Maura's unease grew. Why was he so secretive?

"Well, Mr. Trotter," Maura began pointedly, "there's a pub over in Ballynaross that lets rooms. That's about twenty minutes from here. It's called Fitzpatrick's."

John took the hint; he could hardly have failed to. "Yes, I think I noticed it as I drove through. You're right, it is late. Perhaps I could come in and ring them—tell them that I'm coming? My cell phone died on me."

"Of course," Siobhan answered. She didn't know what Maura's problem was; the Leeside was a public house, wasn't it? Mr. Trotter had every right to come in. She was getting tired of everyone protecting her all the time.

John asked, "Are you sure that Mr. Doyle will be a while yet?"

"Yes," Maura answered firmly. "I'm sure we all agree it would be better if you came back in the morning."

John hesitated. This was a delay he hadn't foreseen. The man owned a pub; John had naturally assumed the pub would be open when he arrived. All day long on his way here he had been trying to frame the words that would tell his daughter who he was. He had pictured himself walking into the Leeside and taking the uncle aside first, to "soften the blow," and then speaking to the girl. Now here was the girl without the uncle. John realized, for his twenty-five years in auto sales had made him a student of human nature, that Maureen's brother might very well be hostile and resentful toward him. He further realized that this young couple, from their protective attitude, were obviously close friends of Siobhan and that they considered her someone in need of that protection. He looked at Siobhan, who stood regarding him with guileless and friendly eyes, very like the eyes of a child. Doubts about what he was doing assailed him once again, as they had innumerable times since he had purchased his plane ticket. Siobhan was speaking to him, she was unlocking the front door.

"Mr. Trotter, please come in and use the phone. I'll look up Fitzpatrick's number for you."

Maura and Brendan, of one mind, started inside as well, but they all stopped as John spoke. "Wait . . . wait, please. Look . . . you might not want me to come back in the morning once . . . once you know who I am."

He paused and Brendan asked jokingly, "Inland Revenue, are you?"

John smiled slightly and then resolutely turned to face Siobhan. "Siobhan, your mother was Maureen Doyle? Who was killed in an IRA bomb attack in Comagh?" Siobhan nodded, surprised. "That's what I thought. Well, Siobhan . . . I knew your mother. In fact, I more than knew her. We were . . . pretty close for a time."

Maura suddenly knew exactly what John was going to say. She went swiftly to Siobhan's side, linking arms. Siobhan didn't seem to notice as John spoke slowly and carefully, his eyes on her face. "I think it's quite probable that I'm your . . . your natural father."

For a second Siobhan didn't understand. Then her knees

began shaking and she was suddenly very grateful for Maura's strong arm. Shivery and light-headed, Siobhan stared at Mr. Trotter. She felt dazed and rather sick but not for one moment did she doubt his words. Somehow, in her heart of hearts, she knew the truth of it.

CHAPTER 12

> The lough waters
> Can petrify wood:
> Old oars and posts
> Over the years
> Harden their grain
> Incarcerate ghosts
>
> Of sap and season.
>
> —SEAMUS HEANEY

Kee and Katie had almost reached the Leeside. They'd stayed behind to visit for a while with Sean and Bettina. By one accord Katie and Kee had decided not to make love tonight. Both recognized that this evening was a turning point in their relationship. They were on the threshold of something unprecedented, something exceptional. Both wanted to proceed with care and vigilance, but both wanted to proceed.

They noted the strange car in the yard as Kee drove Katie's Rover up to the door. The lights in the pub were all on.

"What's this then?" Kee asked mildly.

"Maybe Maura and Brendan came in for a nightcap," Katie suggested.

"But that's not their car."

"I can see Maura sitting at the bar." Katie pointed to the window.

"Oh, right. Well, I'd best go in and see what's going on."

He turned to her and no more words were necessary. They kissed, a soft lingering kiss, unlike any they had shared before. It was the only kiss between them that had not been a precursor to sex. But it felt wonderful, so much so that they kissed again. Then they smiled at each other and Kee climbed out. Katie slid over into the driver's seat and gave a little wave as she drove off. Watching the Rover disappear, Kee thought to himself that he wasn't quite sure what was happening here, but it felt pretty damned terrific.

. . .

Maura sat alone in the bar. It was almost one o'clock. Brendan had gone home to check on Niall and make sure that he had put Triona properly to bed, not sprawled out on the sofa asleep while he played video games. Siobhan was in the sitting room with John Trotter, learning, for the first time in her life, about her origins and about her father. Maura had offered, even expected, to be present at that conversation. But Siobhan had assured her she wanted to hear Mr. Trotter's story alone. Maura had at first been dismayed, then proud that Siobhan wanted to face this difficult situation alone. But Siobhan agreed to Maura's offer to stay in the bar until Uncle Kee got home. Both women shied away from thinking about Kee's anticipated reaction to the appearance of John Trotter.

Maura poured herself a whiskey. She felt she needed it. She had offered one to John Trotter but he declined. He and Siobhan had gone quietly into the sitting room, like a doctor and patient about to discuss a difficult diagnosis.

Siobhan's seeing life now, Maura thought wryly. She's in

the thick of it. Since she didn't go and seek it out, it must have decided to come to her. Maura drank to that.

She heard a car door slam. Oh, God—Kee was home. Maura jumped off her stool and stepped outside, shutting the door after her. Katie's Rover was disappearing down the drive.

Kee exclaimed, "Maura, love, what are you doing here? Is Siobhan okay? She's not sick or anything?"

"Siobhan's fine," Maura replied quietly. "She . . . she has a visitor."

Kee frowned. "A visitor? At this time of night? Who the hell . . . it's not Tim Ferris, is it?"

Maura shook her head. "No, it's not Tim. Maybe you'd better sit down, Kee. But out here—not inside."

"Are you daft? It's a bit cold out here to be sitting around. Who's in there?"

Maura hesitated and Kee looked alarmed. He started forward but she planted herself in front of him, heart beating fast. After all, she'd known Kee all her life. She'd just give it to him flat.

"The man inside is named John Trotter," she began, and then stopped as she looked at Kee's face. The name hadn't meant anything to Siobhan but it was very obvious to Maura that it did mean something to Kee. He froze and fixed a stare onto her face.

"What . . . what name was that?"

Maura's eyes narrowed. "John Trotter," she said with precision. She saw it in Kee's face that he knew exactly who the man was. "You know—John Trotter. Siobhan's *father*?"

"Jesus. Jesus Christ."

"Yes, you might want to talk to Jesus right now. God in heaven, Kee! You selfish *bastard*. You've been lying to Siobhan all these years—haven't you—about her father being dead?"

"No! No, I didn't! I thought he *was* dead. I was sure of it."

"I don't believe you," she said levelly.

"Bollocks on what you believe, Maura!" Kee ran his hands through his hair. "Do you mean to tell me that they're in there talking? The two of them? Alone?"

"For more than an hour now."

Kee bent over, hands leaning on his knees. He spoke as if to himself. "Sweet Christ. What the hell is he doing here? Why now, after all this time? The bastard." He straightened up and took a step toward the door. "I'd better get in there."

Maura refused to move. "You be decent, do you hear me? They're getting along grand."

Kee glared at her and didn't reply. He strode past her and went inside. Maura followed on his heels.

. . .

In the sitting room John found himself talking easily to this small pale girl who had Maureen's features but none of the same look about her. Maureen had been provocative and confident, while this girl was quiet and restrained, and innocent. She sat across from him, listening with her hands tightly clasped in her lap. Her friend had draped a deep blue shawl over Siobhan's shoulders because she'd kept shivering even after they sat down by the fire.

John told Siobhan about his relationship with Maureen; how he had been young, away from home, lonely and scared.

"A few days after she told me about the baby I was wounded, shot in the arm. I was near the end of my posting so they shipped me home to England. And then, well . . . I did write to your mother, but the letter came back. I confess I didn't try too hard after that. I was getting married, you see. It was all such a mess.

"When you're twenty-three and in over your head you often make the wrong decisions. I wish now, of course, that I had tried to find you, tried to contact you somehow. We could have written, or rang each other once in a while. Or I could be just talking ridiculous nonsense." He sighed. "I suppose it was best, the way it happened. You've been happy with your uncle?"

"Oh, yes," Siobhan answered automatically. She still felt a bit dazed and also confused, not so much by what Mr. Trotter was saying but by the thought that Uncle Kee might have lied to her. Had Uncle Kee known all these years that her father was alive? She looked at this dapper, middle-aged man who was regarding her anxiously through his tortoiseshell-rimmed glasses. She felt a wave of kindness for him; as naïve a soul as she was, even Siobhan realized how incredibly difficult it must have been for him to come here and do this.

"You don't really have to explain why you didn't keep in touch," Siobhan told him. "I think it's very understandable." She thought of the lie to Tim. "I know what it's like to be taking the easy way out. People just do things."

Her clemency amazed him. He expected at least some bitterness, some reproach, some finger of blame. There was none. "I feel like I'm getting off pretty lightly here," he told her. "You're being very forgiving and I'm not sure I deserve it."

"I don't know how else I should feel. I think it was nice of you to come."

How like a child she sounded, he thought. "Well, I'm very grateful to you."

There was a short silence. Then Siobhan said, "I don't think Uncle Kee will be very . . . I mean, he might be a bit angry with you."

John nodded resignedly. "Yes, I know, and more than just a bit. I expect that."

"You've never met him, have you?" John shook his head and Siobhan sighed. "He's awfully big."

Although this remark should have alarmed John, he found

himself laughing. "So I might get my just deserts in the form of a black eye?"

Siobhan smiled, she couldn't help it. "I don't think so, not really. But heaven only knows what he'll say!"

At this moment the door to the sitting room opened. Kee and Maura came in, and John Trotter stood up. Siobhan stood up, too, and involuntarily stepped closer to John.

"Hello, Uncle Kee," Siobhan said quickly. He ignored her, but she planted herself in front of Trotter. Her uncle thrust a pointed finger at the guest.

"Is your name John Trotter?"

John stood his ground but it wasn't easy in the wake of the big Irishman's obvious wrath. Maybe his joke about getting a black eye wasn't so funny. "Yes. Yes, that's who I am."

"You fecking bastard." Kee breathed heavily. He took a step closer so that Siobhan was forced to lean back toward John. "What in the bleeding hell are you doing here?"

"Uncle Kee!" Siobhan spoke more loudly and sharply than she had thought possible, and placed a hand on his chest. "I will have you remember your manners, *please*."

"My *manners*? This man gets your mother pregnant and then deserts her and I'm to remember my manners? Just because it's twenty-seven years later?"

"I'm asking you to do just that, yes," she replied firmly, as she maneuvered him a step or two backward. Siobhan was determined to not have Mr. Trotter made to feel uncomfortable or unwelcome.

"Jesus, Siobhan," Kee said with exasperation. "You don't know what you're saying. I suppose you've just been chatting away in here with him as if there's nothing wrong, nothing *immoral* in him coming here! And WHY have you come, will you tell me that? To make some big confession? To atone for your sins? Why, are you dying of cancer or something? At least that'd be justice!"

"Uncle Kee!"

"It's all right, Siobhan," John said quickly. He looked squarely at Kee. "No, Mr. Doyle, I'm not dying. But I'll admit that my . . . my motives are selfish ones."

"Selfish! You're an expert in that area! You disgusting piece of—"

Maura again planted herself in front of Kee, and poked her finger into his chest. "*Keenan Doyle.* If you don't shut up for two seconds and let the man say what he's come all this way to say, I'll call Brendan and Niall to come over and sit on you, I swear to God so I will!"

Kee flicked a cold gaze at her. "Maura, go home. This is a family matter."

Siobhan said quickly, "No, Maura, don't go." The last thing she wanted was to be alone between these two men.

"Don't worry, love," Maura said stoutly. "I'm not going anywhere, unless, of course, Kee wants to try and throw me out."

Kee glared at her and there was a tense pause. Then they all heard a voice call from the pub. It was Katie.

"Kee, where are you? We forgot all about your gifts in the backseat! I've got them here—" She pushed through the kitchen door and saw the four people in the sitting room, framed like a tableau.

"Hello?" she said uncertainly, as she stood in the doorway, her arms full of packages.

There was silence for a few moments. Katie met Kee's eyes and saw that he was white-hot with anger and holding himself in check with difficulty. This surprised her; she had known Kee for fifteen years and had never seen him really in a rage. Siobhan was pale and wide-eyed, Maura standing next to her looking defiant. And a small, well-dressed man was standing in front of the sofa, looking down at the floor. Finally Maura spoke.

"Katie, this is John Trotter. Mr. Trotter, this is Katie O'Farrell, a friend of ours."

Mr. Trotter raised his eyes and smiled slightly at the absurdity of the situation. "How do you do, Miss O'Farrell."

"Hello, Mr. Trotter," Katie replied. She flicked a questioning glance at Kee but still he was silent.

Maura continued resolutely: "Mr. Trotter is Siobhan's father, Katie. Her birth father."

Katie looked at Kee again and raised her eyebrows. For some reason she wasn't terribly shocked, but then not much surprised her anymore. But she could well imagine what Kee's reaction was on meeting Siobhan's father. The man must have been here when she brought Kee home. She put the presents down and advanced into the room.

"It's a pleasure to meet you, Mr. Trotter." Katie offered her hand. "I would imagine this was a bit of a surprise to everyone?"

He smiled, rather a charming smile, and replied, "Yes, indeed."

Siobhan said, "Mr. Trotter and I were having a wee chat. Then Uncle Kee came home and . . ." She paused awkwardly.

Katie nodded. "Right. I can imagine the rest. Well, it's late. Mr. Trotter, I've a proposition. Why don't you come home with me to my farm? I can give you a bed for the night."

Kee's entire body reacted to this suggestion and he started to speak. Katie continued firmly. "As I said, it's late, and it's been my experience that people say things they usually regret at this time of night. I'll bring Mr. Trotter back in the morning when everyone has had a chance to get some sleep. It's been a very long day. What do you say, Mr. Trotter?"

John glanced questioningly at Siobhan. She said softly, "Yes, please come back in the morning. Please. Thank you, Katie," she added, almost in wonder. Who would have thought that Katie would understand?

Kee took a deep breath, looked around at all of them, set his jaw, and left the sitting room. His thumping up the stairs was eloquent.

"Well," Katie began, "that was a dramatic exit. Is this the Leeside or the Abbey Theatre? Let's go, Mr. Trotter. I assume that's your car outside? Right. You can just follow me then. It'll take about fifteen minutes to get to my place. I'll have him back here at ten o'clock tomorrow, Siobhan."

After Katie and John left, Maura and Siobhan sat at a table in the pub, exhausted. Maura asked, "Are you all right? How do you feel about all this?"

Siobhan shook her head. She felt dazed as she said, "I don't know. It's very strange. He . . . he seems very nice." She didn't know what else to say.

"I thought so." Maura put her hands over Siobhan's cold ones. "Don't try to sort it out tonight. Go to bed and have a rest. Katie's right. It'll all be easier to deal with in the morning. Don't let Kee talk to you about it tonight. You both need some space."

Siobhan agreed. She wasn't sure she could even look at her uncle tonight. In one way he had loomed larger than ever, in his wrath. But he had also diminished in her eyes, just a little. That he had kept this from her . . . she couldn't begin to process the implications of it. Not yet.

"Thanks, Maura. And thanks for staying. It made it easier. How will you get home? Or you're welcome to sleep here."

Maura stood up and stretched. "I'll ring Niall's cell and make him come and fetch me. The lazy sod can get out of bed for once and let Brendan sleep."

. . .

Kee Doyle stood at the window of his bedroom watching the taillights of Katie's Rover disappear for the second time that night, followed by the red pinpoints of John Trotter's rental car. A few moments ago his huge bulk had been trembling, overpowered by a seething mass of hatred, disgust, and frustration. Hatred for John Trotter, disgust that the man had actually been welcomed under his roof by Siobhan, and frustration that this unholy situation had been thrust on him and he felt little control over it.

But as the car lights faded his boiling blood cooled, and he felt utterly drained and dazed with exhaustion. Katie was right, he thought dully. He'd best get to bed. Kee walked over to his dresser and caught sight of himself in the mirror. *I look all of fifty tonight.* He shook his head. *John Trotter, of all people. Jesus. I'm not sure I believe it still. But he's really here. He really is.*

A flash of honesty assailed him. How *could* he have kept the truth from his little Siobhan? It was a terrible decision. Why hadn't he just seized a moment and told her? What a fool he'd been. For her to find out like this was the worst possible way. God damn the man for forcing this on them!

Siobhan's quick acceptance of Trotter shocked him; she usually didn't trust people. An uncomfortable thought followed. Had her sense of trust in himself been damaged? He might have to deal with that, explain things to her. He had always just skirted the truth of it, let her believe the assumption that her father was dead. Really, he had reasoned, it had been for her own good. Knowing that her birth father was out there somewhere would have frightened Siobhan. He'd convinced himself there had been no reason for her to be knowing, for her to be having any uneasiness. He'd only wanted to protect her. He himself had forgotten the man's existence. No . . . no. That last was a bald-faced lie. Just as he'd lied to himself about Maureen, about who she'd become and what she had done. Consorted with an enemy soldier. Gave comfort to the enemy. Slept with the enemy. And even borne him a child—the child Kee loved as his own.

Kee leaned down and pulled open his bottom drawer. He took out a small metal box from under some sweaters and set it on top of the dresser. Slowly he opened it and, rummaging through the pile of old letters, withdrew a yellowed envelope addressed to him in official handwriting. It was postmarked twenty-five years ago. He took it out and unfolded the thick paper inside. Siobhan's birth certificate. "Name of Mother: Maureen Nora Doyle. Name of Father: John Thomas Trotter. Occupation of Father: Lance Corporal, British Army." The name of John Trotter had not appeared on the list of those killed in Comagh, but it had stayed etched in the ice of Kee's memory for twenty-five years.

PART FOUR

SIOBHAN AND THE
REST OF THE WORLD

CHAPTER 13

The hills have vanished in dark air;
And night, without an eye, is blind.
I, too, am starless. Time has blurred
The aeons of my life behind.

—STANDISH O'GRADY

Before going to bed Siobhan sat in front of her computer, trying to e-mail Tim about what had happened. She felt as if Uncle Kee's birthday party had taken place in another century. She was exhausted but keyed up, experiencing a confusion of different emotions that she couldn't begin to sort out. The strength of her present feelings frightened her. A bizarre visual image came to her, of emerging from a cave and being buffeted by swirling gale-force winds from all directions. But she had no desire to go back inside the cave. She was determined to deal with this the best she could and not allow Uncle Kee to brush her aside and "handle it" for her. And she was grateful to Katie for defusing the tense situation downstairs. The newness of feeling gratitude toward Katie was one cause of her confusion. She remembered what Bettina had said: *Maybe it's just a habit we've fallen into, not liking her.* It was the easy way out.

After sitting and staring at the computer screen for twenty minutes, unable to type a word to Tim, Siobhan made a decision. Looking up the phone number he'd given her so many weeks ago, she went quietly downstairs to call him, hoping her uncle wouldn't hear her.

"Hello?" The sound of his voice, so close it seemed as if he was in the next room, fluttered her heart.

Her small voice spoke. "Tim? I . . . I'm sorry to ring you . . ."

A short silence, then, incredulously, "Siobhan? Is that you?"

"Yes, it's me . . ."

Her strained voice signaled trouble to him. "Are you all right? Has something happened? Is Kee all right?"

"Oh, yes . . . I mean, we're all grand. I mean . . . Something *has* happened."

To her dismay and shame she began to cry. Siobhan had wept little since she was a child; up until recent weeks she had had little emotional stake in her own life. But now the tears came as delayed shock completely overwhelmed her.

Tim was consumed by sympathy and helplessness. "Oh, Siobhan. Please, whatever it is . . . Please, can't you tell me about it? Please, Siobhan. Take some deep breaths." He wished desperately that he was there, that he could take her in his arms and hold her small body close to his. What could it be? What could have happened? He heard her trying to get control of herself. What wouldn't he give to be with her at this moment. What wouldn't he give? At the same time a part of him was exultant; she had called *him*, had turned to him when she needed someone.

Siobhan finally began speaking, not much more than a whisper. "I'm . . . I'm better. I'm sorry. I'm so sorry. What a stupid thing . . ."

"No, no. But what is it?"

"My . . . my father is here. My real father. He didn't die

with my mother. He's alive—he's always been alive. And now he's here. He came to find me." Her voice held a faint note of wonder.

Tim felt the shock of the news, but more concern for her. "My God, Siobhan, that's . . . amazing. But, well, kind of wonderful, too, isn't it? I mean, it's a shock for you but he must have wanted to find you. Do you know what happened? Why he waited so long to contact you?"

The calm tone of Tim's voice helped Siobhan considerably. She told him John Trotter's story and in the telling of it, she found herself accepting it all over again. It made such sense to her that the young soldier would have reacted like that.

"How do you feel about meeting him? What's he like?"

"He's nice," Siobhan found herself saying. "I think I like him. But Uncle Kee is so angry with him, so hateful . . . so hard and unforgiving."

Tim assumed this was the real reason for Siobhan's distress. "Yes, I suppose he would be. I'm so sorry, Siobhan. That must be making things very difficult for you."

"Yes. I don't know what . . . what to say to him."

"Well, it's a shock for Kee, too. He had no idea your father was alive either."

Siobhan's voice dropped to a whisper again. "I'm not sure. I think maybe . . . I think Uncle Kee did know he was . . . alive all those years."

This made Tim pause, then he asked, "Siobhan, what makes you think that?"

"Because . . ." Again her voice faltered and she took a deep breath. "Because of the way he said the name. The first thing he said was 'Are you John Trotter?' Like he recognized the name straight off."

"Well, maybe he did, but he still could have thought the man was dead."

"Tim, the names of all the victims were printed in the newspaper. Uncle Kee's got a copy of the article—he's kept it all these years. Anytime I asked, he was always on about how both my parents were killed in that bombing. The name of John Trotter isn't on the list."

"Are you sure?"

"I've read those names over and over all my life. There were twelve people killed that night and I used to wonder which of the men was my father. Uncle Kee always said there was no way of knowing which man it was. I used to pick out a name and pretend that this one or that one was my father. I would dream about the names. I've never seen or heard the name John Trotter before tonight—but Uncle Kee has. I'm sure of it."

Here was the real cause of her pain. "Oh, Siobhan. Try not to jump to conclusions, please. This is too important. You two have to talk it out. I know it's hard but please try."

"Yes, I know. I'll try. I'm not going to think about it any more tonight. In one way, I think . . . well, it was all such a long time ago."

Tim quoted an old Gaelic saying: "*Taréis gach beart is fearr a thuigtear é.* (It is afterward that events are best understood.) Please remember that. And it is still important, no matter how long ago it all happened."

"Thanks so much for listening."

"That's what friends are for," he told her. "Siobhan, I'm glad . . . it means a lot to me that you called. Anytime you want to talk, I'm here. I'm always here."

. . .

The next morning Katie and John Trotter sat eating breakfast in Katie's big farmhouse kitchen. Soon after she bought the place, Katie had built a huge addition onto the original stone house so that the room which for one hundred fifty years had been both kitchen and living area for families crawling with children was now a large eat-in kitchen used by one woman. John thanked her for her hospitality.

"Your arrival and offer were a godsend. I hope things will be a little easier this morning."

"Don't bet on it. I'd like to help you, John, and I'm thinking the best way to do that is to tell you something about Kee and Siobhan Doyle."

"Yes, I would appreciate that."

She poured them both more coffee. "We'll start with Kee—although my opinion of the man isn't completely objective because I happen to be in love with him." John raised his eyebrows. She continued. "More fool me, right? But that doesn't mean I'm blind to the man's faults—far from it. Kee Doyle is proud, stubborn, shortsighted, a bit selfish, and a grudge-holder. He was devastated when Maureen went off to live her own life away from him and the Leeside, and completely shattered by her death. And then to find that she died partying with British soldiers, and had a child she never bothered telling him existed? He was her bloody brother—why couldn't she have come to him? Why did she just drop off the face of the earth?" Katie sounded irritated with the long-dead girl. She sighed. "But he'd always seen her through a bit of a rose-colored lens, you know?"

Katie paused and took a drink of coffee. She shook her head. "I've heard a lot of talk about Maureen over the years from folks that knew her. And there's no getting around that she was one for the lads. She liked flirting and teasing and having a good time."

With a rueful smile John said, "She certainly did."

"Are you knowing about the Magdalene Laundries?"

John nodded. "I do. They were horrible places."

"A mild description. Then you know that girls considered

'bold' were often sent there by their families and were kept virtual slaves by the oh-so-caring nuns and priests who ran the bloody places. Well, apparently there were rumors and rumblings about 'that fast Maureen Doyle who should be sent away to the laundries to learn her lesson.' Kee had just turned a blind eye to the kind of company his sister was keeping. But it all came to a head when she ensnared the son of a well-to-do shopkeeper in Carnloe and the boy's mother went to the parish priest about her. Soon after, Maureen hightailed out of here, going up to the North. Kee's never forgiven himself for what he sees as utterly failing his sister.

"So, with Siobhan he was keeping her close at his side, in part to make up for all that. He doesn't go quite so far as to consider Siobhan his property—he's not cruel or abnormal. And in many ways they have quite a good relationship. But what happened was he created a little shadow. Siobhan is the most introverted, underdeveloped, removed-from-reality person I've ever known. She's hardly been away from the Leeside all her life. She lives in a very narrow world of ancient poetry and Uncle Kee, who she thinks walks on water."

John was quiet for a few moments, digesting this intimate family history. Then he said, "But the pub—I mean, it's pretty hard to live and work in a pub day in and day out without seeing some of the raw realities of people's lives. I'd say it's impossible."

"Oh, she's *seen* life, all right. But she's made herself an onlooker. We have our share of alcoholics, God knows, and we've had a few wife beaters and drug dealers, and mothers who neglect their children. We've got people who gay-bash or Jew-bash or black-bash or whatever feckin' bash—and Siobhan's heard and seen it all. Hell, when she was eighteen or nineteen she helped a woman hide from her husband who was coming after her with a billhook. Siobhan shut the woman in their kitchen and lied as cool as you please to the man. But she just doesn't consider herself a part of it. It's as if she thinks of herself as being another species. She's a curious creature—and Kee is absolutely crazy about her."

John cleared his throat. "I suppose they really do have a father-daughter relationship."

"Completely."

John sighed. "I should have thought this out more. It was too impulsive of me to just show up out of the blue. Maybe I've made a big mistake."

Katie leaned forward. "Don't you believe it. Two people more in a rut than the Doyles I've never seen. I think they need this. I think they need to be waked up and shaken up and shown life beyond the door of that bloody pub. As far as I'm concerned, I think it's grand that you're here, John Trotter."

. . .

Maura phoned Father O'Grady early that morning. She knew it was interfering of her but she didn't care. She thought it was important that someone completely objective be at the Leeside at ten o'clock when Katie was set to deliver Mr. Trotter, and Maura's Catholicism told her, who better than the priest? Even after a night's sleep she doubted that Kee would be willing to calmly sit down and talk with Mr. Trotter like a sensible person. Kee's grudges were carved in granite. Maura arranged to pick up Father O'Grady at nine and bring him to the pub. That way he would have time to talk to Kee and Siobhan before Mr. Trotter arrived. The priest had been quite interested in the appearance of the long-lost father and had agreed with Maura that his presence might help keep things fairly calm. Actually, Father O'Grady was doubtful of that, knowing Kee Doyle as he did, but he wasn't about to pass up a chance to witness a drama like this. He could dine out for weeks afterward on this story.

When Maura and the priest arrived Kee was outside, restlessly tinkering with an old chest freezer. He'd had a hellish night of little sleep and fighting an urgent need for that blessed oblivion he knew whiskey would give him. Already in a black mood, Kee was not pleased to see Maura and infuriated by the sight of Father O. Before either of them were able to get out of the car, Kee threw down his wrench and strode up to the driver's-side window.

"We're not selling tickets to this, Maura, thank you very much. You and him are not needed here."

"I think otherwise," Father O'Grady said, not at all put out by this dubious welcome. "You've got yourself a bit of a family crisis here, Doyle, and in these cases an arbitrator can help a good deal."

"In these cases? You sound like a bloody social worker. This isn't Dublin or Galway, you know, O'Grady. We're used to handling our own problems without—"

The priest interrupted serenely. "I've never known you to be a blusterer, Doyle. You've always seemed to me to be a fairly reasonable man. Don't let me change my opinion about you."

"I don't give a flying—" Kee broke off as Siobhan came outside to join them. Maura gave her a quick hug and was relieved to see that Siobhan looked rested and even excited. She obviously wasn't letting her uncle's black mood affect her.

Siobhan was embarrassed to see Father O'Grady. She didn't know him well and was keenly aware that she and Uncle Kee were not regular churchgoers. She didn't think he needed to be here but guessed that Maura thought his presence might help. Maura was someone who believed the church could usually help with most things.

Uncle Kee was speaking to Father O. "I don't think it's unreasonable of me to consider this a private family matter."

"Not at all," the priest replied. "You've every right to feel that way. But you're not the only person this concerns. The way you think the situation should be handled isn't necessarily the way it should or will be handled. So let's just see how things go, shall we? For you, I advise less talking, more listening."

Kee rolled his eyes in frustration. Siobhan asked quickly, "Would you care for some tea, Father?"

"No, thank you very kindly, Siobhan."

At that moment Katie's Rover came into view, followed by John's rental car, and the four people stood in silence and watched them come. For John Trotter it felt rather like a prisoner arriving at his trial. They swung into the yard. Katie jumped out of her vehicle and quickly walked over to John's. She said with some humor, "I see Father O is here. I suppose Maura brought him. She probably thought it best the priest be here so Kee doesn't deck you. But don't worry—he won't."

"I'm not really worried," John lied, getting out of the car. "I just hope he accepts the idea of my wanting to have some contact with Siobhan—if she wants to, of course."

"If she wants to, that's all that matters, don't you think?"

They walked together toward the waiting group, Katie saying, "Good morning all. Here's the man of the hour, *safe and sound.*" She gave Kee a pointed look. "Hello, Father. This is John Trotter, whom you've heard all about, I should imagine. John, this is Father O'Grady, our local priest."

The two men shook hands and as John greeted Siobhan and Maura, Katie went over to Kee. She said in a low voice, "I know you're angry with me for taking him home but I honestly thought it best to let things settle overnight."

Kee looked at her a little impatiently and said, "All right, all right. It doesn't matter."

"Then calm down. You look like dog growling at someone on his territory."

"I'm calm enough." Kee took a step or two toward John, who greeted him politely.

"Good morning, Mr. Doyle."

Kee wasted no words in greeting. "Siobhan's told me your side of the story, Trotter."

"That was good of her, although I planned to tell you myself. And it's not 'my side'—it's what happened, it's the truth," John said with admirable calm. "I admit what I did was wrong. I'm not hiding from that—I hardly could after coming all this way to see Siobhan."

"Right. I'll ask you this, then. Why did you come? Why did you rake it all up?"

John hesitated and looked around at the interested faces. He decided the only thing to do was to continue being honest. "I think it was because I was lonely," he began diffidently. "I wanted another person in my life. My wife and I are divorced now and our only son is focused completely on his career. I had stopped . . . connecting with anyone. No one really needed me. I was feeling a bit useless, I suppose. I'll be fifty on Boxing Day this year, and felt my life was at a standstill. Well, I was just marking time, wasn't I? I've often thought about Maureen over the years, a 'what-if' kind of thing. And then when I read about Siobhan—there was an article in *The Telegraph*—I started to wonder about her. One day I knew that I had to come, I had to meet her, even though it might be a rather stupid thing to do. I confess I didn't really think things through. I just came."

There was silence for a few moments and Siobhan smiled at him so sweetly that he felt no embarrassment for what he had just said in front of a group of strangers.

Kee said accusingly, "It seems to me you're good at not thinking things through. Did you have to abandon my sister? I keep coming back to that. What I'll never understand or forgive is how you couldn't commit to Maureen once you got her pregnant. Couldn't you have married her?"

John looked at him levelly. "Would you have tolerated a British soldier for a brother-in-law?"

Kee blinked, then said, "It's what Maureen would have wanted that mattered. I was here for her and would have stood by her."

"Forgive me for saying it, but Maureen did what she wanted—always. She didn't fancy marrying me." He paused and a look of pain came into his eyes. "To be honest," he continued, "I was beginning to really care for her. But she kept me away—didn't let me inside. It was all on the surface with her, wasn't it? Casual. Even when she told me about the baby. She was very calm, telling me she'd handle it, pretty blunt about not wanting my help. What I mean is she made it quite clear she considered herself done with me."

Kee sneered. "And that suited you just fine, didn't it?"

"No, not really," John shot back. "But at the time I fell in with what she wanted—just because it seemed the easiest. For me, it always comes back to that."

"So you just took from her what you wanted and then you—"

"Hey, she took from me too, right?" John interrupted sharply. "It was a two-way street, believe me. Maybe I should have been more honest with her about the feelings I was starting to have—I don't know. But at least she was honest with me, right? *You're* the brother she couldn't tell about having the baby."

Kee flushed an angry red. "Why, you little white-nosed—" And before Father O'Grady could make a move to intervene, Kee landed his giant fist on John's neat, small nose.

John stumbled backward and fell to the ground, holding his

nose. "Shit!" he exclaimed. Maura went to help him; Siobhan covered her mouth with her hands, staring at her uncle.

Father O'Grady started forward toward Kee but Katie got there first.

"Right! That's it!" Katie's voice cut through the air and she grabbed Kee's arm. "You're coming with me, Kee Doyle—now."

"Katie! What the hell! Take your hands off me, woman—"

"You'll come now and that's flat. If you argue about it I'll make you regret the day you ever met me, Keenan Francis Doyle. We're going down by the lough to cool off."

Everyone watched in amazement as Katie hustled the huge angry man around the corner of the building and out of sight.

Father O'Grady heaved a sigh and said, "Mr. Doyle is a rather emotional man."

Maura murmured, "Only lately. Siobhan, why don't we all go inside?"

. . .

Kee crashed with fury through the dry heather and grasses and Katie followed. After a few minutes he turned around. "That was goddamned interfering of you, Katie O'Farrell!"

"I thought perhaps by now I had special privileges, including 'interfering,' as you call it, in family matters."

Kee looked a little ashamed at this remark. "Well, maybe so," he allowed grudgingly. "But this isn't over, my girl. I have a hell of a lot more to say to the man."

Katie nodded, hands on hips. "That's what I thought—and all with the same wrecking-ball charm. But I'm going to tell you something now, Kee, and you'd better listen. This doesn't really concern you."

"What?"

"This is between Siobhan and John. Your only role in this

whole situation should be to help Siobhan deal with it. And that you are *not* doing. You're just blathering. And it's making it harder on her. There's no point in berating the man for something that happened over a quarter of a century ago."

"It happened to *my* sister!"

"Exactly. Not to you."

"This is personal—to *me*. He did it to my sister, Maureen, who I loved and still love."

"Yes—your sister. About whom you've always had this 'walk on water' view. Unlike every other person I've spoken to about her. She was a lover of life, Kee—and of men. She slept with John Trotter because she wanted to."

"Katie, watch yourself. I'm not—"

"No, you watch *your*self! You've sown plenty of wild oats in your day. You can't deny that to *me*. Don't you come all over the righteous brother of the wronged maid—this isn't the nineteenth century and it's not as if Maureen didn't know what she was doing. You know why she went to the North—she was running scared. She knew she might be heading for the Magdalene Laundries, didn't she? Admit it. People around here had been talking and thinking she needed to be thrown in there to learn her lesson, right?"

Kee went pale with rage. "I'll not have my sister's memory destroyed, by God I won't! Goddammit, Katie! Don't ever bring that up to me—"

Katie spoke with deadly calm. "It's not me that talks about it, Keenan Doyle. Everyone in the district tells the story. Not in your hearing, but it's local gossip right enough. She would have landed in the laundries for her flirting ways."

Kee drew a sharp breath. "I never would have let that happen. Not there—not to that hellhole. My God, Katie!"

Katie hesitated, then spoke more gently. "I know that—and

I'm sure she did as well. But she wanted to leave, wanted a life in a different place, away from here. You've just never really been able to admit that to yourself."

Kee was silenced for a few moments. Then he said, "But—a British soldier! A goddamned British soldier—"

"Oh, here we go! I'm not going to listen to that shite! Does it really matter who he was? He was Maureen's choice. Would you have preferred it to be some Provo? Would that have made it better?"

"Katie, I'm the least political man you'll ever know."

"So you keep telling me. Listen to yourself! He was a young, scared soldier away from home who did what millions of other soldiers the world over have done. This is the oldest story known to men and women, and well you know it."

"It doesn't make what he did any more forgivable," he replied sullenly. He was calmer now.

Katie said with exasperation, "It gave you Siobhan! Would you have wanted that to be different?"

This made him pause. "What are you saying?"

"I'm saying that without John Trotter, Siobhan wouldn't exist. I'm saying that it's too late for anger. There's no place for it in this. Other emotions, yes. But not anger. It'll help no one, least of all Siobhan. It's *Siobhan* that matters, Kee."

Kee looked at her with dark unsettled eyes. His head told him he should be annoyed with her, even angry. But it felt so good to have her here, understanding him, understanding Siobhan, and wanting to help because she loved him. He was flooded with the realization that his need for her was absolute. Suddenly he took her in his arms and her surprised heart leapt. "Were you always this smart and I missed it entirely?"

"There's a lot of things you've missed about me," she said softly. "Now keep holding on because I've got something else to tell you. What John really wants is to keep in touch with Siobhan. Write to her, ring her once in a while, maybe a visit or two. But only if Siobhan is willing. He made that clear. You'll not cause problems about that, will you?"

Kee looked off into the distance at the enclosure of hills he had known all his life. Katie saw his face take on a sadness and he sighed.

She said gently, "You've had her all her life, Kee. It's time to share her. She needs other people in her life."

"It's just . . ." He swallowed hard. "It's hard realizing I'm not enough anymore. It's a stupid way to feel—and selfish—but there it is."

"It started happening before John appeared on the scene, my love," she said gently. "If I'm any judge, there's someone else who might be wanting part of Siobhan—maybe a big part."

Kee looked down at her and nodded resignedly. "I know. Tim Ferris."

Katie looked at him searchingly. "She's growing up, Kee. Just a little late, is all. That's really what it comes down to."

"I know they e-mail each other every day . . . I did mind. I suppose I still mind. But it's mostly fear. My little *alannah* doesn't know anything about men, anything about that side of life. I just don't want her to get hurt," he whispered.

Katie's throat constricted. "I know, my darling, I know. That's the hardest part. That's why you've kept her in cotton wool all these years. And cotton wool is grand—for stopping up bottles."

She looked at him and saw, for the first time, his dear eyes brilliant with tears. She pulled his head down and held him very tightly for a long time.

CHAPTER 14

Tastes, instincts, feelings, passions, powers,
Sleep there, unfelt, unseen;
And other lives lie hid in ours—
The lives that might have been . . .

—W.E.H. LECKY

Siobhan and her father strolled along the lough shore. It was the same path she had taken with Tim. John asked if they could go for a walk together, just the two of them. He had to leave right after lunch to catch his flight home and he wanted the chance to talk to her. The aftermath of Kee's punch to John's face had been anticlimactic. Siobhan and Maura had administered ice and sympathy, Siobhan apologizing at least every two minutes until John begged her to stop.

Katie had ushered in a disgraced but faintly defiant Kee, who apologized formally. Just as formally John accepted and the two men briefly shook hands. Siobhan's relieved, happy smile made the embarrassing moment easier to bear for both men. Father O'Grady beamed on them, somewhat cynically, and murmured about "bygones" and "counting our blessings." Katie glared at him and took Kee into the cellar to choose a wine for lunch. Even Maura was a little disappointed in her man of the cloth.

As they now walked along, John told Siobhan one or two stories about her mother, funny little stories that made her laugh. Sheltered though she may be, Siobhan was very familiar with pub culture, and since John and Maureen had spent almost all their time together in pubs and nightclubs, Siobhan did appreciate the humor in the stories. She liked John very much and was more than appreciative of his desire to meet her. She was still bemused at the idea that this man thought her existence was significant enough to him that he had sought her out, an emotionally challenging thing to do that was completely self-motivated. But there was still no real perception that this was her father—her *father*. In her mind the only person who could ever answer that description was Uncle Kee. But she felt relaxed and valued in John's company.

Siobhan and John paused in their walk as she spotted an otter swimming in the lough. She pointed it out to him. "I never get tired of watching them," she said softly.

After studying her face for a few moments John asked, "You really love it here, don't you?"

"Oh, yes," Siobhan began her standard reply, "I can't imagine—" She stopped suddenly, realizing she was about to recite her standard mantra: *I can't imagine being anywhere else.* But now she knew it wasn't true anymore. Disturbingly, she reflected that perhaps her old habit of repeating it over and over to herself had been her way of struggling to make it true.

"Yes?" John prompted. "You can't imagine what?"

"Well, I . . . In the past I've always felt that there was no other place in the world but here. No other place where I could . . . be happy."

She paused and John asked, "But you don't feel that way anymore?"

Siobhan looked troubled. "I don't know," she replied simply.

"Have you been thinking about it? Has something happened that's made you change your mind?"

"Not change my mind, exactly, just start thinking . . ."

"Do you mind telling me about it?"

"No, I wouldn't mind, but it's nothing, really. You couldn't be interested."

"Now why else would I ask?" Two of John's strongest assets as a car salesman were patience and quiet persistence. He was prepared to use them now.

Siobhan hesitated. She'd confided in people so rarely in the past, but lately the desire to do so was strong. Maura, Gwen, and Bettina—and now John. For some reason she felt John was safe. He had the unusual advantage of being completely objective while at the same time having a very personal interest in her. The giving and receiving of confidences did not come easily; it was a skill that people honed as they moved through life, through relationships. Siobhan saw now that people divulged different things to different people for different reasons. She thought about her recent conversations with Gwen. She had always been comfortable revealing private thoughts and feelings to Gwen; she'd assumed it was because Gwen was an outsider, like herself. But maybe it stemmed from the fact that Gwen moved in and out of Siobhan's life. The transient nature of their contact created few emotional demands. Whereas confiding in Uncle Kee or Maura or even Bettina created more complex layers within her relationships. Siobhan remembered reading or hearing somewhere that people will often reveal secrets and innermost thoughts to total strangers sitting next to them on a train much more easily than to the people who mattered in their lives.

Siobhan realized she'd been quiet for some time now, and glanced up at John. He smiled quite kindly, and asked, "Well? What's the verdict?"

Siobhan simply liked him, that was the verdict. Meeting him was, in a way, very similar to Tim at first meeting. He simply didn't feel like a stranger. She began speaking.

"Well, there is . . . someone. I met a friend, a new friend, this summer. A . . . a man from the States. A teacher. He teaches Irish literature at university there."

"Is it the man from the article?"

"Oh, yes, I forgot. You've read about him."

"And you're interested in him?"

"Y—yes." She was feeling shy now. "He's so interesting. We just seem to be . . . we enjoy talking about things." She blushed and John smiled.

"Well, there's nothing wrong with that, you know. How does he feel about you?"

"But that's just it, isn't it?" Siobhan replied desperately. The floodgates were opened. "I don't know. How can I know? I'm not even sure what I feel is . . . is . . . well, I mean, is it love? How can I know that? It's so scary and confusing. I've never . . . done this before. How in the name of heaven do people *know* when they love someone?"

She looked at him, flustered and confused, almost panic-stricken. He placed his hands on her shoulders; it was the first physical contact between them. They hadn't even shaken hands when they met. Since John was small he was only a few inches taller than his daughter.

"Oh, Siobhan," he said with a kind smile. "That's a question, isn't it? Possibly the hardest question in the world to answer— because the answer is different for everyone."

"That's what Gwen said," Siobhan told him in wonder.

"And who is Gwen?"

"A friend. A traveler."

"Really? And what did Gwen say?"

"She told me that love has as many faces as there are faces

on God's earth. And if when you're not together there's an empty place deep down inside, then that's a love for a lifetime."

John's eyes were a little sad. "I like that. I'm afraid I didn't have that kind of love with my wife. But I wish I had."

"I don't . . . trust myself . . . to really *know*, you see."

"Yes, you do. You do, really. The problem is that people let too many other things get in the way, so that listening to their hearts is impossible. There's too much . . . outer noise. Don't agonize, don't analyze—just listen. The honesty is always there inside us."

Siobhan nodded, appreciating the beauty of his words. Then she glanced down at his hands on her shoulders. He dropped them, sensing she was a little uncomfortable. John sighed, then decided to take the plunge.

"Siobhan, I know your real father is Keenan—and that's as it should be. I mean, he raised you, he loves you and you love him."

Siobhan felt frightened suddenly but didn't know why.

John continued: "But I'm very glad I met you, very glad we could talk to each other like this. I . . . I'd really like it if we could keep in touch. Write to each other and maybe ring up once in a while. Would that be all right with you?"

Siobhan's heart quickened with uncertainty. She looked out over the lough, her dear familiar lough, which was so important to her. The surrounding hills had always encircled her, protective and secure. But now the real world, which had left her untouched all her life, was crashing through the door. First in the disquieting person of Tim Ferris and now, more disturbingly, in her father. Siobhan's brain began to wrestle with unfamiliar dilemmas. Would they both demand things from her she couldn't give? What if she took her first steps outside her narrow world and stumbled irrevocably? How could she give them parts of herself and not lose herself doing it? Other people obviously could but she could not. She didn't know how. So she was better off staying as she was. *Better off? Why not be honest with yourself? You've no choice but to stay as you are.*

John again studied her face during the silence and knew she was struggling with his proposal. She was uncertain of herself, this pretty young woman, uncertain and, he suspected, newly searching to find herself. He hoped very much she would agree to a relationship, and decided he would consider it a sacred duty to help this daughter of his come out of whatever shell it was that she, or others, had created for her. He felt somehow responsible. John continued gently.

"Would it be all right if I just wrote to you once in a while? You wouldn't have to write back if you didn't want to."

Siobhan, without looking at him, replied in a whisper, "I'm not sure. I don't know what I want. I'll . . . I'll think about it. I'd better go help Maura with the lunch."

She started to run away but John, though disappointed, was not to be put off entirely. He was a patient man.

Siobhan barely opened her mouth during lunch and kept jumping up to get things. Maura couldn't understand it; Siobhan went off quite happily with John for their walk. The group consisted of Siobhan, John, Kee, Katie, Maura, and Father O'Grady. Everyone felt it would be easier to have as many people around as possible until John left. Conversation was general, carried primarily by Katie and Maura, helped occasionally by John and very occasionally by Father O'Grady. The priest contributed mainly charming smiles and a healthy appetite. Kee was preoccupied, Siobhan unsettled.

When John said goodbye and offered his hand to Kee, the big Irishman hesitated only briefly before returning the hand-shake but he said nothing, only nodding politely. John took both Siobhan's hands in his and would have liked to kiss her cheek. But he only smiled his goodbye and then quickly got into his car and drove away. Siobhan immediately went back into the pub, followed by Maura.

Kee turned to Katie. "Well, was I polite enough for you?"

"I could have hoped for more but I think I can call it a victory."

"Oh, a victory? For whom?"

"For me, of course, and my expanding influence over you."

"You are a hideously devious woman. I don't know why I even talk to you."

"I do."

The priest felt it was time to break in on this conversation. "Katie, would you be so kind as to give me a lift back? I have an appointment at half two."

"Sure enough, Father. Let's go. I've got ponies to exercise. I'll be back tonight," she told Kee.

"I know."

. . .

In the kitchen Siobhan and Maura started cleaning up the lunch things. Siobhan seemed calmer now but still distracted. Maura bided her time and made small talk about Triona. Suddenly, in the middle of a story about Triona drawing on her bedroom wall, Siobhan blurted out, "I don't think I can!"

Maura looked at Siobhan calmly. "What is it you can't do?"

"I can't keep in touch with him . . . with . . . with my father. Write to him and that. I *can't*."

"Why ever not? Tell me."

Siobhan didn't answer, she just stared out the window. Maura began to feel uneasy; her friend looked so . . . stricken. Then Siobhan spoke in a whisper that chilled Maura.

"Her soul had such desire
For what proud death may bring
That it could not endure
The common good of life . . ."

Both women stood still, Siobhan as if in a trance and Maura shocked and confused by Siobhan's words. Then Maura breathed out. "Siobhan, what is that? What are you saying?"

Siobhan suddenly flung open the back door and fled. Maura lurched after her but it was no good. She watched from the open door as Siobhan ran like a desperate animal up the hill, farther and farther, not stopping or pausing, just running—running away. Maura went slowly back into the kitchen and sat down. Dear God, she thought, whatever is the matter? What did she mean by those words? *Dear God, please tell me how can I help her, my poor dear Siobhan.*

She heard Kee's voice outside calling to Siobhan and a few moments later he came into the kitchen. "What's got into Siobhan? She running up that hill like there's no tomorrow."

"Oh, God—don't say that," Maura burst out. "Don't say *that.*"

Kee stared at her. "What the hell's going on?"

Maura took a deep breath. "Kee, what poem is this from—something about her soul having desire for a proud death and couldn't endure the good of life."

Kee looked at her strangely and his face was pale. "Why do you want to know that?"

"Because Siobhan quoted that to me right before she ran out."

"Jesus. Why would she . . . I don't believe it—"

He suddenly started for the door. Maura jumped up and caught his arm.

"What's it from?" she demanded desperately.

He turned a troubled face toward her. "A poem called 'That the Night Come.'"

With frightened eyes they stared at each other and then, as one, ran outside and up the hill where Siobhan had gone. She was out of sight now but they spotted Blasket grazing placidly so they knew she was still on foot. They got about halfway up and Maura had to pause to catch her breath. They split up then, both calling her name, both trying not to panic, both bathed in the sweat of fear.

Kee crashed through the bracken for the second time that day, cursing himself, cursing John Trotter, cursing God and the world. If anything happened . . . but she wouldn't do harm to herself—she wouldn't. Not Siobhan. Her gentle spirit wouldn't let her. She was upset, that's all. She just needed to blow off steam, right?

Maura found herself shivering as she stumbled her way through the rough terrain. She was cold, inside and out, and in between shouting for Siobhan, her lips moved in constant prayer to Our Lady. Maura didn't really believe Siobhan would . . . would do anything to herself, not really . . .

It was Kee who found her. He had struck off to the left, away from Carnloe, and when he finally breasted the hill and started down the far side he heard something. It wasn't the sound of weeping exactly; rather it was the sound a small child makes when lost or afraid of the dark. He followed the sound until he came upon her, sitting among the brown grasses and withered wildflowers. She had her knees drawn up to her chest with her arms wrapped tightly around them.

"Siobhan! Siobhan, love—you had us scared half to death."

He saw that she was shaking. He dropped down beside her and enfolded her in his arms. He rocked her back and forth, listening to her whimpering subside, and was taken back in time to that night in the Comagh police station when the sound of her crying had so devastated him.

He began speaking in Irish. "*Seo, seo, a linbh. Nach féidir leat insint dom faoi? Cad atá ag cur bhuartha ort?*" (Now, now, darling. Can you not tell me about it? What is it that's upset you?)

Siobhan laid her forehead on his strong arm and gave a great sigh, so that her whole body shuddered with it.

"It's . . . my father. He wants to . . . to keep in touch with me."

"Oh, aye. So that's it. Don't you want to?"

She shook the head resting on his arm. "No, I don't think so."

Kee looked out over the horizon. From this side of the hill the sea was visible, today a strip of pale green against the dove gray sky. His conversation with Katie fresh in his mind, he swallowed hard and asked his niece a question that was very difficult for him: "Are you sure? Are you sure you want to turn the man away?"

Siobhan raised her head and looked at him. "It's like . . . he's just some nice man I met. He could never really be my father. But . . . but he might want to try. And I don't want that." She shuddered again. "It'll just be so much easier if we don't keep in touch. Everything will stay the same then. That's what I'm wanting. Everything to stay the same," she finished almost pleadingly.

Kee studied her face. To be truthful he couldn't help feeling relieved and a little complacent. If this was how she really felt . . . John Trotter could recede back into the tunnel of history from whence he came.

"All right, all right," he said soothingly. "No one's going to have you encourage the man if you don't want to. What would be the point in that?" Just then they heard Maura calling Siobhan's name. "Oh, God. I forgot about Maura. Let's go, love. She needs to know you're safe."

They scrambled to their feet and Siobhan asked anxiously, "So it's all right then?"

"Yes, love, it's all right. You're not to be worrying about Mr. Trotter anymore."

. . .

Tim couldn't understand it. Siobhan had suddenly stopped e-mailing him. She sent him a brief e-mail the day after their phone conversation, saying that she had enjoyed meeting her father but didn't think she'd pursue things with him. It was an odd, cold little message, which she ended by saying that she was going to be very busy in the next few weeks and wouldn't be able to write regularly anymore. She would just have to see when she could find the time. It distressed him, and made him very uneasy. He waited two days, then called the Leeside. He called midmorning Ireland time and no one answered. Then he called again that night, during pub hours, and Katie answered. She was friendly and chatted for a minute or two, but Siobhan wasn't there, she was babysitting for Triona. She'd tell Siobhan that Tim had rung.

Siobhan never called him back. And he sent half a dozen e-mails to her before she replied, unsatisfactorily:

> Sorry it's taken so long to get back to you. Things are busy just now. The woman on Inishmaan won't see me—I think she's going a bit demented. She's not recognizing me anymore. I don't know what else I can do. We'll just have to wait and see for now. Siobhan.

Tim stared at his screen. She was withdrawing from him. And he suspected he knew why.

For some time Tim had had a growing suspicion about the poems Siobhan had given him. The more he studied them, the stronger his conviction was that they were fake. There were elements, such as cadence and overly sophisticated phrasing, that had eroded their authenticity in his mind. At first he had considered the possibility that Siobhan had made some errors in translation, but knowing her abilities, he doubted that. He was almost sure that the poems dated from no earlier than the late nineteenth century, but it was the authorship that really intrigued him. They were exquisitely written and, he believed, by the same person. He wondered if the entire book was authored by the same writer. He still wanted to see the book, just to get the rest of the poems.

Tim suspected that Siobhan must have come to realize, or had known from the beginning, that they weren't authentic ancient poetry. And now she didn't know how to tell him. She was probably frightened and unsure of herself and instead of reaching out to him and being honest, she was pulling back. Maybe she felt as if he had entrusted her with some sort of sacred quest and she had failed him. *Maybe she thinks the only reason I'm keeping in touch with her is because of that goddamned woman and her goddamned book.*

He decided not to press, to give her some time, but it was a difficult and frustrating decision. If only he could see her in person . . . But it was no good thinking of that. Unfortunately during the upcoming midsemester break he was committed to a seminar in Chicago at which he was one of the main speakers. He regretted that, but there was nothing to be done about it. He began to think he might manage a quick trip over to Ireland at the start of the Christmas break, before the actual holiday. Yes, he decided, he would definitely do that. Only then would he know if he had a chance, if the daydreaming and wondering about Siobhan was fruitless or . . . a promise of things to come.

CHAPTER 15

That crazed girl improvising her music.
Her poetry, dancing upon the shore,

Her soul in division from itself
Climbing, falling she knew not where . . .

— W. B. YEATS

Siobhan sat on the lough wall, her favorite place to be. She'd spent a lot of time here over the last few weeks since her father left, searching for her accustomed contentment. But it eluded her. She felt strangely suspended in time and place, removed from everything and everyone familiar. It was as if the life she'd known for twenty-five years didn't fit her anymore, or she didn't fit it. Siobhan had done little soul-searching during her life but now it occupied her constantly, almost obsessively. Siobhan constantly asked herself, Why is this happening? Why did she feel so displaced? Struggling to find real answers, she realized it all started with her father's request to establish a relationship. She had felt afraid. But afraid of what? Of . . . expectations. What if they found no place they could connect? What if he got to know her and found her lacking, that she simply didn't have much to offer? That thought brought her to Tim. She was backing away from Tim for the same reason. Expectations. What could she possibly give him? Nothing—nothing of value. Nothing . . . nothing. The more she ruminated, the darker the path before her became. She was intuitive enough to know that she couldn't continue like this.

Now in this moment, a resolute calmness settled on her. Siobhan followed her thoughts to what she assumed was a natural conclusion. Because she was certain she had nothing to give the real world, in the persons of Tim and her father, she wouldn't try. Was that it? Yes, because it was too terrifying to try. Why? Because failure would be too much to bear.

Backing away from Tim and ignoring her father's overtures were the least complicated ways out of her deception regarding the book and handling her inadequacy. The path of least resistance. They were all three better off like this, she assured herself. What she was doing was best for everyone in the long run. She would have to ignore Tim's voice inside her head. She told herself she just had to wait until her own world felt comfortable again.

More difficult were her feelings of fundamental betrayal by Uncle Kee. Why, *why* had he lied, telling her that her father was dead? It seemed so cruel—and he was never cruel. Siobhan knew she should ask him, confront him about it, but she didn't know how. Tim had said to wait until she'd heard Uncle Kee's side of the story, but he hadn't offered it. Initiating that conversation seemed too threatening, and too difficult. So she took the easy way out and did nothing . . . nothing except begin an instinctive retreat back toward the familiar, insulated shell that was patiently waiting for her.

A few days later Siobhan was washing the windows in her uncle's room. She paused, as she often did, to look at the picture of her mother on the big dresser. But this time there was a difference. It had been years since she had taken it in her hands and pondered the pretty, cheerful, open face under the glass. Was it a "come-hither" face, as she'd heard flirty girls had? Maybe it was. But it was also a face lit from within, an unguarded face, a happy face. From her distant memories came the faint echo of her mother's laugh, generous and lyrical. Her mother had been a happy person.

Siobhan heard a car come into the yard and glanced out the window to see the green postie van lurch to a stop. She opened the window and called down, "Morning, Andy. Can you be leaving it all on the bar?"

"Righty-o."

Siobhan closed the window. Letters. Her mother would have written Uncle Kee letters. It suddenly occurred to Siobhan that he had probably kept them and that they were most likely right here in this room. Why had she never thought of it before?

Turning her back to the window, Siobhan surveyed the room with cold calculation. Her uncle was in Ballynaross. She felt no compunction about searching for the letters and reading them. They were written by her mother, she had every right to read them despite the fact that they'd been written to someone else.

Reaching out to the top dresser drawer Siobhan's hand hesitated for only a thin moment before firmly pulling it open. Underwear, socks, sweaters, and shirts were neatly replaced after her small hands had carefully searched for what she was seeking. Finally in the bottom drawer, she took out a small metal box with a feeling of inevitability.

Inside, lying on top, was her birth certificate. *Susan Maeve Doyle*. The name looked very strange and staring at it, Siobhan tried hard to remember the echo of "Susan" in her mother's voice, tried to pull out from the recesses of her brain any sense of connection with that name. But there was nothing. Two spaces down was another name—John Thomas Trotter. Yes, she thought grimly, it had been a mistake to keep that from her. Underneath was a small pile of folded letters and a few cards wrapped in old rubber bands. Siobhan took out the bundle and replaced her birth certificate inside the box. Closing the lid, she returned the box to the drawer and arranged the sweaters on top of it once more. Stepping across to her own room, Siobhan thrust the bundle under her mattress just as her uncle came home. By the time he came upstairs to find her, she was washing the windows in his room, no different than every Tuesday.

. . .

Later that afternoon Siobhan rode Blasket around to the far shore of the lough, the letters tucked inside her bulky sweater. Sitting on a sun-warmed rock, she tried to remove the old dried-out rubber bands that held the bundle together but they broke apart in her hand. Carefully she tucked the pieces into her pocket, planning to place them back in the box so it would look as if time had finally caused them to snap.

She held the first folded letter in her hands for a long time before opening it, silently asking forgiveness from her mother for this breach of privacy. Her resolve had not weakened since the morning when she had taken the letters, but she felt that it was her mother's privacy, not her uncle's, into which she was intruding.

Belfast, 27 April
Dear Kee—

This is a grand place Belfast is. The people talk funny—fast you know. Sometimes its hard to understand. I miss you but its grand here. Im hoping to get a job in a tea shop thats looking. Its down the road from a house that was bombed but not bad. Ive made a friend Elain—shes a Prod but doesnt care that Im RC caus Im from the country. Shes taking me to the Prod disco tomorrow nite. She says just not to say Im RC or it would cause trouble. Im living with her and her brother now, they have a room in the back. Tomorrow nite will be grand. Im going to meet some of their friends. I have enough money for now.

All for now. Il write again soon. Take care of yourself.

Love, Maureen

Armagh, 5 August
Dear Kee,

I left Belfast like I said I would. Theres too much fighting there—its all the boys think about. And some of the girls too. I hope this is better but its smaller and it might be hard to be finding a job. There's a fish & chips shop that Im hoping for. So maybe you could be sending me a little? Just to tide me over. Il be finding something soon. If not, I might try Comagh next. A friend of mine is from there but she came with me here, and there's a church dance tonight. The priest is nice they say. Shes RC too. Im still going to Mass every Sunday so dont worry about me. But if you could send me something that would be grand.

Love, Maureen

Armagh, 12 December
Dear Kee,

Things are grand here. I work at a chippie shop and there
nice people. Lots of free food too. My friend went home to
Comagh cause she wasnt finding a job. Im going to dances
and things at the church—Father Michael is nice but no
Prods allowed. Things are more quiet here but a girl was
killed for going around with a soldier—a Brit you know.
I knew her a little—she was nice. It was in the paper. But
dont worry about me. Im living with a lady who works at
the parish—she has rooms. Me and another girl Mary get
along okay. Father Michael found the room for me. I just
have to help with some things and pay her what I can. I go
to Mass every Sunday, so things are grand.

Its busy here for Christmas so I cant be coming down to
see you. Its allot of money too. Maybe Il come down after
Christmas if I make allot. So Happy Christmas! I will light
a candel for you.

Love, Maureen

There were five more letters within the next year. After that
there were only two or three birthday cards, and then nothing.
There was a poignancy to that paper silence; Siobhan could feel
the desolation her uncle must have felt in losing that vibrant
voice. Had her mother been selfish in her happiness? Yes, most
certainly. But it hadn't been Maureen's fault that her brother's
need of her had been so basic, or that he had found solace
inside a bottle. The heart and soul of a place, Uncle Kee called
her. Had the Leeside lost its heart and soul when Maureen left?
Uncle Kee had felt it so. But perhaps he never grieved his mum

and da . . . so losing Maureen was just more than he could bear. Yet the Leeside lived on; too many people had lived in it and loved in it over the centuries for one person to take away its soul. It was Uncle Kee who'd lost something—he had lost not only his family; he had lost an ideal.

Siobhan wondered if her mother would ever have brought her back home to the Leeside. Would she have finally decided that the two of them needed the stability and security waiting here for them? No, it wouldn't have happened. She was sure of it. Siobhan considered, for the first time, what her life would have been like had her mother lived—if "Susan" and her mother had continued to drift from pillar to post, barely skirting poverty, because of her mother's need for freedom. She shuddered. Some "what-ifs" were too frightening to contemplate and her mind closed on this troubling new question, banishing it forever. But before disappearing, it gave birth to a disloyal thought. *I'm sorry you died. But I wonder if, just maybe, it was better for me that you did. I think Susan died, too, but then Siobhan was able to be born.*

She jumped up and quickly climbed onto Blasket's back. As she rode back to the pub her uncle came out and watched her approach. He looked troubled.

"Siobhan, there's a letter for you. From London."

Filled with apprehension, she dismounted and stood uncertainly. London. It could only be from John Trotter.

Her uncle hesitated, then asked, "Are you wanting to see it?"

No. But she replied, "I suppose so."

Uncle Kee jerked his head. "It's inside on the bar."

Siobhan was uncomfortably aware of the presence of her mother's letters under her sweater as she slowly walked inside. She looked over her shoulder at her uncle. He was watching her, then deliberately walked off toward the shed. Siobhan didn't know if she was glad or not. Did she want privacy just now? Maybe it was better if she opened John's letter alone. She looked at the envelope resting innocently on the polished surface of the bar. More letters. How odd it was that it had arrived today, the day she had found and read her mother's letters. But this letter wasn't from the past. It might appear innocuous but it was demanding her full attention and response with a clarion call.

Siobhan walked around the bar and got a sharp knife. She carefully slit the envelope open. There was a card inside. No letter. It was a thank-you card with a picture of a pink rose. She opened it.

Dear Siobhan,

I wanted to write and thank you for your warmth and hospitality. All the more, since I landed on your doorstep completely out of the blue. I sincerely hope my visit didn't cause any trouble between you and your uncle. I wouldn't wish that. I also want to give you my address, which is written below. I hope you are well and happy, and I want you to know that I'm grateful for the time we were able to spend together.

Very sincerely,
John Trotter

Siobhan read the card twice. She noticed that he was careful not to ask her to write back or to ask permission to contact her again. The card was brief and gracious, and nonthreatening. Siobhan looked at it for a few moments, thinking about the unspoken claim it was making on her. Then she walked over to the large fireplace and opened the fireguard. Only the past that's well buried beneath your own life was safe, she thought stonily. The recent past was too disruptive. She threw the card into the fire.

The thick, shiny paper caught slowly, browning around the edges first, like one of her own meat pies, she thought vaguely. As the top edge began to blacken in earnest, Siobhan's eyes were drawn to the words *I hope you are well and happy.* A tiny flame was licking around them. Suddenly she seized the fire tongs and fished the card out, dropped it onto the hearth, and stamped the flames out with her shoe. She stood staring at the half-burned card, fragile now in its damaged condition. Siobhan was horrified at what she had done. How could she have assaulted such an honest, inoffensive message? She might not want a relationship with John but his sincerity did not deserve this. Siobhan picked up what was left of the card and placed it carefully back into its envelope, with the return address neatly printed. Making sure Uncle Kee was not yet heading back inside, she went upstairs and replaced her mother's letters, along with the dried bits of rubber band, in the metal box. Then she went into her room and put the remains of John Trotter's card between the pages of a book of ancient Celtic stories.

. . .

A week went by, then another. Siobhan struggled on. Her only defense against the pain of removing Tim from her life was to retreat back into herself. This was a comfortable and familiar place, especially when she returned to spending the majority of her time daydreaming, fantasizing, and reading her ancient poetry. But, unlike her lifetime habit of fantasizing about ancient heroes and other romantic figures, she fixated on Tim.

She now had a definite flesh-and-blood romantic man to take center stage within her passionate poetry and folklore. This was different. This was . . . intoxicating. *Tim as Princess Créde's lover, lying beside her, spinning poetry, kissing her flowing hair, her cheek, her neck* . . . Siobhan found herself trembling. But she misinterpreted it as the trembling of fear rather than the trembling of desire. Again and again she revisited legendary tales of love in her mind, envisioning Tim in the roles of hero, poet, warrior, prince . . . lover. She felt strange stirrings that made her light-headed.

Siobhan had one small mirror in her room, a tiny square hung above her dresser, in which only her face was visible. She'd never needed to look at her whole self in the mirror, to see how she appeared to others. But she began to think about nakedness, both physical and emotional. She wondered what it would be like to have someone else—Tim—see her naked, and how that might make her feel.

Most often she fixated on the medieval Irish legend of Cormac and Gormlai. Their union had been a celibate alliance, he a man of God and she a virgin awaiting the spiritual fruits of this chaste marriage to reveal to her a vocation to the veil. Late one night, Cormac walked past his wife's chamber quietly, as it was very late and he had no wish to disturb her. He paused and glanced into her room, surprised that there was a light still burning at the late hour. Through the curtains he beheld a sight that froze his eye and plunged him, with frightening intensity, into the toils of temptation.

His wife stood completely naked in her chamber, her body glowing sensuously in the flickering golden light of the candle. Her long plait of hair that might have served to cloak her body cascaded down her back so that her breasts were revealed in their perfect roundness, their curves accentuated by the soft candlelight. *Look, look!* He felt the Evil One tempting him at his elbow, forcing his suddenly lustful eyes to continue their staring. Then her supple body leaned forward and the candlelight was extinguished.

His temple burned and throbbed with the intensity of his passion, the suddenness of its assault. Almost drunkenly he reeled from the doorway, deploring that he had been outwitted by the Evil One. He had taken pleasure in the sight of his wife's nakedness. His marriage vows had promised an inviolate and spiritual union, yet the first time temptation thrust itself at him, he had surrendered instantly. But as he struggled with his emotions, the same thought kept occurring to him over and over: "I saw my own wife." The idea amazed him. *Could* it be wrong for him to behold his wife's body, since they were one flesh in the eyes of God? Even if seeing her caused such intense desire? He thought of her grave smile, her low melodious voice that always made him think there were drops of honey in the roots of her tongue. There had been times in their marriage when he had had to resist his natural inclinations, but always his spirituality had triumphed. But this . . . this was different, this fierce fervor. *Oh dear Christ, help me!* his mind cried out. *Gormlai, Gormlai, my love!*

For Siobhan, that a man as saintly and resolute as Cormac could be so drawn into the dominion of sexual passion simply at the first sight of his wife's nakedness was a revelation of the power of her own body, the power it might have over Tim. Siobhan read and reread the scene of marital voyeurism, her mind expanding each painful detail, casting herself and Tim in the roles of Gormlai and Cormac, modifying, altering, fine-tuning like a stage director. She took the story one vast step further as Tim in the guise of Cormac succumbed to his spousal desire, caressing her breasts, hips, thighs. Her imagination exploded in sexual ecstasy even as she felt her body's sexual awakening. She didn't encourage it physically but didn't shy away from it. She welcomed it.

Night after night, disturbed and aware of her strange disconnect from the lough, Siobhan sat in the back window of the pub, looking at it through the glass, or stood in the open doorway removed from the lough's once familiar aura, and fixated on her fruitless obsession. Fanatically she convinced herself that this apparition could be her reality. The pain of a true relationship was too much to bear. Her familiar world no longer held her in the palm of its hand; even her cave of old was closed to her. She could not go back. So she began to dig a new dark hole, not of detachment but of fantasy. Down and down she descended into her realm of unreality with her imaginary Tim.

. . .

"Siobhan!" Her uncle's voice cut through her layers of preoccupation. "What's up with you lately, girl? I've asked you three times to fetch some soup and sausage rolls for those folks over there."

So fogged in was she by the borders of her fantasy world that his annoyance did nothing to pierce it. Siobhan sleepwalked into the kitchen, gathered the customers' order, and served it with only the surface of her attention.

Tonight she was engulfed once again by romantic legend. She and Tim were cast as Aileen Aroon, the beautiful daughter of the fourteenth-century house of Leinster, and the handsome poet-chief O'Daly, whom she adored: During his long absence her parents thrust another suitor upon her, and the candlelight of the feast of celebration danced in her unsettled mind. Aileen, in a turmoil of despair over her impending loveless marriage, wandered through glowing, music-filled rooms full of her parents' drunken guests. The face of her beloved O'Daly floated before her and the sound of his voice in her ears was sweeter than any music. She slipped down a darkened passage, the silvery threads of her ice-blue gown shining like holy raiment. Then a hand caught her wrist as she passed. She began to cry out but the face that emerged from the darkness belonged to her own true O'Daly! Dressed as one of the musicians at the feast, he had eluded her parents' sentries and come to spirit her away—her brave, darling O'Daly. Together they escaped into the night . . .

Siobhan's spiral downward into fantasy continued.

· · ·

Maura was desperate to talk to Siobhan. Her friend had avoided her ever since that day on the hill. Siobhan took care of Triona one evening but hurried away as soon as Maura and Brendan got home. Maura decided to call Siobhan and ask her to babysit, only this time she'd stay home and make Siobhan talk to her. She could see that Siobhan was desperately unhappy and was withdrawing more and more into herself. This was all the more discouraging because Maura had been so hopeful with Siobhan's slow blossoming after the advent of Tim Ferris and John Trotter. But now it was as if her friend had taken a giant step backward and she wasn't going to retreat any farther if Maura could help it.

· · ·

Siobhan developed the habit of riding Blasket to the far side of the lough every afternoon. It distanced her from the Lee-side and seemed to soothe her restlessness. Today the expanse of water stretched like a faded gray coverlet over a vast bed,

like the hopeless resting place of a dying woman. It reminded
her of Gwen. Instead of dismounting Siobhan hesitated and
turned her eyes to the final hill, the one whose far side part-
nered the sea. Impulsively she urged Blasket up and up, sensing
his surprise, for this was not a familiar trek. His hooves found
the sure places among the rocks as they climbed toward the
thick oyster-gray sky. There was a rare reluctance in his pace
and Siobhan's impatience grew as Blasket ignored her persua-
sions to hurry.

Finally they breasted the hill to the smooth top ridge. Below
was the sea, impossibly huge, smudged with the slate-colored
shapes of the Aran Islands. Beyond them, over the rim of the
world, was America and Tim. The distance was unimaginable,
like the spatial emptiness between two planets.

Siobhan was transfixed by it but Blasket tossed his head and
shifted his hooves restlessly, bruising the untouched grasses.
This horizon was too unfamiliar, too strange—where were his
folds of hills and cozy knolls? He had no interest in this place.
Twice he made a move to edge back down into the valley and
twice Siobhan resisted. In this time and place the two of them
were not in harmony.

Siobhan's fascination was tinged with despair. So much
emptiness separated Tim from her. To it she was adding her
own, swelling its size even more. How could such an emptiness
be bursting with things like sorrow and longing? How many
people had stood on the western shores of Ireland and poured
these same emotions into that void? A number only God could
know. And the western winds returned nothing to them but
hopelessness.

It is a whisper among the hazel bushes;
It is a long, low, whispering voice that fills

With a sad music the bending and swaying rushes;
It is a heart-beat deep in the quiet hills.

Twilight people, why will you still be crying,
Crying and calling to me out of the trees?
For under the quiet grass the wise are lying,
And all the strong ones are gone over the seas.

Something deep within Siobhan stiffened. She had made her decisions about Tim and John Trotter; she *would not* give in to second thoughts and lamentations. Those were for other people. She was separate and apart, and content to be so. The Tim that existed only in her mind could be made to do and say what she wanted. So that relationship was safe.

She turned her head and saw the lough and the Leeside below her, as if through the wrong end of a telescope, tiny yet sharply defined. With the merest hint from her thighs Blasket gratefully began the descent back into the valley, his legs reinvigorated with each step. When they reached familiar ground again she could feel his body energize with the pleasure of it and they bounded ahead, pony and rider together.

· · ·

One evening at sunset Siobhan walked along the lough shore with her imaginary Tim. In her mind they discussed eighteenth-century ballads, the lovely aching of them. Oblivious of her surroundings, she missed her footing on a slippery rock and received a nasty jagged scrape to the bone on her inside ankle. She sat down abruptly, wincing with pain. Her breathing became shallow and rapid as she raised her eyes to where she had imagined Tim was standing—where he would have been standing if he were really here. But he wasn't. He wasn't really here. If he was, he would help her. He would put his arms around her and help her to walk; he would bathe the wound in cool lough water and bind it gently; he would pick her up in his arms and carry her tenderly back to the Leeside. Her breath was coming in small gasps. Where she looked for him now were only earth, water, and sky. Elemental things, she thought obscurely. Only fire was missing. No—not missing. The fire was inside her: a deep burning need for a Tim who was not here but thousands of miles away. She broke down and sobbed, consumed by the grief of reality.

. . .

Maura biked in haste to the Leeside. Kee had called her and said Siobhan was pale and silent this morning. She wouldn't come out of her room. Something was very wrong but she wasn't talking. Could Maura come? Maura could and did. She routed Niall out of bed and told him to sit with Triona while she had her breakfast. Then he was to take Triona to her play group down the street. After that he was to come straight back—*straight back*, mind—and do up the dishes. Maura was out the door before he had a chance to grumble but she knew he'd do as he was told.

She rode around to the kitchen door and leaned her bike against the building. Opening the door, she went into the kitchen and heard Kee's heavy footsteps coming down the stairs. She met him at the bottom.

"What's going on then?"

Kee's face was serious. "I don't know. I've never seen her like this. She won't talk to me."

"I'll go up."

Siobhan's door was open. She lay in bed looking at the painting that hung over her mantel. It was of a sleepy Irish cottage tucked behind a low stone wall, and everything was bathed in golden light. She used to believe, on days when the sun poured into her room, that the real sunlight merged with that in the painting, making the picture awaken and come alive. But not today. What was sunlight after all but a brightness that hurt the eyes and revealed the vulnerability or hardness of everything? That's all sunlight did for the world.

"Siobhan?" Maura spoke sharply and loudly. The girl in the bed turned her face tiredly and looked at her friend standing in the doorway. Siobhan's milky skin was pallid, her dark eyes sitting within blue shadows.

"Hello, Maura. What are you doing here?"

"I'm here because Kee's that worried about you," Maura replied briskly. "What's the matter with you? Are you sick?"

Siobhan shook her head. Maura came and sat down on the bed. She spoke more gently. "Come on, then. You know you're going to tell me anyway so it might as well be now as later. I can't always wait for you to come to me. What's put you in such a state? You're pale as a ghost."

"I feel like a ghost. As if all my insides were gone."

"But why?"

The small colorless voice answered. "It's Tim. I was stupid and I lied. And lied and lied. Whatever there was—or could have been—between us is totally dead forever."

"I can't believe that. I can't believe it's as bad as all that. Tim cares for you—I know he does."

"Not if he knew the truth about me. It's all been in limbo anyhow."

"But what's it all *about*? What did you lie to him about?"

The tale of the fictitious old woman with her fictitious ancient book came out in a tired monotone; Siobhan sounded like an old woman herself in the telling of it. Maura's heart sank. Her poor, poor Siobhan, resorting to such a childlike ruse to capture Tim's attention and friendship. But when he learned the truth Maura was afraid that the damage not only to Tim's heart but to his ego might be irrevocable. She knew how much importance men, particularly American men, placed on their careers.

As Siobhan came to the end of her story, she added, "I can't bear it if he knew the truth, but he has to know the truth. I see that. And then it'll all come crashing down, the ending will be definite."

"You don't *know* that," Maura tried to reassure her.

"I do, and you think so, too—that I've ruined it. I can see that you do. If only I'd known it would hurt so much—I had no idea. I could never really appreciate the ancient love poems before—not really. I just thought they were full of beautiful imagery and the words were so expressive. If I'd only known. Do you know how I feel? How can a poem from the tenth century—so long ago—know how I feel? But it says so exactly:

"Great love of a man from another land
Has come to me beyond all else:
It has taken my bloom, no colour is left,
It does not let me rest.

"Those words are so old—but so eloquent right here, right now. I think all along I've been hoping, deep down . . . Oh, God, I've been weaving all sorts of fantasies about him. I'm so ashamed. Imagining all kinds of things . . ." She turned her head away.

Maura took her hand. "My God, Siobhan, all women do that about men. It's perfectly natural. What you're imagining is a natural part of being a woman."

"Not this."

"Try me," Maura challenged knowingly.

Siobhan moved her head and looked at Maura. She hesitated and just then Kee came into the room. Maura groaned inwardly. He looked at her questioningly.

"It's about Tim," she said simply. "Siobhan has been telling me that things aren't going very well. There's been some . . . miscommunication."

"Has he been lying to you?" Kee asked sternly.

Siobhan answered tiredly, "No, it's me that's lied to him."

"Oh." Kee looked a little uncertain. "I'm sorry, Siobhan. I know how much you like him."

"Or maybe I love him. I think it might be that. I don't know."

Kee felt the pain and frustration of a parent whose child's hurt can't be kissed away. He sighed. Katie was right. Trying to protect Siobhan from all this was wrong—and impossible. You might as well try to protect your child from the passage of time. "Are you wanting to stay in bed today?" he asked lamely. "It's all right if you do. Maybe that would be best."

Maura frowned at him. *Oh, that's a great way to handle it*, she thought. *Treat her like she's still five years old.*

Siobhan looked at her uncle's anxious, unhappy face. Suddenly she knew this was wrong. Staying in bed was ridiculous—and it was ridiculous for Uncle Kee to allow her to do it. He meant well, but his concern was misplaced. It simply showed he wasn't willing for her to grow up. Well, she *was* grown up. She couldn't feel this way if she wasn't. She sat straight up in bed and threw off her covers.

"Treating me like a child isn't going to help anything, Uncle Kee. I'm going to stop acting like a child, too. If Tim . . . if he doesn't care about me anymore it's my own fault. And I've just got to live with it."

She saw them both staring at her with amazement, and this gave her courage.

"Uncle Kee, I'd like to be talking with Maura some more."

"Right." He nodded, then stood there a few seconds longer as both women stared at him. "Oh, right. Right." He turned and made a confused exit, like some comic stage uncle.

Maura smiled and shook her head, looking pointedly out the window. "I'm just seeing if there's anything interesting out there, since it seems today that pigs can fly."

But Siobhan didn't smile. She drew her knees up to her chest and wrapped her thin arms around them. When she spoke her voice was small and hollow.

"Maura, I'm not normal, am I? I mean, I could never be married and . . . and have children . . ."

A huge wave of pity engulfed Maura for her friend. *Please God, help me say the right thing.* She swallowed hard.

"Siobhan, dearest Siobhan. You couldn't be more wrong. That's just not true. You mustn't believe it could be true."

"But it is true." The forlorn voice was almost a wail. "There's just not enough in me. I'm nothing but a scared, ignorant child. How could I make anyone happy? I wouldn't know where to start. I don't know anything except things out of books—always books! I'm stupid and . . . and closed up like some clumsy crippled fist . . ."

She was sobbing now and Maura, who had not seen Siobhan cry since they were both in grammar school, wrapped her arms tightly around her grieving friend and rocked her gently. She crooned like she did when Triona was hurting, and thought to herself: *Well, it's a start. Siobhan's waking up—and it's a painful time when the blood finally starts seeping into those arms and legs. But thank God for it. Her isolated little heart's opening up at last.* Siobhan started to calm down and Maura leaned back to look in her face.

"Siobhan, listen to me. I think I know you better than anyone—yes, even better than Kee. And you're not clumsy or stupid. God forbid. Scared—yes. But who isn't? We all are, sometimes. And ignorant? Maybe, but that's fixable. You just have to learn—one day at a time like the rest of our lot. No one's an expert on life, believe me. Everyone makes mistakes. *Everyone.* The thing is to get in there and just have a go! And you've got people around you who are desperate for you to try. All of us—maybe not Kee, though he means well enough—but all the rest of us. And that includes your father—and Tim."

Siobhan took a few deep breaths and Maura saw with relief that her friend's eyes held a look of hope. "Do you . . . do you really believe that?"

"I do indeed. When have I not been speaking the truth to you! But you know, Siobhan, Tim is the first man you've ever noticed. I can't tell you how you can be sure he's *the* one. I don't want you to be hurt. Maybe you and he, well . . . you're so inexperienced at this. There might be someone else in your future."

Siobhan's voice was low and intense. "I'm so scared, Maura. It's . . . it's so important. Everything to do with people's feelings is so important. It's much easier to just pretend. Make up a life for myself. But that's wrong, it's *wrong.* And not enough. It's *not* enough. I know that now. But when you love someone, I mean, how can I make sure . . . well, that it comes out the way I want? How do people do that? I don't know if I could bear it if it doesn't."

Maura didn't know, either, but gave her friend an encouraging hug even as she felt a chill of fear for her. "You'll bear it—if you have to. Pain isn't always a bad thing. It helps us to know we're alive. And how to make it work out? You do a lot of thinking and planning—and a lot of praying." *And so will I,* Maura thought.

CHAPTER 16

God be with the times when I
Cared not a thraneen for what chanced
So that I had the limbs to try
Such a dance as there was danced . . .

—W. B. YEATS

The next morning Siobhan came into the kitchen after a hill ride on Blasket. Breathless and exhilarated, she spotted her uncle on the phone through the pub doorway. His serious face gave her a chill of apprehension. Less tentative than she would have been in the past, she went and stood next to him, an inquiring look on her face. That look changed to surprise as her uncle spoke a name she did not expect.

"That's bloody hard, Turf. I'm sorry as hell. I hope she's not too uncomfortable."

"It's Turf? What's wrong? Is it JoJo? Did she lose the baby?"

"Hold on, Turf." Her uncle covered the phone's mouthpiece with his massive hand. "No, darlin', JoJo and the baby are grand. It's Gwen. She's been placed in a Galway nursing home. She has TB."

Siobhan looked out the window toward the lough. Gwen in a nursing home.

"Oh, God," she said.

"Apparently she knew she had it for a time now but didn't tell anyone, even Turf. He's pretty cut up about it. Poor sod, I know how I felt when my mother went through a long dying." He turned back to the phone.

And so the grieving begins again, Siobhan thought helplessly. She couldn't imagine September without Gwen, who was such a vibrant part of that transitioning landscape. No more yellow-and-blue caravan, no more box of treasures, no more rough, kind wisdom. Siobhan's sense of loss was keen; she felt as if Gwen had already died.

"Gwen wants what?" Her uncle's surprised voice cut through her thoughts.

"Just a minute." He handed the phone to Siobhan with raised eyebrows. "Turf says he has a message for you from Gwen."

Siobhan was apprehensive as she took the phone. "Yes, Turf? Hello."

"Hey, Siobhan. I've got a message from Mum. She wants you to take her caravan."

Siobhan felt blank surprise. Uncle Kee was watching her closely, arms folded.

"Her caravan?" Siobhan echoed, and his eyebrows lifted again.

"Aye," Turf answered, "that's what she said. We've sold the pony but she's not wanting the caravan kept here. Will you take it until . . . until her time?"

"But why me? Why not one of the other travelers?"

"I don't know why and I'm not asking. I only know she told me in so many words that I was to have it at the Leeside. But if you'll not take it—"

"No, I want it! Of course, I'll take it."

Her uncle leaned forward with a look of disapproval. "The caravan? Gwen wants us to take her caravan?"

Siobhan nodded at him. "Yes, to keep here until she's . . . passed on."

He held out his hand. "Give me the phone."

Siobhan stared up at him, holding on to the phone protectively. She swallowed. "I won't. You'll tell him no."

His eyebrows rose. "Maybe. Let me talk to him."

Siobhan spoke deliberately into the phone, watching her uncle's face. "Turf, where are you?"

"We're in the caravan park about half a kilometer north of Upper Salthill. At least for the time being, until they tell us to shift."

"We'll find you. We'll come and get the caravan tomorrow." She quickly hung up the phone.

Uncle Kee threw up his hands in exasperation. "Siobhan! This is ridiculous."

An alien stubbornness surged through her as she prepared to face down her uncle.

"Why? Gwen wants me to bring it here."

"I'm sure it's a lovely gesture, darlin', but we can't have that thing here."

"It's not a *thing*, it's her home. And she wants to have it here."

"But why, for God's sake? Why here?" He looked really upset.

"I don't know but I'll not refuse it, Uncle Kee. Not from Gwen. I can't."

He shook his head. "I'm not comfortable with this."

"I don't care." Siobhan spaced the words out, as if speaking to a half-wit. "I will do this."

Her uncle stared at her and moved back a step. "Siobhan, what's gotten into you?"

She felt an exhilarating thrill of achievement as she answered, "I don't know. But she's a friend. And she's *dying*."

"Who's dying?" asked Katie's voice.

Both of them looked toward the pub doorway where Katie stood expectantly. "Who's dying?" she repeated, glancing back and forth at their faces.

Kee turned his head with impatience and answered shortly, "Galway Gwen. Turf just rang us. She has TB."

Katie came into the room. "Oh, I'm sorry. That's a shame."

There was silence for a few seconds, then Kee turned back to Siobhan. "I'm not agreeing to this, young lady. I'll not take you tomorrow and that's flat."

"Young lady?" Katie repeated derisively. "Is she still twelve, then?"

Again the impatient turn of his head. "Katie . . ."

"Yes?" There was palpable danger in her inflection.

"Oh, bloody *nothing*." Kee banged out through the kitchen door.

Katie sighed. "Another dramatic exit. What am I getting myself into with this man?" She sat down on a barstool and asked, in a surprisingly gentle voice, "All right, Siobhan. What's tomorrow and why won't Kee take you there?"

Siobhan was eager to discuss Gwen's behest and did so with more enthusiasm than Katie had ever seen in her before.

"Gwen's been such a good friend—and you know the traveler tradition, Katie. The caravan will only be here until she . . . dies. Then we burn it."

Katie nodded. "So Kee's refusing to take you? I wonder why he's so against it," she mused. "Oh, well. It doesn't really matter what he thinks. Certainly you must go. I'll take you."

"Katie! Are you sure?" Siobhan was overwhelmed by the offer.

"Of course. My Rover won't have a problem handling it, and besides . . ." Katie paused and, to Siobhan's further astonishment, actually looked self-conscious. "Well, I mean, I've got to start winning you over, haven't I? Since Kee and I are together now. I know you've never liked me much, Siobhan."

There was a long silence as both women contemplated the importance of Siobhan's answer.

Siobhan said softly, "I didn't really know you. But I think that's changing."

Katie nodded, her mouth compressed as if to push tears away. She swallowed and replied in a voice modified from her usual confident tone. "Yes, that's changing."

. . .

Katie pulled up in front of the Leeside the next morning at nine o'clock sharp. Luckily the day promised to be fine, with the arrival of a luminous blue sky and sweet breezes from the south. Katie raised her eyebrows as she saw Kee accompany Siobhan outside and approach her car door. She rolled down her window.

"Morning, Katie. I've decided to go along with you two. I can do the driving on the way back when we're hauling the thing."

Katie gave an unladylike snort. "And who asked you?" she challenged. "Get up here in front with me, Siobhan," she added, as Siobhan was about to sit in the backseat. "Thanks and all that, Mr. Doyle, but Siobhan and I will handle this just fine. It's to be a girls' day out, so it is."

"Now, Katie—"

"Look at my face, Kee. We don't want you, so there you are. Now go nurse your wounded ego. We don't know how long this'll be taking, so we'll see you when we see you."

Katie was steadily closing her window during this speech,

which she now punctuated with the final push of the button. Kee mouthed "Fine" through the glass and rolled his eyes as he stepped back.

Siobhan sat in the front seat, the exhilarated sensation once again filling her tiny body. She sat up very straight. Katie glanced over at her as the wheels sprayed gravel.

"Good morning, Siobhan. Are you ready for this?"

"Oh, yes. I feel wonderful." Her voice sounded slightly surprised.

Katie laughed. "That's grand. Me, too. I shouldn't feel this good after giving the man I love a dressing down, but I'm perverse that way."

Siobhan smiled slightly and shrugged. "He just likes to have his own way."

Again Katie glanced at her passenger. "But him getting his own way all the time, that's changing, I'm thinking?"

"Yes," Siobhan agreed quietly, "that's changing."

Katie smiled straight ahead. "Bloody brilliant," she murmured.

. . .

On the way to Galway they didn't talk much at first. Katie played Celtic rock on her car stereo and sang along with relish. In the past this might have, almost certainly would have, annoyed Siobhan but she remembered her conversation with Bettina. After all, what was Katie doing but enjoying life? The world was here, all around. Why not taste it, smell it, sing it? In living large Katie was doing harm to no one; it was her natural approach to life. And it was one of her attractions for Uncle Kee, Siobhan felt sure. Trying to understand Katie didn't mean liking everything she said and did; it meant recognizing that she made choices that were right for her. And that was worth respect.

This was a new idea to Siobhan and, completely without guile, she asked Katie impulsively, "Katie, you're happy, aren't you? You're a happy person?"

Katie stopped singing in mid-note. She looked slightly comical as she turned an astonished face toward Siobhan.

"I'm sorry," Siobhan said quickly. "That was personal."

Katie laughed. "I don't mind you getting personal, Siobhan, far from it. But give a person some warning, for God's sake. I'll die from the shock of it."

"Sorry," Siobhan said again. There was a pause as Katie turned down the volume of the music. Siobhan wondered what kind of answer Katie would give.

"Am I happy? God, what a question. I'm certainly happier these days than I have been for a long time. I'm happy in that a lot of things in my life are going well, and I'm grateful for that. I learned a long time ago that realizing how good you have it goes a long way toward being happy. There, how's that?"

Siobhan nodded. "It's nice. Being happy doesn't mean everything's perfect, does it?"

"It certainly does not. God help us if it did."

They were stopped at a crossroad. Siobhan watched a mother walk across with two small girls who skipped happily, holding her hands.

She said thoughtfully, "I think in many ways you're a lot like my mother."

"Your mother?" Katie seemed startled.

"Yes. You know—enjoying life, enjoying people. Not settling for what you don't want or being, well, bored."

"Oh."

"Maybe that's why Uncle Kee likes you."

Katie laughed slightly. "Maybe."

Siobhan swallowed hard but she was glad the next words

found their way out of her mouth. "Maybe that's why Uncle Kee loves you."

She felt Katie's sudden stillness and the car slackened speed for a second or two.

"Oh." This time Katie breathed it. "Do you think . . . no, I won't ask it." She paused, then spoke softly. "Thank you, Siobhan. That was hard."

"Not as hard as I thought it would be," Siobhan replied honestly.

The Land Rover bounded ahead with new energy.

. . .

When they reached the outskirts of Galway near suburban Salthill, Siobhan was fascinated with the sights outside her window. She had only driven through Galway twice before in her life and had never stopped in the city itself. It had just been, in her uncle's mind, a place on the way to someplace else, an abbey or ancient dolmen, or Yeats's home. Siobhan mentioned to Katie that she had never been to Galway, really *been* there, just as Katie was about to take the turn into Salthill.

"What? The hell with that then." She swung back into the Galway-bound traffic, not without a few angry words and gestures flung her way. "We've plenty of time. We'll go into the town center, down by Bridge Street, and walk around a bit."

Siobhan looked at her, half fearful, half hopeful. "Really?"

"And why not? We'll browse the shops and maybe get a bite to eat. Okay with you?"

"Oh, yes."

Siobhan saw the town as curiously foreign, the air charged with strange energy, and the people with their quick pace and conversation like a different species. Akin to what she had felt on meeting Tim, there was a novel excitement and anticipation, coupled only with slight apprehension. She was glad of Katie's company and appreciated the way she let her go at her own pace. Katie, for her part, was content to watch Siobhan wander, was intrigued and touched by the wide-eyed absorption. Siobhan was content to window-shop and people-watch—she especially enjoyed the buskers—until she stood in front of an old bookshop.

"Could we go in here, do you think?"

"Anything you want."

So many books. They covered every surface, walls, floors, chairs, windowsills. For Siobhan, a manna of knowledge yet to learn, explore, share, interpret. The pervasive smell of paper dust, warmed wood, and worn leather bindings made her light-headed, a little drunk. She climbed halfway up a narrow stairway, then sank down on a step, looking down at Katie with luminous, dazed eyes.

Katie laughed. "This might be a bit too much for you, all in one day! Maybe we should get a quick snack and head out to find Turf. What do you say?"

"I want to get a book for Gwen. I brought money." Siobhan lifted a hopeful gaze up the stairs toward the poetry section.

"Well, now, that's a lovely thought. Go to it, then. I'm just going to nip across to that women's shop that had those grand shoes in the window. I'll be back."

Siobhan perused the vast poetry shelves, silently greeting old friends, brushing inquisitive fingers across unknown bindings. She'd never been in a bookshop like this before. Her uncle ordered a lot of books from catalogues and online. In Clifden there was a store that sold books but it was small and stylish, a book boutique for tourists. Nothing like this place, which felt like an infinite haven for the mind—limitless in its possibilities and protective of the sanctity of the written word.

Siobhan noticed two young women sitting cross-legged on the floor in one corner, looking like they belonged there. How lucky they were to be able to come here anytime, every day if they wanted. Her ears caught the words "those two poems by Heaney," and she moved a bit closer to eavesdrop.

"I can't *believe* she wants that by tomorrow—I have no idea where to even *start*."

This was said in an American accent by the girl on the left, who had Asian features, as well as short black hair streaked with blue.

"It'll be great," her Irish friend assured her. "Just write a lot of lovely bullshit."

"But I *like* Heaney! I just can't dissect him, you know? And I have to get a good grade on this one. But this study guide is total *crap*—it's not helping at *all*." The American girl shut the book that was on her lap and caught Siobhan's eye. She smiled crookedly. "Sorry. Are we being too loud?"

"Oh, no," Siobhan answered. She hesitated, but couldn't resist asking, "You have to write something on Seamus Heaney?"

"*Yes*. My professor wants this essay on a comparison of these two poems but *I* don't see any connection between them."

"You like Heaney?"

"I totally *love* him! But I just like to listen to the language, you know? Kind of let it wash over me or something. I can't *explain* it. But I hate *dissecting* him."

"Can I ask which two poems they are?"

"Sure. 'Blackberry-Picking' and 'Death of a Naturalist.'"

"Oh, yes." Siobhan nodded knowingly.

"You're familiar with those?" the girl asked eagerly.

"Oh, yes," Siobhan repeated.

"Well, then, I *ask* you!" The girl threw up her hands. "A comparison between those two?"

Her Irish friend smiled up at Siobhan and asked, "Would you like to sit down?" She gestured at the floor space in front of them and moved her massive backpack out of the way. "Once she gets going," the friend continued, "she'll talk your ear off, she will. You might as well get comfortable."

"Shut up, Nuala," the American girl said with a smile.

Siobhan sat down slowly, without speaking. She didn't feel shy, exactly; in fact, she was experiencing an odd sense of déjà vu, as if she had done this before. But she hadn't, of course, since she'd never been here and had certainly never sat down with college students. She wondered vaguely if she had dreamed something like it, or else why would it feel so familiar?

"I'm Nuala, by the way," the Irish girl said, "and she's Caitlin from Wisconsin."

"Hi," Caitlin said.

They both looked at her expectantly, with bright friendly eyes.

"I'm Siobhan."

"Hi, Siobhan," Caitlin said, and opened her backpack. "I've got the book with the poems in it." She began rummaging.

"Oh, I know them."

Caitlin stopped and looked at her. "You *know* them? You don't mean you know them by heart?"

"Well, pretty much that," Siobhan admitted. Was that strange?

"My *God*. That's *amazing*. How do you do that?"

"I just . . . I read a lot."

"Jeez, I *guess*. Well, okay. I'm supposed to write an essay highlighting the similarities between these two poems, but to me they seem so *different*. I mean, one is about picking blackberries, and the juice and the colors and references to ripening. And then the berries spoil and get all gross. This poem is totally *awesome*, by the way. But the second poem tells about watching all these frogs and how he would collect the frog spawn—and then the frogs, like, rise up and become like a revengeful army or something and freak him out." Caitlin gestured expansively. "So, one is about berries and one is about frogs. Where are the similarities?"

Siobhan felt an almost primal urge to help this girl better understand these poems, to communicate her own appreciation of their themes, their subtleties, and yes, their similarities. She could feel her excitement building as she listened to Caitlin's surprisingly penetrating summaries. This girl unknowingly was halfway there, but she was starting with a barrier of preconceived ideas. Siobhan felt it was her job to break down the barrier.

Siobhan didn't hesitate for a moment. "Well, for starters, that was a grand summing up. Now, they're both about nature, right?"

"Well, yeah, I guess so."

"And were you noticing how both poems sort of have two parts, the first part where Heaney writes so vividly about what he loves about the subject—the beauty and taste of blackberries or his fascination with the frogs. Then the second part of each poem—because they're very alike in structure—talks about how things go 'off.' The blackberries rot and the frogs become terrifying. Do you see?"

Caitlin's expression became speculative as she nodded slowly. They talked for half an hour and Siobhan reveled in it. She saw the light go on in Caitlin's brain as the girl began to understand the points Siobhan was making and, better yet, the points she herself was able to make. It wasn't at all the same as talking to someone like Tim about the poetry, Siobhan thought. It was better. It was waking up a person's mind to the poetic language's limitless possibilities.

"Siobhan?" She heard Katie's voice behind her. "How are you doing?"

Siobhan turned her head and saw Katie regarding her with surprise. Immediately she felt a little guilty. How long had she been sitting with the girls? She scrambled to her feet.

"Sorry, Katie. We just got to talking."

Caitlin was unrestrained in her gratitude. "That was *amazing*. Thank you *so* much."

"It was fecking brilliant," Nuala said.

Caitlin continued: "Oh, my God, you're like some *angel* sent from heaven or something."

Nuala laughed. "Caitlin, get a grip. Yeah, God really cares about how well you do on this essay. Come on, we'll be late for class."

The two girls stood up and grabbed their backpacks.

"You know what I *mean*," Caitlin told her. "Siobhan's a much better teacher than the prof I have, that's all. Are you a teacher?"

Siobhan was startled at the question. "Oh. No. No, I'm not a teacher."

"You *totally* should be. Thanks again, Siobhan. Maybe we'll see you around."

The girls waved a quick goodbye as they clattered down the stairs, Siobhan looking after them.

All this time Katie had been uncharacteristically silent. Now she said, "Nice girls. Have you picked out something for Gwen?"

Siobhan felt guilty again; she'd forgotten about Gwen. "Oh, no. Not yet. But I was thinking of a Yeats collection." She went back over to the poetry shelf where Yeats resided. Finally she settled on a leather-bound volume.

"I know Uncle Kee said she likes Heaney, but he's not very

comforting, is he? I mean, Yeats is so rich with personal insights into life's journey and aging. Don't you think?"

"You're asking the wrong person, Siobhan. Poetry's a closed book to me, no pun intended. You know best."

"I do?"

"Certainly." Katie nodded her head firmly.

Siobhan held her head a little higher as she paid for the book, and then Katie took her down to Quay Street for gourmet coffee and walnut scones. Siobhan looked around with interest at all she saw, the dark mahogany booths, the stylized posters of Italian and French cuisines, the smartly dressed women with their designer jeans and clunky jewelry.

"So," Katie began after they'd been served, "you were talking about poetry with those girls?"

"Yes, it was grand," Siobhan replied eagerly. "They were so friendly. That Caitlin, she was an American."

"So I gathered. You seemed to have helped her."

"I know." Siobhan was a little self-conscious about Caitlin's effusive gratitude. But even more full of wonder that the girl should have thought she was a teacher. "I just helped her see what she wasn't able to be seeing on her own."

"Well, that's important, isn't it?"

"But it was only—" Siobhan stopped. It had been important, to Caitlin and to herself. She nodded slowly. "Yes, it was." Siobhan smiled. "Wasn't it a thing, her thinking that I might be a teacher?"

"You are. At least you were today."

Siobhan was completely taken aback by this. She sipped her coffee, hanging on Katie's every word.

"A teacher helps people understand things," Katie went on. "And you did just that. They help people expand their way of thinking, don't they? You did that as well. That's a teacher.

You're a teacher. You just didn't get paid for it. At least that's what I'm thinking."

Siobhan was a little dazed. "It felt good, helping her," she said thoughtfully.

"Yes, I could see that," Katie said with a smile.

. . .

Katie found the caravan park easily but they had to do some searching to locate Turf's family, for the park was crowded with traveler vehicles. He, in turn, was on the lookout for the Leeside's old van, not the Range Rover. But they finally spotted each other and Katie pulled in next to the battered camper. Gwen's caravan was just beyond.

Turf looked a little skeptical as the two women got out. His children clustered around, glad of any distraction.

"Where's Mr. Doyle?" Turf asked.

"He wasn't needed," Katie answered blithely.

"'Tis a heavy old caravan," he warned.

"Have you ever hauled a trailer with four Connemara ponies inside? Each weighing about five hundred pounds? I have."

Turf gave his slow smile. "Right you are then."

"And I brought extra chains and a convertible hitch just to make sure we can hook it up right. Let's take a look."

While Katie and Turf examined the logistics of the hookup, Siobhan asked Turf's son Dan if she could see the new baby. There was a chorus of agreement and she was propelled into the beige camper. Used as she was to the interior of Gwen's caravan with its grime but peculiar orderliness, Siobhan was appalled by the cluttered chaos and sour sordidness of the camper. JoJo was sitting on a stained padded bench, feeding a robust baby from her ample breasts. She greeted Siobhan politely enough but chased the children out with a few choice curses. Siobhan did not attempt to make small talk as she felt stifled and swallowed by the fetid atmosphere. She wanted to get out.

Siobhan briefly touched the baby's hand and congratulated JoJo, then asked if she minded about the caravan.

"That old thing? Nasty place. I'm glad to be seeing that back of it and that's the truth. Although it'ould been nice if we could have sold it to get a bit of cash. But she made Turf vow he'd burn it, so there you are. Oh, do you have to be going? Well, see you around."

Siobhan filled her lungs with the outside air that, even carrying the taint of petrol fumes, smelled positively pristine. She walked slowly toward Gwen's caravan and stood looking at it, the worn pale blue trim, the painted yellow sides hewn by wind and rain into a boatlike hull. Strange to think she could climb the rickety steps whenever she wanted to, feel the slickened boards beneath her feet, and be surrounded by the familiar snugness of the barreled walls and ceiling. With one difference. Gwen would not be there.

She stood quietly watching as Katie backed the Rover toward it until Turf gestured at her to stop. Katie jumped out and she and Turf managed, with seemingly little effort, to hitch the old caravan to the waiting Rover.

"Right." Katie wiped her hands on her jeans. "I think that's it, Siobhan. Are you ready to go?"

Siobhan stood very still, her eyes almost pleading with the closed Dutch door to open and reveal the face she knew belonged there. "I need to see Gwen." It was a statement of fact.

Katie studied Siobhan's set face. "You mean you want to see her at the nursing home now?"

"Yes."

"Well, I'm not sure . . . I'd rather not haul the caravan through town. How far is it, Turf?"

"I'll take her." Turf stood looking at Siobhan with an odd expression, as if knowing her thoughts better than she did. "I'll take you, Siobhan."

She turned toward him gratefully and they headed for an old sedan.

"Siobhan!" Katie opened the Rover's door and took out the bookshop bag. "Your present."

"Oh!" Siobhan again felt instant gratitude. "Thanks. You're not minding, are you, Katie?"

Katie shook her head. "Take your time," she replied gently.

As Siobhan took the book from her their eyes met, and they smiled understandingly at each other.

The drive to the nursing home took place in silence. Siobhan was weary; after the emotional high at the bookstore she was now overcome with depression at the thought of the visit ahead. After they parked and entered the long, low red-brick building, Turf stopped and touched Siobhan on the arm.

"She's not too bad most times, Siobhan. She's lost a bit of weight and, well, you'll see."

Fear clutched at Siobhan's stomach and she balled a clenched fist inside her pocket. The other hand, white-knuckled, clung to the bookshop bag she carried close to her chest. She could not imagine an ill Gwen, a cowed Gwen, a Gwen brought down by the double blow of terminal illness and dormancy. The sealed white walls of the long hallway couldn't absorb the dead light spewing from the fluorescent fixtures. It seemed to Siobhan that the light darted back and forth, searching for last breaths.

Turf stopped in front of a plain smooth door with no handle, marked 147.

"Mum and another lady were sharing this room, but that one died a couple of days ago." He pushed the door open and preceded Siobhan into the room, for which she was grateful.

"Hello, Mum. I've brought Siobhan to see you," Turf said, with no hint of coyness or false cheer.

Siobhan saw Gwen turn her head toward them in the dim light. The ruddy complexion was now replaced by the ash-gray of terminal illness. The cheeks were more hollowed, the wrinkles deepened into fissures, like a landscape suffering from drought. But the eyes, the dark, wise eyes were still alive, still held the true Gwen within their depths. It was on these that Siobhan concentrated as she came forward and sat in a chair next to the bed.

"Well, missy." The voice was also mercifully the same, strong and raspy. "This is a surprise. It's the caravan that brings you to Galway, I'm thinking?"

"Yes. Thank you for wanting me to take it."

"You'll appreciate it. And it can end its days in the loveliest of places, the middle of a grand emptiness."

Siobhan smiled a little. "Yes."

"Unlike myself, who'll be buried in a pauper's grave or cremated or whatever the hell they do with us flotsam and jetsam."

Turf stirred slightly, standing by the window, which was shuttered against the bright day.

"Ah, well," Gwen continued, "it doesn't matter. My body's been of little real use to me for quite a time now."

Siobhan asked, "Where do you want me to put the caravan, Gwen?"

"Well, that's up to you, missy, but I've always fancied that little clearing off to the left, at the edge of the long grasses, before the hill rises. That's where my husband and I camped overnight more than a few times, thanks to your uncle and grandmother, bless 'em."

"All right." Siobhan felt a choking, tight pain in her throat from tears that wanted to come.

Gwen studied her knowingly. "If you've a mind to shed tears over me, little miss, go ahead. I count myself lucky to have known you and your family."

Siobhan did cry then, with little gasping sobs. Turf began to move about the room restlessly, rubbing his neck, touching the taps on the sink, fiddling with the cord for the window blinds.

Gwen watched Siobhan with compassion. "I'll think on these as tears for the ending of a friendship but not of pity. Never that. You might as well grieve for me now. I'm trapped by the sheets of a government bed, even as the road pulls at me from outside this room . . . I'm already dead. The stillness has killed me."

At this, Turf blundered out of the room, as if he couldn't listen anymore. Finally Siobhan was able to sigh any new tears away, and she stared with swimming eyes at the pencil-thin rods of sunlight falling onto the bed covers from the shuttered window. She swallowed hard.

"Why—why don't you want the window blinds open? To see the outside? Isn't it worse to have it all closed up in here?"

Gwen turned her head sharply away for a minute, then replied, for the first time with bitterness. "I can only stand it with the window closed. It's easier when I can't be seeing what I can't have." She stirred restlessly under her covers. "These tiny streaks of sun are like daggers to me. But . . ." She paused and the strong voice took on a hairline crack. "But when the sunlight is moving off the bed to the floor, it's worse because I can't touch it."

The two women sat for a time then, how long neither of them knew. Finally Turf came back into the room, a bit sheepishly with eyes that betrayed weeping.

"How are you two doing?"

"Take Siobhan away, boy. She needs to get my caravan to its final resting place."

"I brought you a book of poetry," Siobhan said quickly, taking the book from its bag. "It's not Heaney, because I thought, well . . . it's Yeats."

Gwen smiled then. "It's a thoughtful girl you are. I'll enjoy it. Put it on the table there."

Siobhan did so, and stood up. "Well . . . goodbye."

"Goodbye, missy, and promise me you'll pass some time visiting my old home before it goes up in smoke. It just might be giving you some ideas about traveling, and wouldn't that be a thing."

Siobhan managed a smile. "Yes." She paused and then said, "Read the poem called 'The Hawk' first."

"I will."

. . .

The drive back home was accomplished without problems, Katie's Rover stoic in its task of pulling the heavy caravan. Siobhan said little and Katie respected the girl's need to be alone with her thoughts. She had been touched by the emotional farewell between Turf and Siobhan, with her anxious for the assurance that he and his family would still stop at the Leeside every September.

"Aye, we will, so. I'll be thinking more of that as Mum's final resting place than anything here in town. You and Mr. Doyle can expect us as long as we're welcome."

"You'll always be welcome. And of course you'll come to us when . . . when . . ."

Turf nodded, looking at the ground. "Aye."

Siobhan kept watching the old caravan in the side-view mirror, hoping it wasn't minding this chained indignity. She sensed it would miss the company of the horses that had pulled it over the decades. Maybe Blasket would temporarily adopt it and take to lying in its shadow and cropping the grass at its doorstep. She hoped so.

They were only a few kilometers from the Leeside when Katie asked, "Where are you going to put it, Siobhan?"

Siobhan answered, echoing Gwen's request, word for word, "In the little clearing off to the left, at the edge of the long grasses, before the hill rises."

Katie glanced at her. "Okay."

Katie expertly backed her load onto the very spot that Siobhan had pictured. Kee came out and after a brief greeting, helped Katie undo the chains and hitch, then stood back to look at the new arrival.

"Actually it looks oddly at home here," he commented.

"It's been here before," Siobhan replied.

"That it has, on this very spot."

"Yes."

Kee looked a little ashamed as he avoided looking at his niece's tired face.

"How was Gwen? Did you see her?"

"Gwen's . . . done. She's just waiting."

Kee nodded, then spoke hesitantly. "I'm sorry I was so against bringing the caravan here, love. It was . . . I don't know. Superstition, I think. Burning Gwen's caravan at the Leeside is pretty personal. We've a responsibility to do it right, so that her . . . her spirit is put to rest and not unsettled. Preserve her tribe's harmony."

Katie asked, with a seriousness that surprised Siobhan, "Are you afraid she'll haunt the place? If the tradition isn't satisfied?"

Kee shrugged. "Something like that."

Siobhan laid a hand on his arm. "We'll do it right, Uncle Kee. We love her."

· · ·

Later that night, after the pub closed, Siobhan wrapped her blue shawl around her shoulders—her grandmother's shawl knitted by Gwen—and went out to the caravan. It was very dark so she brought a flashlight with her. Kee had set up the uneven steps and Siobhan climbed these now, opening the half doors. The flashlight gave the barreled interior a ghostly aura, as if the spirit of Gwen had already taken up residence.

Sitting down on the top step, she gathered her shawl tightly around her, gazing out over the lough, which was once again her friend. Somehow the caravan had healed the spiritual rift between her and the lough. Wrapped in the stillness, Siobhan gradually became conscious of a rocking sensation beneath her, a phantom movement of decades of migration, the residue of wanderlust, the fierce need for what was just over the next rise. She thought of Gwen, lying in her alien bed, and of the poem she'd told Gwen to read.

> *I will not be clapped in a hood,*
> *Nor a cage, nor alight upon wrist,*
> *Now I have learnt to be proud*
> *Hovering over the wood*
> *In the broken mist*
> *Or tumbling cloud.*

Yes, thought Siobhan, this is a wondrous place. But even the wind that loves it is free to move on.

CHAPTER 17

O too late I knew,
Although the blame was mine,
Her voice could not be softer
When she told it in confession.

—AUSTIN CLARKE

Kee and Katie rode out on one of Katie's bridle paths, cantering at a fairly brisk pace until Kee called out for mercy. He wasn't in nearly the shape that Katie was and, although she was careful not to push him too hard, sometimes she got carried away.

"Hold up there, woman! I've got to be able to walk when we're done, you know."

"All right, all right. We'll slow it down. God knows I don't want a man with weak legs."

"My legs are grand. In fact, if you want to get off that animal for a wee bit I'll show you."

"And why should I want to get off for a 'wee bit'?"

"Oh, that's nasty, that is."

Katie laughed.

Their mounts walked side by side as Kee smiled at his lady. "You put me in mind of poetry, Katie, m'love."

She smiled back. "What doesn't?"

He replied by quoting Heaney: " '*There was a time when I preferred the mountain grouse crying at dawn to the voice and closeness of a beautiful woman.*' "

"Well, thank you very much. I take it that means you don't still prefer the grouse at dawn over me?"

"Not unless I've a gun in me hands, darlin'."

"Again, thanks very much."

Kee didn't miss a beat with his next sentence. "And seeing as how I do prefer you, at dawn or any other time, what about marrying me?"

Katie's horse broke rhythm for a moment or two as she slackened the reins. She hesitated before responding. "What about the grouse then? Maybe you'll be wanting them again."

"Some things are much more rarely found than grouse—so when you do find them you'd better grab on."

Although it's difficult for two people to kiss while on horseback, Kee and Katie more than managed it. After a few pleasurable moments Kee pulled away slightly and caressed her cheek. He said ruefully, "You're knowing that I'm coming with some baggage, darlin'—still fighting the good fight with the bottle, for one. And I think on the past way too much for my own good, God knows. And Siobhan . . ." He paused.

Katie asked, "What about Siobhan, Kee?"

Kee looked thoughtful and shook his head. "I don't know. The girl's been . . . unsettled lately. I've been thinking on what we could do about her if we were to get married. The living arrangements might be a bit difficult. She can't live alone at the pub, Katie."

Katie hesitated for a moment, then sighed. "I know that. Well, maybe for a time I could live with the two of you at the pub and just commute to the farm every day."

Kee was amazed. "You would do that?"

"*For a time*, mind. Until we get something sorted out. But I don't want Siobhan to feel like I'm stealing you away as soon as the deed's done."

"But you'd really live at the Leeside for a bit?"

"I would—but don't let it go to your head."

"I love you—but don't let that go to *your* head."

. . .

Later that evening Kee and Siobhan were alone in the pub. A couple of regulars had come and gone and there was a cold, gray rain falling. Siobhan was preoccupied and quiet; Kee was finding it difficult to broach the subject of his marriage to Katie. But the longer he put it off, the harder it would be. He was surprised at how apprehensive he was. Would Siobhan feel betrayed or even abandoned? She and Katie were getting along much better but that didn't mean she'd welcome Katie with open arms. Siobhan was changing; she was coming out of herself, just as Katie said she might be, but seemed more distracted and discontented. Would his marriage encourage her to emerge further, give impetus to her search for autonomy? Or would it be a setback and cause her to feel more insecure? He wished he knew. But he had to tell her. This was his life— his and Katie's. This was *real* life—not the kind he and Siobhan had been living all these years behind this bloody bar . . .

His thoughts were interrupted by Siobhan. She spoke quickly in Irish, as if that was the only way she could get out the words. "*Uncal Kee, cén fáth go raibh tú ag ól an mhéid sin sul ar tháinig mé a chónaí anseo?*" (Uncle Kee, why were you drinking so much before I came to live here?)

Kee looked at her in surprise, then pushed aside the inventory list he was working on. After a moment he shrugged.

"Disappointment, I think. Unfulfilled dreams. Loneliness. Self-pity. That last is an easy coat to slip into." He paused and rubbed his chin, rough with its end-of-the day stubble. "Sometimes I think that's why I don't like Niall Curry. He reminds me too much of myself at that age."

"You gave up a lot for me."

"No, I didn't, love. I gave up a lot for Mum and Maureen. Coming home from university was hard—it felt like taking a giant step backward in my life. But they needed me. Then Mum died and Maureen went away. So I was here alone."

Siobhan stared at the taps without seeing them. "I've always thought of her as Maureen—your sister. Not . . . my mother. Why is that?"

Kee felt a wave of sympathy. "I suppose it's because you were so young when she died, and because you hear me talk about her as Maureen."

"Did you drink to help convince yourself that it was right to be staying here?"

Kee raised his eyebrows. "Aye, maybe. That's a perceptive question, Siobhan."

She persisted. "Could you have sold the Leeside and gone back to school?"

Kee smiled wryly. "In theory. But in practice, never. I could never sell this place. We're stuck with each other, thank God. I did consider hiring someone to come and manage it for me. But there just weren't many people in the world I'd be trusting to do that."

"And you'd never live anywhere else?"

Kee hesitated, thinking of his conversation with Katie. He answered slowly. "Maybe I could. But I'd still never sell. Our family has been here for six generations."

Siobhan lifted troubled eyes to his. "Why did Maureen go away? Really?"

He was taken aback. "What do you mean?"

"I heard—a long time ago—that she was headed for the Magdalene Laundries in Galway. That she was known as a fallen woman. That the priest was coming to get her."

He felt his old anger stirring. "Who told you that? That's a . . . well, not a lie, exactly. But I'd never have allowed it. And she knew that. The way it worked was no woman ever went to the laundries if there was a male relative ready to . . . to take care of her."

"To keep her in line, you mean."

Her uncle looked at her sternly. "That's enough, now. She wasn't a fallen woman, for God's sake. She was never in danger of—" He broke off and, irritated, he turned his attention again to his inventory list.

Siobhan watched him in silence for a few minutes, but his severity didn't intimidate her, not like it used to. She took the next leap.

"Uncle Kee, did you know my father was alive all this time?"

His hand dropped the pen on the bar. He straightened up and deliberately faced her. "Not to say 'know'—I didn't know either way. But . . . but I did know that he wasn't killed with your mother."

They were standing at either end of the bar, its long surface like a road between them.

"How did you know that?"

"Because his name was on your birth certificate and that name wasn't on the list of victims."

"So . . . so you could have found him if you had tried?"

"I don't know. I didn't try."

Her voice dropped to a whisper. "Why didn't you try?"

Kee let out a great sigh, the sigh of a man finally releasing the last secret in his soul.

"I didn't want to," he replied with resignation. "I just didn't want him in your life—or mine. I didn't want the trouble of it. I was so grateful and relieved to have gained your trust and love, don't you see? I knew what it meant to have a child completely dependent on me. It scared the hell out of me at first, if you want the truth, but we were a family, ourselves."

Siobhan knew she had to ask it. "Was it . . . was it because he was British?"

"I'd be lying if I said no. That was part of it. I suppose when it comes down to the bone, I was prejudiced—and still am. But any stranger would have been . . . unwelcome."

"But if he'd been Irish?"

"I don't know. You see, what if . . ." Suddenly his face contorted with pain. "What if he had wanted to take you away?" he whispered. "I couldn't have survived that." He covered his face in shame as he began weeping and Siobhan, who had never seen her uncle cry, was at first frozen with shock. Then a wave of compassion drowned out all other emotions. She went forward and buried her face in his chest, feeling his huge body shake with emotion. They stood that way for a long time.

Siobhan finally said gently, "You won't lose me, Uncle Kee. You'll never lose me. I . . . I just needed to tell you that it hurt me that you lied. And to tell you that I've decided to get to know him—my father, I mean."

Kee nodded and wiped his face. "I was thinking you might."

"Try not to mind. It would be easier for me if you could accept it."

"I'll accept it—I can't be happy about it. But it's all right with me. You're a big girl and these are your decisions. That'll take some time getting used to for me, but I'll work on it." He took her small face in his hands. "The very last thing in this world I want to do is hurt you. I'm sorry, love, I'm so sorry." He paused and took a deep breath. "You're right about Maur . . . about your mother. She did need to leave the area. She wanted to anyway, but people were talking and I was uneasy about it. But it was still . . . hard when she went away. I want to start looking ahead inside of behind, Siobhan. You've got a new person in your life now, and I . . ." He paused, and she finished it for him.

"And you've got Katie."

He looked at her searchingly and nodded. "Yes. I want to marry Katie, Siobhan."

For the first time, she smiled. "That's grand. I think you should."

. . .

Siobhan decided the time had come to tell Tim the truth about the book. Although the thought of doing so was very frightening, she remembered Maura's words clearly, that everyone's scared. *"No one's an expert on life . . . Everyone makes mistakes."* She'd made a mistake and it was time to fix it. This was what adults did. She felt better after she made the decision to call Tim. She'd make the call after Uncle Kee went to bed. He and Katie were definitely a couple now and Siobhan was relieved at how little she minded. She had come to realize that some of Katie's qualities, like her take-charge attitude, were valuable. She could have hugged Katie at the end of their day in Galway, she had been so encouraging, so supportive. Siobhan knew she and Katie would never look at everything the same way, but that wasn't important. It was easy to see that Katie really loved Uncle Kee and he loved her. Nothing else mattered.

Siobhan lifted the receiver and slowly dialed Tim's number. She felt slightly sick to her stomach but her talks with Uncle Kee and Maura gave her courage. Everyone made mistakes— the important thing was to admit them. If people really cared about you (it was at this point that Siobhan's courage got a little shaky; did Tim really care for her?), they forgave you. Even if they didn't understand, they forgave (didn't they?). The number was ringing now. It was seven o'clock in the evening, his time. It was the twenty-seventh of November and in the west of Ireland the weather was wet, cold, and windy. Siobhan wondered if it was cold where Tim was.

· · ·

It *was* cold in Minnesota. A freak Thanksgiving storm had dumped fourteen inches of snow and frigid cold had followed it. Most people still had leaves to rake in their yards but now the leaves were buried and not to be seen until spring as sodden, dead masses of brown. But Tim had escaped from it all. The phone in his empty house rang hollowly until the answering machine kicked in. Siobhan, after having nerved herself to talk to Tim, hung up in dismay without leaving a message. The thought of him not being there hadn't even occurred to her; this was their normal online time. She hesitated, then dialed his cell-phone number, but again got voice mail. She'd awaken early tomorrow to try again, she decided firmly. Proud of herself for this resolve, Siobhan went to bed feeling hopeful.

It was just past six o'clock in the morning when Tim landed at Shannon Airport. To his dismay he found his cell-phone battery was dead, and had to wait until he was through customs to call Siobhan from a pay phone and tell her he was in Ireland, was on his way to her. He was surprised to find the line busy and wondered who she could be talking to at this early hour. He hesitated, then decided to wait five minutes and try again. Exactly four minutes and fifty-nine seconds later he dialed again. He heard her soft voice answer the phone.

"Hello, Leeside."

"Hello, Siobhan? It's Tim."

There was a long silence. He became anxious—was she upset that he called?

"Siobhan? Are you there?"

"Yes . . . I . . . yes, I'm here. It's just such a surprise. I just tried to ring *you*."

So that's why the line had been busy, he thought with relief. She'd wanted to talk to him. "You were calling me? Why? Well, never mind—you can tell me when I get there."

"Get here?" her voice echoed.

"Yes," Tim said eagerly. "I'm here. I'm at Shannon. I'll rent a car right away and come up. I should get to the Leeside around ten o'clock or so."

Siobhan sounded confused. "But . . . why are you coming? Don't you have classes?"

He hesitated. He didn't want to go into his feelings for her over the phone. "Well, it's . . . it's the book. I want to come over and meet with that woman. I'd like to at least see the book and talk with her. You can help me arrange that, can't you? If I can get a look at—"

"No—no, stop." Siobhan interrupted him. She gripped the receiver until her knuckles were white. Why oh why hadn't she told him sooner? He'd hate her now—he'd hate her.

"Siobhan? What's wrong? Look, it'll be okay. I know it's been kind of difficult for you. It'll be best if we go together. Maybe she'd appreciate a gift or something—"

"There is no woman!" It was a cry of despair. "There is no woman."

"What? Do you mean . . . did she die?"

"Oh, God in heaven—no, she didn't die."

"Well, then what are you—"

"I made her up!" Siobhan cried in desperation. "There never was any woman! There never was any book! I made it all up . . .

I made it all up . . ." Siobhan breathed quickly as she listened to his dazed silence.

He asked confusedly, "But how . . . how can there be no book when I've got those poems you gave me? Where did the poems come from?"

Her voice was a frightened whisper. "They're my poems. I wrote them."

"*You* wrote them? My God. You wrote them."

"Yes."

"Siobhan . . . why did you do all that? I mean, lie to me about—the woman and everything? Why did you make it all up?"

Still she whispered, her heart pounding with anxiety. "I don't know. I don't know. It just . . . happened. And then I couldn't stop. I just wanted to . . . to be friends."

"Well, I knew they weren't twelfth century, I had figured that out, but—"

This startled her. "You knew that?"

"Well, of course. After I had studied them closely."

"But if *you* knew they weren't authentic, why didn't you tell me?"

"Well, I didn't . . . I mean, I thought if I just . . . if you might be . . . Oh, shit. Look, Siobhan. I'm going to rent a car and come up, okay? We can't talk about this over the phone. Is that all right?"

His voice sounded impatient to her anxious ears.

"Yes, it's all right. Come."

Siobhan hung up the phone with a shaking hand. She felt as if her whole future was about to be decided in the next few hours.

CHAPTER 18

A shadowy tumult stirs the dusky air;
Sparkle the delicate dews, the distant snows;
The great deep thrills, for through it everywhere
The breath of Beauty blows.

—A.E. (GEORGE W. RUSSELL)

Wrapped in her blue shawl, Siobhan sat on the top step of Gwen's caravan waiting for Tim. She told her uncle that Tim was on his way to the Leeside to see her. Uncle Kee looked concerned but only nodded and said, "I'll stay out of your way." She was grateful for his respect of her privacy.

After breakfast was over Siobhan went to sit on the lough wall. The early morning began softly but gradually the wind grew sharper and she watched birds flying to shelter. She would wait in the caravan, Siobhan decided. She'd be out of the weather there. Not only that, but she felt uncomfortable talking to Tim by the lough wall, where they had first met. She didn't want the lough to be witness to today's encounter, with its uncertainty of outcome.

Siobhan set the two half doors ajar and sat with the darkened interior behind her. She'd been here now for a long time, thinking very deliberately about everything that had happened since she'd first seen Tim sitting on that same lough wall more than three months ago. The voices of Tim, Uncle Kee, Gwen, Maura, Katie, Bettina, and even Caitlin the student moved in and out of the forefront of her mind, like isolated musical notes seeking the right melody. She herself couldn't discern it; the forces of discord and doubt were pushing and pulling the voices into a chaotic swirl. How could she gather them into some sort of meaningful rhythm? Was there something missing from the voices in her mind, some vital nebulous key?

A sudden cool gust of wind swept around the open caravan door, enveloped her, then swirled around the dusky space behind her and was gone. Siobhan stared straight ahead, stunned into stillness. It was as if the wind had blown away the chaos and awakened her mind to the missing piece of the puzzle—her own voice.

. . .

Tim made good time from Shannon and arrived after barely two hours on the road. His heart increased its pace along with the car's engine as he surged over the rise and viewed the Leeside in its perfect setting for the second time. But today he had no desire to turn the car around and leave the place in peace.

And he noticed there had been a change. Off to the left, nestled in a clearing, was a yellow-and-blue barrel caravan. The colors were so vibrant and unexpected, it looked as if an artist had come along and decided to paint it on the dulled November canvas. Tim's eyes found Siobhan sitting in its open doorway even before she stood up and watched him drive into the yard.

Getting out of the car, he was keenly aware that this was going to be an important conversation to them both. He had no idea how to begin, no clear plan. He had simply gotten on a plane and come.

Siobhan watched Tim walk toward her. She stayed where she was at the top of the steps. She knew what she wanted to say, just not how to say it.

"Hello, Siobhan."

"Hello."

Tim gestured toward the caravan. "I like the new addition."

"Me, too."

"It's cold to be sitting outside."

"I don't mind it."

A vigilant silence followed, as each searched for an opening. Siobhan saw the uncertainty in Tim's eyes and it helped her know how to begin.

"I'm sorry for lying to you. It was wrong, and stupid."

"No, no. Don't apologize. It shows that you . . . Well, anyway, it doesn't matter."

"It matters. But thank you."

"I wasn't honest with you, either, and I'm sorry for that. I mean, as soon as I suspected the poems weren't authentic I should have discussed it with you."

"What would you have said?"

Tim shrugged. He was standing at the bottom of the steps, looking up at her. "I don't know," he answered. "The problem was—" He looked into her eyes. "The real problem was that I loved . . . the poems so much. They're wonderful, Siobhan."

Siobhan felt a deep sense of pride at his words. But there was something else. "I wonder," she began, "I wonder if I was wanting you to figure it out the whole time."

He looked alert at this. "Why do you say that?"

"I don't know. If I had really thought it out, it was certain to happen."

He shook his head. "It took me too long. I wasn't . . . being objective. I know now that I allowed my . . . personal feelings to cloud my judgment. My feelings for you are . . . overwhelming. That's the only way I can describe them. I just know I don't want to lose what we have, Siobhan. I want you in my life."

Siobhan felt a thrill of delight, but it was tempered with pity. He watched her with a rueful expression.

"I simply couldn't separate how I felt about you from my academic method, shall we say. Not something good scholars do. I feel that I let myself down."

She didn't want him to feel badly about himself. "Why should you feel that? You trusted me."

Again he looked into her eyes. "I still do."

Holding his gaze, she took a deep breath and spoke quickly. "Then trust me when I say that I'm not ready."

"Not ready?" Tim didn't understand.

She searched for the right words. "How can I explain what I'm feeling? I need you to understand, I need to say the right thing. About me. I'm just not ready . . . for you. For . . . us."

A hurt look passed over his face. He didn't respond, just kept looking up at her, injured and cold. The air was chilling quickly now, being flayed raw by the biting wind.

Siobhan picked her next words very carefully. "It would be too easy for me to go with you, to give up my place in Uncle Kee's world for a place in yours. Like a trade. I can't be doing that. Not yet. I need to be finding my own place in the world. I know it's not what you're wanting to hear, but can you please try to understand it?"

Tim squinted into the distance, nodding. She could see it was difficult for him to speak and her own heart swelled with empathy. It was hard to see him hurting, but she knew she was right. Siobhan stayed silent as Tim swallowed a few times, then turned his head and smiled up at her.

"Of course I understand, of course I do. I won't say I'm not disappointed. But if I can . . . I mean, I'll still hope that maybe, eventually . . ."

Siobhan spoke softly. "I said not yet. If you can be patient . . . But I can't be promising anything. We'll need to . . . see."

His face lifted to hers again. He expelled a long breath. "I can be patient."

"Thank you."

They stood there looking at each other. It was a solemn moment, a fateful pact of a few simple words.

For Siobhan it was a powerfully sweet moment; Tim would wait for her, but she alone had made a pivotal decision for her own future, and she knew it was the right one.

For Tim it was bittersweet. In his heart of hearts he had hoped to gather her up and take her home with him, had dreamed she might agree to that. But it was not to be.

Siobhan came slowly down the steps with a purpose. She wanted to put her arms around Tim, wanted to know how it felt to hold him against her. She hesitated on the second to the last step; it was here they were eye to eye with each other. Opening her arms wide, she wrapped them tightly around his neck. She sensed his surprise, and for a fraction of a second he didn't react. Then his arms came around her, with a heady urgency. How wonderful it was to hear him breathing, and feel the beat of his heart and the warmth of him. His whole being was a new world opening up for her to explore.

Tim spoke in a husky voice. *"Tabhair geallúint nach dtréigfidh tú créatúr bocht daonna agus nach bpillfidh tú chuig an síbhruíon?"* (You promise you won't desert a mere mortal and return to your fairy mound?)

She answered gladly, *"Ach níl cónaí orm i síbhruíon, is créatúr bocht daonna mise comh maith."* (I don't live in a fairy mound, because I'm a mere mortal as well.)

. . .

Within the Leeside Kee had been drawn to the window to watch the two of them. When he saw them embrace he was overwhelmed by a mixture of gratitude and closure. Tim was a good man. He obviously loved Siobhan deeply—was there any other way to love her?

Kee thought of Katie. He told himself now: *You're a lucky son of a bitch.* The small chip he'd carried on his shoulder most of his life was gone, smoothed away by the generosity of love.

. . .

Siobhan and Tim walked slowly toward the front door of the pub just as Katie's Rover appeared in the lane.

"Oh, Lord, I forgot!" Siobhan exclaimed.

"What?"

"I'm going to lunch with Katie and Maura, at Bettina's restaurant. There's a few things I'm wanting to talk over with them all."

Katie pulled to a stop and got out of her car.

"Well, well! Tim Ferris, as I live and breathe! How are you keeping?"

They shook hands.

"I'm keeping very well, thanks."

Katie nodded, obviously curious but she didn't press. "Grand." She then leveled an appraising gaze on Siobhan's sweater and jeans. "Siobhan, you're never going to Bettina's in that. Look at me, I'm all dolled up in my new pantsuit. Go on, then. Change into something decent."

Three months ago that speech would have made Siobhan choke with resentment. Now she nodded and replied, "Right. I'll just be two minutes." She started inside. "Are we picking up Maura?" she called over her shoulder.

"She's meeting us there, so."

In the doorway Siobhan met her uncle coming out. He touched her arm.

"Everything all right, love?" he asked her significantly.

"Everything's grand." She reached up and gave him a quick kiss on the cheek, then hurried upstairs.

. . .

The women sat around a prime corner table at the restaurant. Bettina joined them after making sure that their order was being given the proper attention in the kitchen.

"Well," she began, after sipping her chilled pinot grigio, "you could have knocked me down with a feather when Siobhan called this morning. It was wonderful to hear from you." In a warm, spontaneous gesture she briefly covered Siobhan's hand with her own.

Siobhan smiled happily. It had been an impulse, calling these three women and arranging a meeting. She had felt an overwhelming desire to share with them her thoughts, and the decisions she had made earlier that morning. Realizing now what Gwen had meant, Siobhan craved the support of the women around this table who were special to her.

"I wanted to talk to all of you about some decisions I've made," she began in a businesslike manner.

"Decisions, is it?" Bettina asked with interest.

"Does one of them involve Tim Ferris?" Katie asked archly.

Maura raised her eyebrows. "Tim?"

"He was at the Leeside when I got there this morning," Katie informed them.

"He wasn't!" Maura exclaimed to Siobhan.

"He was," Siobhan answered shyly. "He . . . wants us to be together."

Maura leaned forward toward her, her mouth open in a small circle. "Wow."

"My, my!" Bettina said.

Maura asked, "But what happened when you told him about the book? You've told him, right?"

Siobhan nodded.

"What book?" Katie asked, a little impatiently.

Siobhan replied, "It's a bit of a long story, but everything's grand about it, Maura. He was brilliant. We can talk about that later."

"You'll talk about it now, if you don't mind," Bettina said mildly. "It all sounds very mysterious. Please, Siobhan."

So the tale of Siobhan's great lie was told, and the two older women took it very much in stride.

"Men need a grand shake-up now and then," Katie declared, and took a deep drink of her wine.

Bettina remarked, "Sure, and haven't we all lied to our man at some time or other?"

Maura smiled wryly. "We have."

Katie echoed thoughtfully, "We have indeed."

At that point the waiter arrived with their food, exquisitely presented as usual. When everyone was served, Katie brought the conversation back to Tim.

"Siobhan, you said that Tim wants you to be together. It sounds like you're not sure."

Siobhan looked at her with wide eyes. "I'm not. And I told him that. I told him I don't want to trade Uncle Kee for him—being taken care of and that. I'm just wanting, well, time. Time to do other things." The three women stared at her with blank amazement. Siobhan looked around at each of them. "I've decided I want to go to university."

Katie sat back in her chair. Maura dropped her fork. "Jaysus, Mary, and Joseph," she said.

Bettina beamed. "That's fantastic, Siobhan. Brilliant."

Maura leaned over and hugged Siobhan tightly. There were tears in her eyes when she looked at her friend. "Siobhan, I'm so proud of you. God in heaven, those pigs *are* flying!"

They all laughed then.

Bettina asked, "Do you know where you want to go? What you want to study?"

"The National University in Galway," Siobhan answered definitely, "into their Celtic studies program."

"Celtic studies?" Katie repeated. "Will you be going as a student or a teacher?" she joked.

But Siobhan answered seriously, "I want to learn to be a teacher. Katie, remember that day in the bookshop? I helped that girl, I know I did. I loved talking to her about it all. It was like it was meant or something. Anyway, I know I want to try. I have to try."

"What about your Leaving Certificate?" Maura asked.

"They have special entrance tests, for older students."

"Can you afford it?" Katie asked bluntly.

"I have my savings. It's more than forty thousand euro."

"Forty thousand?" Bettina exclaimed.

"Well, Uncle Kee's been paying me since I was sixteen, for working in the pub. I've never spent much of it."

"What does he think about all this?" Katie asked with raised eyebrows.

Siobhan looked thoughtful. "I don't know. I haven't told him yet." She sat up a little straighter, a tiny, determined figure. "But my mind's made up. I'm going."

Maura stared at Siobhan as if at some amazing vision, chin resting her in hand. "My God," she said finally, "I feel drained, like I've been present at your birth."

Bettina refilled everyone's wineglass, then raised her own. "To Siobhan!"

The others echoed, "To Siobhan!"

Looking around the table, Siobhan knew she had never been so happy. "Thanks to all of you. You're grand. And, well—I'm as ready as I'll ever be."

. . .

Tim and Kee took a walk on the hills. Battling the wind was a welcome physical release for their pent-up emotions. After the first few minutes, Tim was compelled by some ask-for-her-hand code to say, "Kee, I love Siobhan. She and I have come to, well, an understanding of sorts. I'm willing to wait until she's sure about me. I'll wait for her—I want you to know that." It was such an old-fashioned way to put it, and yet it seemed the right way.

Kee was silent so Tim glanced at him. "Are you okay with that?"

"Does it matter?" Kee's voice was gruff.

"Well, yes, I think it matters a lot. Siobhan couldn't really be happy if she knew you disapproved."

"I don't."

"Oh. Well, that's great. Thanks."

"You're welcome." Kee's voice was ironic.

Tim was slightly annoyed. "I probably sound like an idiot but I'm just trying to make sure things are okay."

Kee stopped walking and faced him. "Why?"

"Why?" Tim was confused.

Kee spoke slowly. "Siobhan is not like other women. Yet now I see her changing before my eyes, and it's a mighty shift that's happening. No, I won't be the one to hold her back. If the two of you love each other, that's all that matters, right?"

"I . . . yes."

"Well, then, man! You should be over the moon, not trying

to smooth the path! You're in love, for God's sake. You should be bursting with the wonder of it!"

"But I am, dammit!" Tim exclaimed, throwing out his arms. "My God, I still can't believe it. She's the most incredible, lovely . . . I can't believe I've found her. If she'll really have me, I'll do whatever it takes to make her happy. She . . . has my heart. I never really knew what that meant before. From the first moment I saw her . . ."

"Though she smiled without intention yet from that day forward
Her beauty filled like water the four corners of my being,
And she rested in my heart like the hare in the form
That is shaped to herself."

Kee looked off into the distance, and Tim's passionate quote echoed in the air. Siobhan's uncle spoke gruffly, "You'll be good to her?"

Tim answered solemnly; this was a pact of a different kind, a sacred trust: "I'll treasure her forever, Kee, I swear to you. Forever."

The big Irishman smiled slightly. "Well, all right, then. Being in love myself I know what it feels like."

Tim nodded. "You and Katie. That's great, Kee."

"Thanks." Kee put out a hand, and they shook firmly. "Good luck to you."

. . .

When Siobhan and Katie returned to the Leeside they found Kee and Tim in earnest conversation. They were discussing the Ossianic Cycle and its controversial Scotch-Irish elements.

Kee broke off to ask them, "Did you ladies have a good lunch, then?"

"We did," Katie answered.

"Yes, it was wonderful," Siobhan said, smiling at the men. It felt good to have Tim here, visiting easily with Uncle Kee.

"What did you have?"

Katie said, "I had the prawns, a whole platterful looking up at me with their beady black eyes, God love 'em. Delicious."

"Ah, Sean's a grand chef," Kee remarked.

Katie looked at him. "Walk me out to my car?"

"Sure, darlin'."

Katie had an ulterior motive in getting Kee to walk her out. He assumed she had also, but not the one he thought. She let him nuzzle her neck for a few moments before pushing him away.

"Kee, I need to *talk* to you."

"Go ahead, I'm listening." He pulled her close again.

She chuckled, but pushed him away firmly. "No, you randy old bastard. *Listen* to me. Can you do that?"

"Always." He kept his hands on her waist and she leaned her elbows on his chest.

"Siobhan's got some things to talk to you about."

"Like what?"

"No, that's up to Siobhan. But I have a confession—something that I've never told you. About my husband."

That surprised him; Katie never talked about her husband. "Oh, aye? What's that then? You're not going back to him, I hope?"

"God forbid." She took a deep breath. "Kee, I didn't leave my husband. He left me. Out of the blue. For a younger woman."

He looked at her in mild surprise but didn't speak. Katie watched him anxiously.

"Well?" she asked. "I didn't tell you because I thought you'd think less of me—"

Kee began laughing.

"Kee!" She punched his chest.

"I'm sorry, love! It's just nice to know that there's a bigger fool in the world than myself. I'll have to thank him someday."

Katie threw her arms around him and they kissed passionately. When they finally broke apart, she said firmly, "You come over later, mister."

"Oh, I will."

. . .

Siobhan waited with suppressed excitement for her uncle to come back. She was so anxious to tell the two men of her decision to go to university she was almost bursting with it. She was also a little uncomfortable in the spotlight of Tim's admiring gaze. But not very uncomfortable—just a little. In fact, she rather liked it.

"You do look excited," Tim finally remarked. "Do you have some news?"

Siobhan nodded but didn't speak for fear it would gush out of her. He smiled.

"Okay, okay, I'll wait."

A few moments later Kee came back inside, and Siobhan said, "Come and sit, Uncle Kee."

"All right, what's cooking? Speaking of cooking, we'll be needing a few meat pies for tonight, love."

Siobhan was just about to launch into her announcement, but his last remark suddenly filled her with dismay. She'd never thought about who would help Uncle Kee in the pub if she went away to school. What kind of a person was she? How could she just leave him here with all the day-to-day work? Worse, was she running away, just like her mother all those years ago?

Hesitating, Siobhan felt doubt overcoming her excitement.

It was a frozen moment as she struggled to come to terms with the consequences of what she was about to say. Or if she could say it at all.

Then her new voice, the one that had emerged this morning in the caravan, spoke quietly in her mind. *Just because you've made an important decision about your future doesn't mean that everything's going to be easy, that there won't be obstacles or problems. But that's what friends and family do, they help overcome obstacles and solve problems. Everyone will try to think of things. It's all right to put yourself first for once. It really is. And you're not running away. You're moving toward something.*

Her uncle noticed the silence and looked up questioningly. "Siobhan?"

Siobhan took a deep breath and lifted her chin. "I want to go to the National University in Galway into their Celtic studies program."

Her eyes were on her uncle's face, but she heard Tim say, "Oh, Siobhan—that's terrific." She sensed Tim turn his head toward Kee, so that they were both looking at her uncle, waiting for his reaction.

Kee looked down at the table. The silence grew to the point where the sound of the refrigerator kicking in made Siobhan jump.

Finally he asked quietly, still looking down, "So, you'd live there, then?"

"Yes. I thought I'd try for a place in one of the halls. Maura will help me."

"And when would you be starting?"

"Next term, in mid-January."

Kee nodded. Then he raised his head and looked into her face, neither smiling or frowning. Though he was looking at her, Siobhan sensed he was really seeing something else. Finally he spoke again.

"Well, I think it's grand. I think it's grand, Siobhan. I do. It'll be brilliant. *You'll* be brilliant. You'll take those professors for a turn around the block, I'm thinking, eh?" He stood up. "And now I'm off to Carnloe. I've a few things to pick up."

He started for the door. Siobhan didn't want him to go; it was too sudden. He was upset. He was opening the door.

"Uncle Kee!" He stopped, half turned toward her. "Uncle Kee, I'm sorry about leaving you here with all of this . . ." She gestured somewhat helplessly at the room.

He shook his head gently. "That doesn't matter, love. We'll sort it out. I'll . . . I'll just miss you, *alannah*. That's all."

The door closed softly behind him.

. . .

Early birdsong scattered through the dark air the next morning as once again Siobhan watched Tim drive away. Now the pit of time apart gapped widely between them. But it was balanced with the delicate and precious gift of needed space. Earnest plans and promises of Skype and phone calls and e-mails had been exchanged. Their goodbye was swift and their embrace passionate. The sound of Tim's voice speaking his parting words of poetry rang in Siobhan's ears as the birdsong grew louder and the day grew brighter.

The misty morning is burning
In the sun's red fire,
And the heart in my breast is burning
And lost in desire.

I follow you into the valley
But no word can I say;
To the East or the West I will follow
Till the dusk of my day.

CHAPTER 19

She sings as the moon sings:
'I am I, am I;
The greater grows my light
The further that I fly.'
All creation shivers
With that sweet cry.

—W. B. YEATS

John Trotter sat on a bench in the commons beneath a beech tree, his new mongrel terrier at his feet. He was reading a letter.

Dear Mr. Trotter:

I hope you'll be happy to hear from me. I wasn't very nice to you that day and I want to say I'm sorry. Of course I want to keep in touch with you, now that we've met each other. As I said to you that day, I think it's great altogether that you wanted to know me. I'm willing to meet you halfway. So, feel free to write or ring me whenever you want and I'll do the same. I'm starting at the National University in Galway in the January term, so you see I'm starting

to "stretch my wings." And, I'm hoping you don't mind,
but I don't think I'll ever be able to call you Da. I've always
liked the name Jack, though, so I was wondering if you
would mind if I called you Jack?

Thanks for being patient with me. I'm not sure if growing up all at once at 27 is easier or harder than doing it bit
by bit—but it's definitely worth doing. Please write back
soon.

Siobhan

She wanted to call him Jack. He felt elated and thankful, and
tried to ignore the tears in his eyes. The only person who'd ever
called him Jack was Maureen. He began to fashion a reply in
his mind.

Dear Siobhan,

There's absolutely nothing to apologize for. As far as
I'm concerned you can call me Jack, John, Hey You, or
whatever—it's entirely your choice. By a funny coincidence,
though, the only other person who ever called me Jack
was your mum . . .

"It's a nice letter," Maura told her, when Siobhan let her read
it. "Life can be such a lotto game—your birth father could have
been a real gobshite."

"I suppose," Siobhan replied, "but then he probably
wouldn't have wanted to meet me."

The two of them were going through all of Siobhan's
clothes, books, DVDs, and anything else she might be taking with her to Galway. Triona was helping, and she enjoyed

playing with some old stuffed animals found in a box in the closet. Siobhan and Maura spent way too much time curled up on the floor rereading some favorite picture books of fairy stories.

Looking at one page, they chanted together, "Up the airy mountain, Down the rushy glen, We daren't go a-hunting For fear of little men!" They laughed, and Maura said, "Remember how scared I was of being stolen away? But you used to tell me that the little people are just, that they only harm those who harm them."

"I believed that with everything in me."

Maura looked thoughtful. "After we got older I used to wonder if we . . . I worried that maybe we had played make-believe too much. If all that had made you, well, a bit too steeped in the folklore."

"Out of touch with reality, you mean. I'm sorry you worried about it—it's part of a past I wouldn't change. We had a brilliant time with it all, didn't we?"

Maura smiled. "We did. And anyway, look where we are now. You're the one who's leaving and I'm staying here. Once that would have seemed strange to me but not now."

"Why?"

"Because it just seems right. People go or stay for a lot of reasons. But either way . . . certain places have the power to keep us tethered to them. This valley is one of those. I stayed home because of Da and Niall, and now I stay because of Brendan and Triona. But over the last few years I've realized the real reason I stayed was because I wanted to. Somehow it's just that simple." Suddenly there were tears in Maura's eyes. "I'm so bloody proud of you, Siobhan. You've your own magic in you—I've always known that. I'm so glad for you, but I'll miss you something fierce."

. . .

A few weeks after Tim's visit, Turf and his family arrived at the Leeside with the news that Gwen had died. Siobhan's sense of loss was not as keen as it would have been had she not already felt the forfeit of Gwen's life that day in the nursing home.

"She's free now," she said to Turf, who nodded awkwardly, his face working to control his emotions.

The children had asked permission to play in the caravan one last time, so it was only Siobhan, Kee, Turf, and JoJo with the baby who sat in relative peace having tea. Talk was desultory at first, JoJo filling in gaps with cooing to the baby and tidbits about the children. Into a long silence, Turf suddenly spoke with apprehension.

"With Mum gone, I'm not sure I can be doing it anymore, Mr. Doyle. Traveling, I mean. I'm not sure I have the heart for it. But I'd feel like I'm letting her down . . . she loved it so."

Uncle Kee spoke with sympathy. "Ah, now, Turf. It's natural you'd feel that way, while the loss is fresh. I know from when my mum died, you feel a bit rudderless. It's hard to get a handle on things, but you will."

"I've been feeling this way for a long while, Mr. Doyle. I knew I was only staying with the traveling for Mum's sake—and because it's all I'm knowing. Same for JoJo here. But it's a fierce hard life—only worth doing if it's all that's in you. I'm thinking we'd be better off in Galway, with me trying for regular carpentry work."

JoJo nodded. "There's a terrible lot of building going on just now. Townhomes and that."

"But it's hard—I feel like I'd be breaking a promise to Mum." Turf looked at them, as if seeking their reassurance, or permission.

Siobhan told him with conviction, "Turf, Gwen knew that

just because you're born into something doesn't mean it's right for you. People need to find their own way."

Uncle Kee said speculatively, "Are you really thinking you'd like to settle?"

"I am."

Uncle Kee looked over at Siobhan, and she knew exactly what he was thinking. She nodded with rising excitement, her heart suddenly constricted with hope.

He continued carefully: "I'm thinking this might not be a time for making big decisions, Turf, but if you want to try settling, would you consider staying here, at the Leeside, to see if it suits you?"

Turf's stunned look, as if he had been offered a glimpse of Eden, made Siobhan's eyes prick with tears. She watched his face as her uncle explained that with her going off to university and his marriage to Katie, he needed someone to live here and help with the work. Her own tears spilled over as she saw Turf's trickling unchecked down his cheeks, and JoJo began sniffling loudly. When Uncle Kee had made his offer, in a voice that wasn't too steady, Turf took a deep shuddering breath.

"Mr. Doyle, before she died one thing Mum told me was that I was born here at the Leeside."

"You never!" Kee exclaimed. "How didn't I know that?"

"It was when you were away at university. She swore your own mum to secrecy, didn't want anyone to be knowing why this place was special to her."

"Well, I'll be damned." Her uncle looked stunned, but Siobhan wasn't really surprised. She had always sensed that there was a unique bond between Gwen and the Leeside.

There was silence for a few moments, then Uncle Kee laughed out loud and slapped Turf on the back.

"Good man, yourself! Welcome home."

To Siobhan, it seemed nothing short of a miracle.

. . .

JoJo, with surprising tenderness, shooed the children out of the caravan just as the gloaming settled in. Turf climbed the rickety blue steps alone for the last time. Siobhan and Kee joined the family, which stood so reverently in their little group; members of an ancient clan, ragged nobles of the road, the last strands of a vanishing way of life.

Young Dan sidled over to Siobhan and Kee. "Da fetched her pots and dishes and that," he whispered. "He knocked 'em apart and buried the bits behind yon shed, Mr. Doyle. Da said—"

"Shut it you," his mother interrupted in a low voice. Dan stopped talking instantly and Kee laid a hand on the boy's shoulder. He felt the hard, small bones through Dan's thin shirt. Kee remembered the day when he and Turf and Dan had walked over the hills, pretending to be "stalking fairies." Suddenly, despite the somber moment, he was filled with joy.

Turf stepped out of the caravan, his pale face sad but peaceful. Kee had placed kerosene at the ready, along with some old cardboard. Turf had said he wanted to get this fire "blazing hot and quick." The two men piled cardboard underneath the caravan against each wheel, followed by a good splash of kerosene. It was ready for the match.

JoJo and Siobhan drew the children back to a safe distance but young Dan was allowed to help his father set the caravan alight.

Siobhan felt suspended in time as she watched the flames grow stronger, hotter, brighter. The lough waters came alive with it, diffusing the light up into the gloaming. Siobhan looked at the faces of the children, unbelievably beautiful in the fire's reflected radiance. She hoped the streetwise darkness within their wide, serious eyes would soften and grow merry within the Leeside's embrace.

She wanted to capture everything in this moment—the vivid colors, the snap and crackle, the smell of burning wood layered over the mossy earth scent, the heat of the flames on her face, and her feelings of gratitude . . . and freedom.

Siobhan sent up a little prayer, not to God but to Gwen's ancestors, asking them to bless this effort to honor her friend's memory, and begging forgiveness if it wasn't quite right. But deep down she knew it was because, as she'd told Uncle Kee, they were doing it with love. The deep heart's core of Gwen's torched caravan glowed white-hot against the blue dusk. Floating and flitting in the sky above were orange-gold embers performing the dance at this tinker's wake beneath the stars.

. . .

Sleep surrounded the Leeside a few days later as Siobhan descended the stairs very early in the morning. Turf and the baby were in their camper but the other children were scattered around their new home on beds and sofas. Bettina was in the kitchen with JoJo teaching her to make the meat pies customers at the Leeside had depended on for decades now. Siobhan stood silently in the sitting-room doorway, marveling at the changed atmosphere of the home she knew so well. The sound and the milky smell of the children's breathing, the little yellow-shaded lamp kept on for comfort, the scruffy toys lying patiently on the floor were so transformative as to render the room completely new to her eyes. It was still her home but now its narrow embrace had expanded exponentially. And for that she was deeply thankful.

Siobhan gathered her blue shawl tightly around her and slipped out the front door for one last visit to her special place. Sitting on the lough wall, she drank in the scene around her with deliberate intensity, intoxicated with anticipation. Soon she would be leaving the Leeside to start a new life, and the moment was sweetened by the knowledge that she knew she was ready.

Taking a deep breath, Siobhan got down off the wall and walked slowly to the water's edge. She needed to say goodbye. Reaching down, she dipped her hand gently into the water, piercing its icy clarity. She spoke silently. *When I see you next, I'll be different and yet the same. So don't be afraid.* The lough water stirred at her feet. As she walked away, the ripples from her touch on the lee side flowed freely outward to the far shore, where they inevitably found their way to the sea.

ACKNOWLEDGMENTS

My parents were and continue to be the core inspira-
tion behind my love of and need for literature and writing. I
miss the fun we'd have had talking about this novel, particularly with my dad, Joe, a warm, magnificent man for whom the
Irish ethos was a living, breathing reality. I'm grateful to the
legendary P. J. Curtis for his generous translations of the story's
Irish Gaelic passages. Words cannot express my gratitude to my
amazing literary agent, Marly Rusoff, who took a chance on an
unknown writer because she "fell in love" with this novel. And
I feel extremely honored to have the unparalleled Nan Talese
as my editor. These two women are superb in every way, and it
means everything that they believe in my writing.

I owe a special debt to my daughter Kate Barrett whose
insightful suggestions always enhance my work. And last,
I dedicate all my writing to my best friend and love of my life,
my husband, Greg Peterson, who is always generous, understanding, and supportive. I love having you with me for each
step of my life (even when we have to retrace them because you
dropped your glasses on the beach).